Edward Upward was born in 1903 in Romford, Essex. He was educated at Repton School and Corpus Christi College, Cambridge, where he won the Chancellor's medal for English Verse and where he and Christopher Isherwood wrote stories for each other about the imaginary village of Mortmere, described in the latter's *Lions and Shadows*. He took a degree in History and English and became a schoolmaster. In the 1930s he was a contributor to *New Country*, *New Writing* and *Left Review* and had a significant influence on young writers such as Auden, Spender, Day Lewis and Rex Warner. His first novel, *Journey to the Border*, was published in 1938.

In the Thirties, the first volume of *The Spiral Ascent*, was published in 1962. Simultaneously with the next volume (*The Rotten Elements*) he published a collection of short stories, *The Railway Accident and Other Stories*. The trilogy was completed in 1976 with *No Home but the Struggle*.

Now retired, Edward Upward lives on the Isle of Wight.

In the Thirties

Volume One of THE SPIRAL ASCENT

Edward Upward

QUARTET BOOKS
LONDON   MELBOURNE   NEW YORK

Published by Quartet Books Limited 1978
A member of the Namara Group
27 Goodge Street, London W1P 1FD

First published by William Heinemann Ltd, London, 1962

ISBN 0 7043 3216 7

Printed in Great Britain by litho at The Anchor Press Ltd
and bound by Wm Brendon & Son Ltd
both of Tiptree, Essex

To Hilda

I

ON THE PADDLE STEAMER half-way across from the
mainland to the island Alan Sebrill was already less oppressed
by his failure to make progress during the last fortnight with
the long poem he had started writing. His fears in the train
down from London that he might waste the freedom he had
gained when he had thrown up his preparatory school teaching job two months before, and that he might never produce
the real poetry he had then believed himself capable of, were
forgotten as he looked at the nearing pier-head above
the glistering water and at summer trees dark behind the
shore. Though he could not yet hope that his visit to
the island might help him to continue writing, he felt
he was reprieved now from anxiety; and before the steamer
arrived against the landing-stage of the pier he was thinking pleasurably of the meeting he would soon have with
his friend, Richard Marple, who had invited him down
here.

The roof tiles of the pier pavilion, as Richard had said in
his letter, were curved like the scales of a fish; and the two
gabled huts, one on each side of the turnstiles at the shore
end of the pier, did in actuality have finials suggestive of
the spikes on Prussian soldiers' helmets. Beyond the turnstiles
a dark crimson open motorcoach was waiting, recognizable
immediately as the one that Richard had told Alan to look
out for, with a bright brass horn fixed just below the brass-
framed windscreen. Alan climbed up to sit on the front seat

1

beside the cocky young driver, who wore a cap tilted so far back that Richard must surely have been right in supposing it to be held to his head by some sort of hat-pin, and who waved to a girl in a kiosk before he drove away from the pier. Under trees along lanes where Tennyson and perhaps Turgenev had once strolled, the motorcoach hurried, while Alan remembered phrases and sentences that Richard had used to recommend the marvels of the place: 'the marine *lueurs* in the sky' (gallicisms, as well as certain americanisms, being in fashion with the two of them at this period); 'from where I sit the underside of the verandah roof looks like an inverted clinker-built rowing-boat'; 'come and live the poetic life at last'; 'your bemused friend, Richard.' Sooner than Alan expected, at a point where the road rounded a beech copse, the bay came into full and close view. To the right was the Britannia public house, mentioned in Richard's letter, with a balcony supported by wooden Doric pillars. To the left, on a shingle bank, Richard was sitting. He scrambled up from the shingle and leapt over a low concrete parapet towards the motorcoach, his legs apart and his arms thrown upwards in greeting. He was so demonstratively glad to see Alan that he seemed not merely to be expressing his own feelings about him but also to be welcoming him publicly on behalf of all the bystanders and of all the houses around and of the sea itself.

'Thank god you've come,' Richard said loudly as the two of them moved off down a sandy side-lane towards his lodgings. 'Oh boy, it would be impossible for you not to be able to write here. This place is utter heaven. . . . But I ought to have told you in my letter – there are certain complications. I'll explain later.'

'I suppose I shall be able to sleep somewhere tonight in this town?' Alan asked.

'Oh yes. I've fixed all that with my landlady, Miss Pollock. You can stay as long as you like. And when you find the

2

effect it has on your poetry I expect you'll want to be here for the rest of the summer.'

'Is yours still going well?'

'Wonderfully, though I've not been attempting any during this last week.'

They came to a small white front-gate over which a hawthorn tree had been trained into an arch. A mossed gravel path curved round an ascending lawn to reach the verandah of the house. Glass doors wide open to the verandah revealed a shadowy sitting-room in which an oil lamp with a white glass shade stood on a bobble-fringed velvety table-cloth. As Alan stepped after Richard into the room he noted that the ottoman and two armchairs were upholstered in red plush; and over the mantelpiece there was a large gilt-framed mirror with swans in green reeds painted on the lower corners of the glass.

'It's marvellous,' Alan said.

'Isn't it?' Richard agreed with a pleased grin. 'But you won't meet Miss Pollock herself till she brings in our tea. She's never to be seen except at meal-times, and even then only for a moment or so. She's rather strange, and very old.'

A few minutes later, when Alan was standing at the window of the bedroom up to which Richard had shown him, and was pouring water from a jug into a wash-basin while simultaneously looking out at a near-by cabbage patch that Richard said was owned by coastguards, he had the beginnings of a new hope about his poem. Trying to think what particular thing outside the window had suggested this hope to him, he spilt some of the water on the washhand-stand; and Richard, who was standing behind him, said with a disproportionately loud laugh, 'Aha, it leaks.'

Alan was startled, momentarily wondering whether the insanity which Richard had often boasted he might one day inherit from both sides of his family had at last come, then asked him to explain the earlier-mentioned complications.

'There were hints in my letter,' Richard said.

'Do you mean Love?'

'Yes, that's it. But what I didn't tell you was that the family were down here for only a week. They went back to London the day before yesterday. The mother invited me to come and visit them any time when I'm back there.'

'Don't you want to?'

'Oh god, yes. I'm utterly in love. The trouble is I don't know how much longer I shall be able to wait. I haven't managed to start writing again since they left.'

'You will.'

'I'm not so certain.'

But Richard soon added, 'I won't put it to the test just yet. I'm not going to try to write for the next few days. I want to show you round this place. I want you to feel the same astounding delight that I've had here.'

'I shall, I'm sure.'

'I'll introduce you to the inhabitants.'

'Good.'

'I'm thoroughly in with the so-called lower classes here – the boatmen, the hotel workers, a bookmaker's clerk, a coast-guard called Mr Hards, a jobbing gardener whom I've privately nicknamed "the Hedger", though his real name is Mr Lillicrap, which is perhaps even better, a Mr Peel who retired from Birmingham two years ago after winning a bit of money in a newspaper competition and who looks every inch the tripper, and a Scotsman who always wears a straw hat but no one knows quite what he's up to when he isn't in the pub, and lots of others. As a matter of fact the mother is a kind of lady's maid, very rafeened, and the father is a broad cockney. The family's holiday is paid for by the rich old woman she works for who comes down to stay here every Whitsun – and who seems rather nice, I must say, though I've never met her. I enjoyed talking loudly to them on the esplanade: it surprised the stuck-up public-school gang staying at the big hotel. I've realized lately that the time has arrived for me to show definitely that I'm against the plus-foured poshocracy, and for the cockneys and the lower orders.'

'I'm for them, too,' Alan said. 'And I've always wanted to get in with them. But I haven't your courage. I am afraid they will despise me. How did you do it?'

'By behaving naturally. They are rather proud of their gentlemanly friend.'

'That's where I always make my mistake. I try to talk to them in what I imagine to be *their* language. But if you introduce me all will be well. I usually make my friends lead me where I haven't the nerve to go alone.'

'You'll do fine, boy,' Richard said. 'And as soon as possible we must get you a girl. There are some promising ones about here. We'll find you someone really beautiful.'

'Good, I'm glad. So long as it doesn't prevent me from starting to write again.'

'You mustn't let it. Though I admit I'm hardly the person to talk.'

That evening Alan met some of the inhabitants. He did not see any of the poshocrats except in the distance, where they appeared as dinner-jacketed or gowned shapes moving among hydrangeas behind the glass walls of the lounge of the big hotel up on the cliff. The hotel lawn descended to the level of the Britannia's roof, which it seemed almost to touch. Following Richard into the bar, Alan was as excited as though he had already drunk several pints. He was introduced first to Mr Lillicrap, the Hedger, a man of sixty with a square-looking front face, a very small chin and reddish swellings of the flesh at the corners of his jaws below the ears. The Hedger accepted drinks but did not speak much, appearing to be very tired. Once, however, he poked Alan in the side of the leg and pointed at the rumpled white flannel trousers worn by a fat man who bustled into the bar and who, on seeing Richard, exclaimed with the heartiest pleasure, 'Well, if it isn't our Dick.' This was Mr Peel, the Tripper. He took an immediate liking to Alan. He talked a lot, affably recommending excursions to various beauty spots, and he laughed often, throwing his head back and shaking. His face was assertive yet undetermined, rather too pale for the grossness of its shape, and he had butcher's curls. He carried a walking-stick hooked on to his arm. He insisted on ordering drinks for Alan and Richard and the Hedger. The barmaid wore ear-rings, was not unfriendly but never once smiled. Her glance was sharp and black. Her hair was black and waved. She hissed slightly when she spoke, though not from asthma. The Scotsman came in, nodded seriously to them but did not join them. He leant a forearm on the bar-counter, and with his straw boater tilted to the back of his head he crouched staring fixedly and without curiosity at Alan. Then the Hedger began to talk, slowly but pause-lessly; and he talked, first, about eggs, having perhaps noticed a few minutes earlier that Alan's attention had been attracted by a bright yellow bottle of advocaat which was standing with other liqueurs on a shelf in front of a long horizontal strip of looking-glass beyond the barmaid's head. The Hedger said that when rats stole eggs they did it in a gang, one of the rats lying on his back and holding the egg on top of him while the others pulled him along the ground; that hedgehogs would climb anything to get at eggs and would suck out the yolk and afterwards break and eat the shell; that a rook would carry off an egg, suck out the contents and leave the empty shell resting on – for instance – the top of a flint wall. He himself had bred white mice and then guinea-pigs 'for research'. He had worked in a stone quarry, with many steps to climb down, slippery and without a rail to hold on to, very cold, so that he had twice had pleurisy. The slow voice steadily continued, and Alan would gladly have listened to it for the rest of the evening, but the Hedger had to stop when the bookmaker's clerk, a young man with a brickdust-red complexion and a stutter, appeared and was introduced to Alan. Later, outside the Britannia, in the middle distance along the broken esplanade and indistinct in the moonlight, there were girls, beautiful even beyond expectation. As Alan and Richard stood looking towards them a boy named George, who worked in the still-room up at the hotel, came and spoke to Richard. Pleasantly monkey-faced, he wore a dull silver-coloured watch-chain hanging from his lapel buttonhole. He spoke about Basher, a man who – as Richard explained soon afterwards to Alan when they had begun to walk back down the sandy lane towards their lodgings – also worked in the still-room and was George's hero. 'And he really is a hero,' Richard said. 'A hero of our time. Whatever else you don't do, you mustn't fail to meet him.'

They did not continue walking for long. Suddenly Alan started to run, and he ran as fast as he could down the hundred yards or so of lane till he reached the white gate under the arched hawthorn. But the excitement which goaded him was increased rather than relieved by the running. Only one thing could ease it, and that would be to find words which might give his friend some inkling of how he already felt about this place and the people here. Richard was running too, though not quite so fast as Alan had been. The gate made a startlingly loud creaking sound as they pushed it open, and they warned each other by gestures to avoid alarming Miss Pollock. They moved with absurd caution, almost on tiptoe, up the gravel path to the verandah. Miss Pollock had lit the oil lamp and left it burning low. Richard went over to the table and turned the small red-gold-coloured wheel that controlled the wick, till the light whitened inside the glass shade. They carried chairs out on to the verandah. Alan said, 'Thank heaven you invited me

7

down here. A place like this is what I've never dared to hope for. Now I shall come alive again at last.'

'It'll seem even better when you really get to know it.'

'I wish I could tell you how dead I've been for months and months until now. Not only before I chucked up the school at the end of March and went home to live with my parents. All through April and May I haven't succeeded in writing a single really satisfactory line of poetry; though I've tried to fool myself into believing that because I've at least made a start on my long poem I've achieved the main thing, and that it will improve later.'

'I thought the opening passage you sent me was very good.'

'Perhaps it wasn't absolutely bad,' Alan conceded, pleased, 'but what I've written since is worse, and I've been writing more and more slowly and for the last fortnight I haven't been able to get ahead at all.' With story-teller's relish, as though he were describing a deliberately imagined experience and not an actual one, Alan added, 'I've had some rather nasty moments recently after waking in the mornings. All the feeling seems to retreat out of my arms and legs and to become burningly concentrated in my solar plexus. I've found a meaning for those lines – "Central anguish felt/ For goodness wasted at peripheral fault." '

'It sounds pretty distinguished,' Richard said, in the admiring tone they still used at this period when speaking of any seemingly pathological symptom that one or the other of them might produce.

'I shan't wake like that in this house. Because here I shall be allowed to write. And I *shall* write.'

'Of course you will. But tell me why you're dissatisfied with the present opening. Let's get to the bottom of that.'

'It's much much too pictorial. There are no ideas in it.'

'I thought there were going to be some Marxian ideas later on in the poem. You said so when you wrote to me at the end of last term.'

'Yes, but Marx doesn't seem as he did before I escaped from the school. He attracted me then because I was in a fury with the anti-poetic life I was leading, and because I saw him as the great repudiator of the whole loathly upper-class mystique on which the school was run. He doesn't seem quite so relevant now.'

Richard looked disappointed, though he had to admit, 'I couldn't make much sense out of *Das Kapital* when I began reading it soon after I got your letter about it. The first chapter was full of entities that Ockham would certainly have razored.'

For some reason Alan wanted to defend Marx against this criticism. 'That's what I thought at first. But later I wondered whether my distrust of Marx's abstractions mightn't be due to the bad influence on me of the logico-positivist philosophic gang when we were up at Cambridge, and whether he mightn't perhaps be dealing with realities and not just with words.'

Richard began to be hopeful again. He said almost coaxingly, 'So you might be able to use Marxian ideas in your poem after all?'

'No, they wouldn't be natural to me. But don't worry: since we've been sitting here I've become certain that very soon indeed – perhaps this evening – I'm going to know how to write this poem. The solution is very near. It's in the night air here.'

From before ten o'clock until after eleven they sat out on the verandah, talking not only of Alan's poem but also of the poems Richard had written since he had been staying here and which he now recited, knowing them – as he usually did know his poems – by heart. Without any envy at all, and with happy admiration, Alan recognized that his friend's work was far better than anything he himself had done or ever could do. He sat looking at the black trees that framed the rising shingle bank and the night sea. Through a spray of thin leaves the orange-coloured façade of the Britannia appeared grey under the moon. He seemed to be able to see also, as from some slight distance away, both Richard and himself sitting there on the verandah, the two young poets; and he had the idea that the picture they formed would not disappear when they returned inside the house, was permanent, would continue to exist long after they were dead.

Next morning they went walking, taking sandwiches with them for lunch. At the bay, as they left their lodgings, the sea-light was reflected in shifting reticulations on the concrete groyne. Almost continuously throughout the day Alan was in a state of elation. All that he saw gave him delight, and he saw with clarity and in vivid detail many things he would not have noticed at other times. As for instance, near the end of the broken esplanade, the tall silver-painted iron lamp-standard whose top was curved over and decoratively curled like a bishop's crozier. Or, along the shore at low tide, sand ridges which resembled chains of buried fish. Or, among lugworms' tangle-coiled sandmounds, the meandering footprints of birds. Or the upper face of the red cliff channelled horizontally by erosion into corridor grottoes and pitted with miniature caves and looking like a section of a rabbit warren or of a wasps' nest. Near by, the apex of an isolated greensand pinnacle was whitened with bird droppings. Richard used the word 'guano'. A dead guillemot, or so Alan named it to Richard, lay putrefying among rounded stones, emitting a smell as of coffee. A top-heavy black protrusion of cliff was streaked vertically with rust-coloured stains, like a derelict battleship, and at its base an under-sand streamlet was betrayed by an above-sand dendritical figure. Richard spoke the words 'ferruginous' and 'chalybeate'. Elsewhere along the cliff-face a shallow hole narrowing downwards to a neck reminded them of the inside of a ship's ventilator. They spoke geological words – more for sound and for poetic suggestiveness than for scientific meaning – such as sandrock, the Perna Bed, mud-flows, blue slipper, the Gault, the crackers. They named the soft rock of one of the cliffs 'the purple marls', not knowing whether they did so correctly or not, and Alan said that if this was the Wealden outcrop there ought to be iguanodon bones here. They thought of similes and metaphors for the movement and appearance of the waves breaking on the shore: the frail circlets of spume; the spume like fine lace curtains undulating in a black wind, or like the shredded fat hanging down over a bullock's heart as seen in a butcher's shop. Then the minia-ture waves detaching themselves from the spent breaker and scarcely having the power of individual motion: these flopped on the sand with pause and dip like the rolling of a metal ellipse, or like the movement of the genitals of a naked male runner. Suddenly and inconsequently Richard quoted from a contemporary American writer: ' "I'm a goner. I'm in love with him, I think." ' The word 'goner' filled Alan with an astonishing joy. It excited him at first because of its strangeness, and next it made him hopefully imagine a time soon to come when he too would be utterly in love, and then it returned once again into his consciousness as a sound, as a word newly coloured and illuminated by what he had just imagined. And many other words that they spoke while they were out walking together went through a similar pro-cess. Memory or some not clearly perceived external object would suggest a poetically interesting word, and the word would make them look closely at an object whose own fascina-tion would then be reflected back on the word, giving it a more than doubled beauty and power. They walked in a rapture of imagery. And Alan thought that no other activity on earth – not even making love – could compare with this savouring of words.

On the second evening after Alan's arrival he met Basher. In the moonlight Alan was standing with Richard and George outside the Britannia. Basher approached from inland along the road out of the village. He moved with bent shoulders and with long fast strides, and he had very long arms that swung in time with his legs. There was something palaeolithic about him, Alan thought. George introduced Alan to him in a tone of voice which made quite clear who was being honoured.

'Enjoying yourself here?' Basher asked, kindly.

'Yes,' Alan said. 'This afternoon we went out in a rowing boat in the bay.'

'Rowing, rowing,' Basher said. 'Ah, I used to be very fond of it myself.' He crouched, and, straightening out both arms, made movements as though pulling at oars. 'Then the sculling . . .' He continued the movements, but this time on coming to the end of each stroke he turned up his wrists as though feathering the blades of the oars. He was evidently giving Alan a lesson in how it should be done.

Richard asked deferentially, 'You know a bit about boxing too, don't you?'

'That's right.'

Basher at once began to demonstrate, head lowered, left forearm forward, legs apart and knees bent.

'Stand firm on your feet – always,' he said. 'I've done a lot of scrapping. Because I'm fond of women. Not just for the sake of going out with them. I believe in giving them a good turn over.'

'Tell us about the women,' George admiringly begged him.

Basher seemed very pleased. 'I was in Samaria once,' he said. 'I was standing as I might be here and an old man with a beard came past. Behind him was about ten young maids walking in file and all wearing – what d'you call 'em? – yashmaks, you know what, hanging down over their noses and mouths. I touched the last one up as she went by. Quicker'n you can say she pulls out a small dagger.' Basher did not explain what happened next, but went on just as though he had left no gap in the story. 'An old woman arranged it with me by sign-language. Afterwards she threw us a towel over the wooden partition. She was an old woman of seventy. She made signs with her fingers that the girl was thirteen. Then I lifted up the old woman. She was the best I ever . . .'

'Show them your tattoo,' George asked.

Basher slipped one arm out of his jacket, rolled up a shirtsleeve, revealed a blue and red tattooed design of girls with prominent rumps and busts and with wasp waists. He worked the bulging muscles beneath the skin of his arm, and asked, 'Can you see them dancing?' Alan couldn't, but answered, 'Yes.' Basher was thoroughly satisfied and, having at last rolled down his shirt-sleeve again and put his arm back into the arm of his jacket, he said, 'I've been a sailor. Been everywhere in the world. Australia is the best country. I've had something to drink this evening. I've just been with a woman I know here. All the doings. I've got no use for any of those contraptions. I just go right through them. She says I ought to wear leather.'

Alan dared to ask, 'What do you think of the people staying up at the hotel?'

'Oh *them*,' Basher said, seemingly with contempt. But he wouldn't say any more about them. Either the sense that Alan and Richard belonged to the same class as those people prompted him to be cautious in spite of his inebriation, or else he didn't really feel and couldn't simulate the absolute disapproval which he must have guessed Alan would have liked to hear him express.

Not till the afternoon of the next day did Alan meet someone who not only belonged to the lower orders but was prepared to show a dislike for the poshocrats. After returning from a walk along the shore Richard and Alan were on the shingle bank when they saw the motorcoach arrive, and among its passengers was a red-faced middle-aged man wearing a check suit whose black and white squares were so large that Alan could only suppose he had hired it from a theatrical costumier's. He wore a cap to match, and a blue bow-tie with big white spots. As soon as he had stepped out of the motorcoach he came and stood on the concrete parapet quite near to Richard and Alan, and he began to address the other passengers in a powerful uncultured voice. He spoke of the pyramids of Egypt, of the British Empire, of a dandelion he had picked that morning and now wore in his buttonhole, warned his hearers that they and the motorcoach they had ridden in would wither away like the grass of the fields. He seemed surprisingly hearty for a religious maniac. When he had finished his short sermon he came and stood next to Richard, but without speaking. At that moment a group of guests from the big hotel, blazered young men and striding girls, went confidently past. In their dress, their voices, their every minutest gesture and facial movement, they represented for Alan what he then loathed more than anything else in the world: they were the loyal young supporters of that power which cared only for outward appearances and ceremonies and which despised the living poets and the truth. Richard dared to ask the maniac whether he hadn't something to say about these young people. At once, and to the alarmed delight of Alan, the maniac shouted after them with coarse scorn, 'Tulips, twolips, there you go, there you go. And all you have is nothing.' He ended with a tremendous bawling laugh. The young people, in a way that Alan could hardly help admiring or at least envying, ignored him. The maniac himself then walked quickly off towards the village. Later Richard talked about him to the driver of the motorcoach, who said, 'I suppose he must have been drunk.'

Three evenings later there was an open-air dance at the bay. A small local brass band, only two of whom wore uniform, brought canvas stools and set them up on the gravel not far from the windows of the Britannia. There were fewer than a dozen couples dancing and some of the girls had to pair off together because there were more girls than men. The dancing was on a sunken stretch of grass below the broken esplanade. Richard and Alan watched at first from inside the bar of the Britannia, but soon they came out and stood on the shingle bank. Alan looked at each of the couples in turn, and he found that several of the girls were beautiful. And suddenly they, and their partners, and the other couples also, seemed more than merely beautiful, were transfigured. The unambiguous emotional music, the soft strong movement of limbs beneath the dresses, the happy seriousness of faces, the pride and the gliding erectness of body and of head, made Alan feel that in these dancers he was seeing the human race as it truly was, sublime, infinitely finer than all the gods and goddesses it had ever invented. No supernatural light shining around these girls and men could, he thought, have given them such a glory as they naturally had now. He was on the point of trying to tell Richard about this when he saw standing at the near end of the esplanade two girls and a young man who were also watching the dancers. The shorter and plumper of the girls had a face that reminded Alan of Rossetti's *The Beloved* in the Tate Gallery. The other had straight coppery hair and eyes that, for no reason he could think of, seemed to him Icelandic. He was aware that he could fall utterly in love with either of them. But the shorter one turned towards the young man and, eagerly catching hold of him by the wrist, led him on to the grass to dance. He had a willing, though rather helpless, look, moved clumsily, and his long black hair was untidy. He might not be her husband yet – her possessiveness would perhaps not have been so ostentatiously avid if he had been, Alan thought – but he appeared likely to be before long. The other smilingly watched them begin to dance. Alan asked Richard, 'Do you know who that girl is over there at the end of the esplanade?'

'No. I'm pretty sure she's not one of the inhabitants. Do you fancy her?'

'God, yes!'

'Go and ask her to dance.'

'She might be posh.'

'Well, even if she is she can only say no.'

'I think I'll wait a bit.'

'She might try to look insulted, but she wouldn't feel it.'

'What scares me is that she might say yes,' Alan explained.

'Come on, boy, she's looking at you.'

'No, I'm not ready. I should seem a complete fool and spoil all my chances. Or, worse, I might find that she was the fool. It's too soon.'

She was in fact looking at Alan – frankly and mildly and with apparent approval. He briefly looked back. The blood thumped in his body. But funk or perverseness made him say to Richard, 'Let's go.'

'Where?'

'Into the pub again. Or, better, back to the lodgings.'

'What about the girl? Would you like me to speak to her for you?'

'No.'

'All right. But promise me that if she's staying here you'll introduce yourself not later than tomorrow.'

'Very well, I promise.'

'Then I shall be able to feel that I've got you properly equipped.'

As they walked away Alan became aware of the pain of the injury which his timidity had caused him to inflict on himself. He was almost on the point of turning back and going to speak to the girl, but the thought of his promise to Richard, which he had every intention of keeping, partly soothed him. Quite soon he was able to remember her without any unhappiness, and even with hope. Then he remembered also the impression that the dancers had made on him;

and something of the exalted admiration he had felt for them began to revive in him.

'What is it that makes them so fine?' he asked.

'That's what I was wondering,' Richard said.

'It can't be just sex.'

'No. Perhaps it's beauty, eh?'

'I don't know.'

'Then it's because they're *living*.'

'Yes, that's partly it. But there's more to it than that.'

Richard was opening the white gate under the hawthorn arch when Alan added, 'I've got it.' He bounded forward up the path, then stopped, waiting for Richard. 'It's because they're doomed.'

'Boy, I believe you're right.'

'It's because in ten to fifteen years' time all those girls will be prematurely middle-aged and ugly. And they're dancing now in defiance of the inevitable rot which will come upon them.'

'Yes, that's it.'

Inside the sitting-room Alan went on, 'The band's rhythm made us obscurely recognize it: the historic tragedy of woman. We weren't looking just at a few local working girls wearing their summer frocks, but at the first or second act played over again in sight of a small bay and still cliffs.' With a sense of rising inspiration Alan added, 'But I see now that there's far far more to it than anything I've suggested yet.'

'What?' Richard urged him on.

'The girls aren't the only ones who are fine. People like the Hedger, and Mr Rudge, and the Scotsman, and Basher, and that maniac in the check suit, they're all just as fine, and, for the same reason: they're all doomed. Most of them have reached the fourth act already. What makes people vile is being successful or comfortably off. That's why most of the hotel visitors are so poisonous. They are the wicked, the devils. Only the doomed are good, and we must be on their side always.'

Richard, excited by this conception, said, 'Our duty is to live among the doomed and in our poetry we must record and celebrate what they are.'

'We ourselves, in our own way, are doomed too,' Alan said. 'We shall always be misfits, not properly belonging to any social class. We shall never settle down anywhere. We must walk the earth. We must descend into hell.'

They found themselves standing in front of the big gilt-framed mirror. On the mantelshelf to one side of it there was a vase of Cape gooseberries and to the other side a vase of honesty; and in its pewter-coloured depths, like a view veiled by faint rain, part of the hallway appeared through the open door of the sitting-room. Above the lincrusta dado in the hallway an engraving of Holman Hunt's *Light of the World* was made visible by the dimly pinkish-golden glow of evening. High against the wallpaper a feathery head of pampas grass intruded, the umbrella-stand in which its stem was based being out of sight beyond the door-jamb. They themselves, more vivid in the foreground, stood half-facing each other, at right-angles, both looking into the mirror. They were of much the same height, both rather short. Richard quoted from Matthew Arnold's sonnet on Shakespeare:

' "All pains the immortal spirit must endure,
'All weakness which impairs, all griefs which bow,
'Find their sole speech in that victorious brow." '

He spoke the lines half-ironically, guarding against seeming guilty of the naïve presumption of likening Alan and himself to Shakespeare, but in spite of, or because of, Richard's irony they were conscious as they looked at their reflected faces that there was suffering and victory in those brows too. They were conscious of belonging, however humbly, among the English poets. Awe came upon them as they continued to look at themselves. They saw not merely the two individual representatives but the ages-old and ever-living greatness which was here represented. They would be true to poetry, Alan told himself, no matter what miseries and humiliations they might have to undergo for it, no matter even what crimes they might perhaps have to commit for it.

Next morning, which was the sixth since Alan's arrival here, Richard came down late for breakfast. Alan had finished his, and was sitting on the red plush ottoman reading Tennyson's *Locksley Hall*. There was a glum frown over Richard's face. Alan said, 'You look as though you've had an all-night visit from a loathly succubus.'

Instead of grinning, Richard said violently, 'I can't stand a single day more of this.'

'Of what?' Alan asked, astounded.

'Of this house, this place.' Richard became a little milder. 'I can't wait any longer. I've got to go to London. When I invited you down here I thought I should be able to stay on and write poetry after the family had gone back, but almost as soon as I saw you in the motorcoach – and for heaven's sake, boy, forgive me for saying this – I had a premonition that even with you here this place could never satisfy me again.'

'I wouldn't have guessed it.'

A bitterness rose in Alan, who wanted to say something hatefully contemptuous about Richard's capriciousness, to call him deserter, to break with him for ever, but who unaccountably was able to say nothing more offensive than, 'How soon will you be going?'

'As soon as I've had breakfast.'

Suddenly Alan recognized that Richard had a right to leave for London, that it was not desertion, that the relation

19

between them had always been one of mutual independence. His anger weakened, and he said, 'Of course you ought to go if it's necessary for your poetry.'

'It is. I'd never be able to write another line here.' Richard remembered something important. 'But you'll be able to get ahead with your poem here, eh?'

'Oh yes.'

'You absolutely must.'

Later, while Richard was upstairs packing a suitcase, Alan became doubtful whether this place and this house would in fact be favourable to his own writing. Perhaps the 'poetic life' he had been invited down here to lead might not seem so feasible after Richard had left. Perhaps even it could be lived only by someone who like Richard had enough private means to be able to go where he pleased when he pleased. Alan, waiting in the sitting-room, began to feel afraid, but he checked his fear by deciding that he would try to restart his poem this very morning, as soon as he had said goodbye to Richard.

After seeing Richard off at the motorcoach stop he returned at once to the house and fetched his notebook from his bedroom and went to sit out on the verandah. He gave himself twenty minutes to begin. During the past two days he had already made up his mind about the sort of detail he wanted in the new opening, and on the previous evening his discovery that only the doomed are good had provided him with what he had most lacked when writing the exist-ing version – a unifying central idea. At the end of twenty minutes, without difficulty, he started the new version. He was helped by a slogan he had made for himself, 'Get it on paper – well if possible, but badly rather than not at all.' By lunch-time he had written five lines. He was surprised to recognize that they were not valueless, that they would cer-tainly do to go on from tomorrow, that they might even be good.

When he had finished lunch he went out to look for the coppery-haired girl he had seen at the open-air dance. He did not find her. But the next day, after writing another five lines of his poem in the morning, he saw her almost as soon as he left the house. She was walking towards the esplanade, and he followed her. She was brought to a halt at the top of the wooden steps by a family coming up from the beach. He stood beside her for at least half a minute, and she saw him, but far from saying anything to her he ridiculously tried to give the impression that he was with her there by mere chance. Although after he had let her go he recognized that this diffidence – like his earlier failure to ask her to dance with him – was a reversion to a former, boyish type of behaviour which he ought long before to have broken himself of, he couldn't bring himself to follow her down to the beach. His next opportunity came two days later on the shingle bank opposite the Britannia, but he was deterred from speaking to her because she was sitting with the other girl and the untidy-haired young man. If there had not been a second open-air dance a week after the first he might never have got to know her.

On the evening of this second dance he began, as he had begun when Richard had been with him, by watching from inside the bar of the Britannia. When he saw her with the other girl and the young man approaching along the road he came out of the bar so quickly that he had to make a detour towards his lodgings and back again in order to avoid walking just in front of them to the dance. They stood as before at the unbroken end of the esplanade, and as before she was left on her own while the young man partnered the other girl. The fear that someone else might get to her first made him hurry towards her. When he asked her whether she would like to dance she accepted with a laugh which seemed meant to suggest that there was no need for him to try to look as though they didn't already know each other.

Soon she was asking him, 'What is it you're so busy at in the mornings on the verandah of that house over there?'

'I didn't know I could be seen from outside.'

'Well, you can be.'

'As a matter of fact I've been trying to write some poetry.'

Before the band had stopped playing the music for the foxtrot which they were dancing he had told her more about himself, his family, his education, his poems and Richard than afterwards it seemed possible to him that he could have done in so short a time. And in the same time he had discovered that she not only liked poetry but had written some, though her main interest was in painting.

'But Iris – that's my sister – is a much better painter than I am,' she said. 'When this foxtrot's over you must meet her. And her fiancé. He's a 'cellist and has hopes of becoming a professional one. He's very nice, though I'm not sure she's wise. By the way, what's your name?'

'Sebrill. And my other name is Alan.'

'Is that your only other name?'

'No. I've also got a rather fancy one chosen for me by my grandfather. It's Thorwald.'

'That's the one I like. I shall call you Thorwald.'

'What's yours?'

'Halscomb. My other is Althea. Perhaps that's too fancy a one for your taste.'

'Not if it's the only other you've got.'

'In the family I'm called Peg, though no grandfather or anybody else gave me the name at birth.'

'That's the one I like.'

The music had stopped and the couples were moving back to the edge of the small grass arena.

'The fiancé's name is Willie,' Peg said. 'Willie Buxton. We're all three of us staying with my aunt at her house, which you can see down there in the hollow. And I'd better tell you now that I've got a fiancé too. Not here. I left him behind in London. His firm wanted him because of some quite important contract they're on, so he thought he oughtn't to take his holiday till later in the year.' Before this information could do its full work on Alan's feelings she added, 'It won't matter. You needn't let it worry you. It won't make any difference to us at all.'

She turned towards him as though they were about to continue dancing, and she looked at him. Then the words 'It won't make any difference' became less ambiguous for him. They might have meant 'We can be friends just the same', but her look gave likelihood to another interpretation. He began to be sure not merely that her fiancé did not matter to him but that soon something was going to happen which he had long ago stopped himself from hoping for. The schoolboy's romantic daydream of meeting a girl who was both marvellously beautiful and genuinely fond of poetry was going to be realized with a completeness which the boy's imagination had been too delicately ignorant to picture. Joy and expectation so bemused him that when Peg took him over to Iris and Willie and in an almost serious voice said, 'Allow me to introduce you to Count Thorwald', he made no attempt by word or grin to disclaim the title, and they must have suspected – if they had seen him come out of the Britannia before the dance – that he was drunk. He was soon aware, however, that they both approved of him. And by the time the dancing came to a final stop the four of them had arranged to go for a walk together the following evening.

The walk was in the moonlight along the path up the cliff. Iris and Willie were in front, but Peg would not go slowly enough to let them get out of sight. Alan kissed her, and she said, 'They won't be with us at all two days from now. They're going away to spend the rest of their holiday with Willie's parents in Hampshire. Iris has been sharing a bedroom with me, so on Wednesday night I shall be alone there.'

'But what about your aunt?'

'She won't know, I hope. That means you'll have to come in through the back door —or, no, it had better be through the scullery window because that has a broken catch and she makes rather a point of seeing that all the doors are locked before she goes to bed. But I want you to meet my aunt. You must come to tea tomorrow afternoon. She'll like you.'

'I'll come to tea. Thanks. And on Wednesday I'll get through the scullery window. You'll let me know what time. Have you done this sort of thing before?'

'Only once. And it wasn't with John, my fiancé. I've managed so far to keep my relations with him fairly respectable, though when provoked he's inclined to go wild and bite. It was with a boy whom I warned beforehand that he ought to listen to Yeats's advice and take love easy as the leaf grows on the tree. Afterwards he wanted to kill himself.'

'I hope I shan't want to do that.'

'You mustn't.'

'Are you in love with John?'

'I'm sometimes not at all sure.'

'Then why do you want to marry him?'

'Because I think he'll be good for me. I need keeping in order. He's just the sort for that. But I am sure I'm beginning to be in love with you.'

Next afternoon he went to tea at the aunt's house. Iris and Willie were there as well as Peg. The aunt seemed amiable but a little crazy. Apropos of nothing that had been said in conversation she informed him without malice that neither she nor Peg's parents were rich. On the Wednesday night just after twelve o'clock he went to the house again. From the road he turned quickly in through the tradesmen's gate and approached the back of the house, aware that there was a good chance of his being seen, if not by the local policeman at any rate by some neighbour who would become suspicious. It surprised him that, far from being afraid, he even felt pleasantly excited by the risk he was taking. The scullery window was easy to open, but when he put his hands on its sill and jumped vigorously up to get through it the toes of his shoes scraped the brickwork below and his arms alarmingly hampered him from bringing his leg inside. He got through and had to step into a slippery sink before putting his feet down on to the scullery floor. Having arrived there, he wondered whether this method of entry had been necessary, whether Peg hadn't wilfully chosen it for him because it seemed more romantic to her than letting him in by unbolting the back door. If so, her romanticism had infected him also and he felt proud of his daring as, following the directions she had repeatedly given him the day before, he went through the kitchen and up the stairs towards the first-floor landing. He went very carefully, but with his shoes on and not too stealthily just in case – as he illogically told himself – he might meet the aunt, whose bedroom was at the far end of the landing. Peg had said that her own room was the first on the left at the top of the stairs. When he stepped on to the floorboards of the landing they gave out an appalling creak. He hurried towards a door and turned the handle. Luckily he did not find himself in the wrong room.

They lay side by side without moving for a very long time. They talked of trivialities, lazily. Bliss came over him like a rising sea. It seemed that he could be content to lie like this all night, as though this alone were the consummation. Only once was anything at all serious said, and by him. 'I have been in love with several girls before now,' he told her, 'and I've slept with several girls before now, but I've never before slept with someone whom I've been in love

25

with.' When they at last did turn and embrace they lay almost as still in one another's arms as they had done side by side, and for almost as long. He postponed movement as though it would have been an affront to her, an impudence, a crudity like overeating. After the climax they stayed awake talking about what they would do next day and what they would do when her holiday was over. She said she would come down at week-ends as often as she could for as long as he was here, and that he must also see her sometimes in London.

'But won't John object?' he asked.

'I shan't let him. He'll have to get used to the idea that I intend to have other men friends – and to have them even after I've married him.'

'Don't marry him.'

She laughed, but with a suggestion of displeasure, as though she guessed that he might mean it seriously – which in fact he did.

There was no excitement for him about getting out of the house in the early morning. Peg expected him to use the scullery window, but he went out by the back door, leaving it unbolted for the aunt to discover and puzzle over if she liked. Opening the tradesmen's gate he again wondered whether he would be seen, but this time the risk gave him a feeling rather of dreariness than of romantic daring. As he walked along the road back to his lodgings he had the thought that many of the romantically tragic love affairs famous in history or in literature would, if they happened today, be merely sordid adventures ending in the criminal courts. He knew now that romanticism was his enemy. He wanted no adventures: he wanted to get married like an ordinary person, but that would be economically impossible for him unless he was prepared to betray himself and give up trying to live as a poet. Therefore what he needed was a bohemian relationship which could become just as permanent as marriage. He decided he would tell Peg this when he saw her again later in the day.

It seemed clear to him at once when they met at eleven o'clock in the morning on the beach that she foreknew what he was going to demand. Her manner was extraordinarily detached, as though she was not the person who had been in bed with him the night before. He found a niche between boulders below the cliff, not less than ten yards from where the nearest other couple were lying. When he suggested they should sit down she agreed with a look implying that somewhere else would have done just as well. He said, 'I wish *I* could marry you.'

'Why?'

'Because I love you and I want to live with you.'

'I love you too. But you're not the marrying sort.'

'We could live together without being married.'

'It wouldn't work.'

'Why not? We have the same kind of nature and interests, and we love each other.'

She was suddenly impressed.

'Yes, you are right. We were certainly made for each other, as they say.'

'Live with me.'

'No. For one thing, I'd prefer not to have to go out to work. And I'd want children, but I wouldn't want to spend all my time on them and the housework. I need leisure as much as you do. And we wouldn't be able to afford it.'

'I would do the housework.'

He put his arm round her and pressed his head into her deep bosom. She made no response, did not stroke his hair, did not move.

'You must control yourself,' she said.

He sat up again; then, avoiding the phrase 'go to bed together', he said, 'If you won't live with me will you promise that we shall be with each other at least once every week?'

She was more than doubtful even about this. 'I don't think I'm good for you.'

'Or at least once every month.'

'No. You're too serious about it. I warned you not to be.'

'Promise not to abandon me.'

'As for abandoning you, I shall have to go back to London tomorrow.'

'But why? You've still got three days of your holiday left.'

'I think I ought to see John again.'

Alone at his lodgings that evening and that night he was unable to defeat his misery and his despair. But next morning after breakfast he succeeded in convincing himself once again that poetry was what mattered to him most, and that nothing must be allowed to interfere with it. If having a woman was essential to him, well, there were plenty of women about and at worst he could get Basher to introduce him to a quickly willing one. He even managed to settle down for an hour and a half in his chair on the verandah and to write three more lines of his poem. This helped to give him confidence for his final meeting with Peg.

In the afternoon, an hour before she was due to leave for London, they went down to the beach again. At first, as on the previous day, she showed reserve towards him, but, finding after they had been sitting for a while together that he made no advances, she abruptly reached out a hand and stroked his hair. He did not respond at all. Then she pulled his head down on to her lap and touched his face with her bosom. In this position he had the thought that if, instead of showing the ordinary feelings of a man called Alan, he were able and willing to show the faked feelings of an ideal poet whom she called Thorwald, he might go far with her even at this late moment. Mightn't he at any rate in the future, by disguising his real longing for her and by pretending that everything was on an ideal plane and that they were only playing a kind of poetic game, manage to provoke her to such extremes in her physical advances towards him that she would, as it were, accidentally gratify his desires? No, he thought, it would not be possible. Then he disengaged himself and sat up.

She looked at him with a sadness that did not seem voluntary. She said at last, 'If only we had met each other two years ago we might have had a wonderful *affaire*.'

The thought of it made Alan feel a regret so keen that if he had had to depend on his strength of will he would have been unable to prevent himself from trying to put his arms round her and from begging for her love. What deterred him was his certainty that at the first sign of any advance by him the longing she now showed for him would disappear and she would be happy to repel him. He leant back, farther away from her. He became aware of the sea behind her. Against it she seemed lonely and pathetic. He did not doubt that she genuinely loved him.

'But we must meet again, in London – often,' she said.

'We'd better not. It would make me too miserable.'

He did not go to the motorcoach stop to see her off. He wanted his break with her to be sharp and complete. He recognized that the only alternative to never seeing her again would be for him to become a 'mere platonic cicisbeo', her pet poet whom she could take about with her whenever she wanted and show to her friends. He could not live – or certainly he could not write – like that.

After leaving her he returned to his lodgings and tried unsuccessfully for an hour to continue his poem. The next day he wrote two lines, and the day after that he wrote ten – which was more than he had yet done at one sitting and more than he was able to do on any of the following days. His average during the next fortnight – excluding Mondays, which he regularly took off from writing – was four lines, but during the third week it declined to two and during the fourth to one. There were consecutive days when he made no progress at all. The anxiety symptoms which he had experienced at home before Richard had invited him down to the island, and which had preceded his total failure to get ahead with the first version of his poem, began to come back again when he woke in the mornings.

One afternoon, when he was lifting the latch of the gate under the hawthorn arch on his way out from the garden towards the beach, he abruptly knew that his poem was no good. And he knew clearly why. Its unifying central idea – that only the doomed are good – was a mere resurrection of an idea which he and Richard had toyed with when they had been at the university together. It was immature and it was silly. It was even a retrogression from the distrust of all general ideas which he had felt when writing the first unsatisfactory beginning of his poem. Fear, similar in its sharpness to the fear he had been having on waking in the mornings, caused him to stand still under the hawthorn after he had opened the gate. But a moment later he experienced, strangely, a certain relief. This, he soon understood, was not solely because he would now be at least temporarily freed from the painful struggle of the last few weeks but also because a plan for a third version of his poem had already been half-formed in his mind before he had recognized that the second version was a failure. As he began to walk up the sandy lane he decided he would do what he had originally intended when he had resigned from the school: he would write a Marxist poem.

After allowing himself five days to think the third version out in detail he tried to make a start on it. He was unable to write a tolerable first line. In his effort to be Marxist he produced nothing but platitudinous abstractions. He decided that he ought not to have expected to be able to start on the new version so soon, and that he needed to give himself at least another week to plan it. One morning, more than a fortnight later, when he was on the verandah soon after breakfast, he knew there was no point in his trying any longer to write. What was the use of his sitting out here in the wicker armchair with his notebook open on his lap when he was sure he would fail – as he had failed for the past ten mornings or more – to put down a single line? He had sat here with his legs up and his feet resting against one of the trellised uprights that supported the verandah roof, the soles of his shoes pressing the jasmine where it bushily intruded through the interstices of the woodwork, his uninventive mind alert only in noting such details as how the tortoise on the sun-warmed doormat gulped and blinked its lower eye-lids, or how, when birds were scuffling once in the virginia creeper out of sight above him, a small brownish feather fell slowly to the lawn. But this morning the time had come, he told himself, when he must see his situation as it was and take the needed action. The months of freedom which he had gained at the cost of throwing up his teaching job, and during which he was to have justified his life by becoming the poet he had felt he could become, must be brought to an end. He had wasted them, and now the most reasonable thing he could do would be to send a letter to the scholastic agency indicating that he was on the market again and asking to be notified of posts vacant in schools.

He got out of the wicker chair and opened the glass doors which led back from the verandah into the sitting-room. Another teaching job, he thought, might not be easy to find. He stood staring into the shadowiness of the room, at the bobble-fringed velvety table-cloth and at the oil lamp on it with the white glass shade. His most recent job had not been the only one he had thrown up in order to be free for writing poetry, and when he had last visited the agency he had been told with a suggestion of severity that he would be well advised to stay at his next school for at least five years.

He stepped from the bright verandah into the room and towards the table, searching the cloth with his eyes, unclear of purpose, not yet fully aware that what he wanted was note-paper for his letter to the agency. Unsatisfied, he turned towards the mantelpiece. The large gilt-framed mirror above this, with white swans in green reeds painted on the two lower corners of the glass, showed him a face for which he could have no sympathy. It was the face, he thought, of a self-fancying spoilt darling, of the overvalued son from a bourgeois home who had been unreasonably expected and had himself expected to do something exceptional, to be different from the common crowd, to be a great poet, a genius, whereas the truth very probably was that he had no talent at all, that he was a pampered young or no longer quite so young shirker who considered himself too good for the kind of everyday job in which he might perhaps have been of some slight use to the community. Alan stood peering for more than a minute at his own image; and the detail of its features – the effeminate eyelashes and the long-lipped mouth – increased his dislike and his contempt for it.

An incipient auto-hypnotic dizziness caused him to stop peering. Then he became conscious of himself not merely as a mirror-image but as someone apart from the mirror. He himself, no longer the reflected object but now the living subject standing here in this room in front of this mantel-piece, was the shirker and the failure. Fear grew inside him. The image, though he still saw it, became as indefinite to him as if it had been visually blurred, and all his attention was held by the feeling of anguished helplessness which was steadily and uncontrollably developing in the very centre of his body. It was like despair made physical: it was like a translation into nervous agony of the thought that now he was wholly lost and abandoned and that his dearest hope in life was finished for ever. A dreadful icy or burning pang, sinkingly prolonged, was somewhere in his solar plexus or heart or stomach. He wondered if he was going to fall to the floor, and he hadn't the power to put out a hand and clutch the mantelshelf. But he did not fall. He continued to confront his meaningless image in the mirror. He was incapable of movement, might perhaps remain incapable of it always. Or if he did at length move, and if he went and found the notepaper, and if he succeeded in bringing himself to the point of writing a letter to the agency, and if ultimately in spite of his rolling-stone record some headmaster or board of governors could be gulled by his academic qualifications or, more likely, by his classy public-school education into offering him a teaching post, could he bear once again to live as a schoolmaster? Could he, after the final failure of what he had seemed born for, go back to a job which injured and exhausted even those who had an aptitude for it and which would bring him only degradation and slavery?

He would very much rather be dead. And, as soon as he had thought that, a change came over him. He was not helpless any more. There was at least one thing he would be able and willing to do. Though the life of joy and poetry he had hoped for was lost to him for ever, this didn't mean he must go crawling through years of humiliation and dishonour. He could 'do that which shackles accident and bolts up change'. He could put an end to 'the soul that should not have been born'. He stepped back from the mirror and turned again towards the open glass doors. He could row far out to sea or he could walk up to the highest part of the cliff. The cliff would be quicker and better. But he must go at once or Miss Pollock might come in and ask him something about meals. He went out on to the verandah, and with vigour and almost with hope began walking down the gravel path towards the small white front-gate.

Above the hawthorn arch the sun was already very warm in the marine sky. His mood of determination was abruptly countered and crossed by another, a nostalgic and woeful mood. The sun reminded him of the time when he had first arrived here, a few weeks before. A pain of grief, very different from but no less physical than the pain of fear he had felt in front of the mirror, struck deeply into him. He thought of Richard's letter which had invited him to come down here to live the poetic life. He remembered his first sight of the bay and Richard's leap of welcome when the motor-coach had come to a stop outside the Britannia. As he opened the gate now and walked out into the sandy lane he was quite unaware of which direction he was taking. Actually he turned left, away from the sea and the cliff.

No one else was about in the lane. He had had his breakfast early – as usual – in order to give himself a long morning for poetry, and the holiday visitors were not yet out of their bedrooms. But even if a dozen bathers returning from the sea had been overtaking him now, he might not have noticed them. He was thinking of the evening of his arrival here. Much more clearly than the lane's red-brown surface that he was staring down at and walking upon he saw the moonlit façade of the Britannia and Richard and himself sitting out late under the clinker-built roof of the verandah. The feeling he had had then of being on the point of discovering how to write his poem was re-created so vividly in his memory that he seemed to be experiencing it directly once again. For a moment he even believed, as he had believed then, that it was not deceptive. But the misery of the succeeding weeks of useless struggle to write began very soon to revive in him, and it discredited and drove out the remembered optimism. He became more convinced than ever – though without recovering the zest he had felt when the idea had come to him in front of the mirror – that the one valid action he was capable of now was to kill himself.

He must go up to the cliff and throw himself over. But if this was what he meant to do, why, he asked himself, had he all the time since he had left his lodgings been walking in an inland direction? The narrow road he had taken led across low-lying ground, reedy, sparsely treed and reclaimed from the sea. Here, in June, he had heard the cuckoo change his tune. Here, to the right of the road and on higher ground, was the milch-goat tethered in the wild garden of the house where Peg's aunt lived. He had come here today not to commit suicide but in the absurd hope that Peg might once again be staying in this house. Absurd, because he knew that she was back at work in London and that she wouldn't be likely so soon after her summer holiday to pay her aunt a week-end visit. And the house itself, with the horizontally striped folk-weave curtains half-drawn behind the closed windows of the bedroom where she had slept during her holiday, gave an impression which – though he didn't know why – convinced him that she couldn't be anywhere inside. But even if she had in fact been staying here this week-end, he thought, what good would he have done by asking to see her? She would never have accepted him again as a lover. And yet she would have been ready enough to accept him on her own terms, as a kind of poetic pet whom she could exhibit to her friends. Mightn't that have been worth his while? It was still possible, even though she was not staying with her aunt now. He could write to her. Wouldn't any sort of relationship with her, no matter how abject, be better than losing her altogether? He quoted to himself as he came nearer to the house: 'Hast thou not given me above all that live / Joy, and a little sorrow shalt not give?' How lucky he had been, in spite of the miseries she had caused him, to have known her. He would write to her and she would answer. He would make no demands, would submit absolutely to becoming whatever she wanted to make of him.

Avoiding the front gate, lest the aunt might see him, he approached the garden fence and walked slowly alongside it, trying to get a glimpse into the downstair rooms through the upper shoots of the untrimmed privet hedge. At one point he had a clear view and he saw nothing to suggest that Peg might be there. But the thought that he could write to her and that she would answer him made her seem physically near. In the air around him there was a tension which increased as he walked on. It was like the tension before a lightning flash or before the expected apparition of the ghost on a theatre stage. He knew that in a moment he would see her, not in reality but with the utmost vividness of which his imagination was capable. And now he did see her. She was standing with her sister and her sister's fiancé at the end of the esplanade in the evening, watching the dancers. But when he tried to view her face in closer detail the picture went out of focus, and soon he was unable to imagine what she looked like at all. Nevertheless the brief apparition, perhaps because it was so real-seeming, made him remember what his relationship with her had in actuality been, and made him recognize how intolerable for him any attempt to renew it would be.

He must put away the idea of writing to her, of offering to accept whatever terms of submission she might impose on him. 'But the idea can never have been serious,' he thought, 'because ever since it occurred to me I have been walking up towards the cliff.' He had been walking up here in order to throw himself over. There was nothing to be hoped for from love. But how little that would matter if only he could write poetry again. How little it had mattered at the time when he had broken with her and had afterwards written poetry. Perhaps even now poetry might still be possible for him. He looked at the leaves of a wayfaring-tree by the side of the chalky path a few paces ahead of him, and their extraordinarily crinkled texture was attractive to him. When he came level with the tree he looked again and found the leaves uninteresting. The sudden hope in him that had allowed him to see them as beautiful had quickly died out.

He knew that he would not be able to write poetry again, and he knew what would happen if he forced himself to go on trying. Already when he woke in the mornings – and he woke very early and did not sleep afterwards – he could hear his heart beating hard and then he could not control the trembling that began in his legs and arms. If he went on trying to write, all he would achieve would be a nervous breakdown. He was defeated, a hopeless failure, and the sooner he was destroyed the better.

He found himself remembering the lines from *Othello* which he had quoted to himself more than once during the past few days. He quoted them again now, aloud, as he walked:

> ' "Had it pleased heaven
> To try me with affliction; had they rained
> All kind of sores and shames on my bare head,
> Steeped me in poverty to the very lips,
> Given to captivity me and my utmost hopes,
> I should have found in some place of my soul
> A drop of patience." '

It seemed to Alan that he too, if any disaster whatsoever had overtaken him other than this actual disaster of his failure to write poetry, would have been able to bear it 'well, very well'. But he had been hit at the one point where he was mortally vulnerable. He had been deprived for ever of the thing he loved most of all. He continued quoting aloud:

> ' "But there, where I have garnered up my heart,
> Where either I must live or bear no life,
> The fountain from the which my current runs,
> Or else dries up – to be discarded thence!" '

He missed out, as not so obviously relevant, the lines 'Or

keep it as a cistern for foul toads / To knot and gender in!'
He went on:

> ' "Turn thy complexion there,
> Patience, thou young and rose-lipped cherubin,
> 'Ay, there, look grim as hell!" '

He was now within a few hundred yards of the edge of
the cliff. The chalkland grass, short as the grass of a close-
cut lawn, sloped downwards before him at a steadily increasing gradient, and only the low sea not far beyond it indicated that somewhere out of sight the land came to an
abrupt end. With the recognition that he could reach the
edge in perhaps two minutes or even less there came to him
also the certainty that he would never be able voluntarily
to throw himself over, that he was no more capable of such
an action than he would have been of jumping from the
bottom of the cliff to the top. He told himself that he would
have to find some other method, less sharply horrifying, less
dependent on crude physical movement, some gentler pro-
cess which could be set going almost by the mere intellectual
effort of wishing. But he did not succeed in deceiving himself for long. Soon it became clear to him that the misery
which had made him want to destroy himself had also rotted
away whatever courage he might once have had, and that,
even if he could cease to exist by merely wishing it, he
wouldn't have the strength to wish. He would never kill
himself. He would go on living in much the same state that
he was in at present until some disease brought him to a
natural death. And at this moment he remembered how he
had suggested to Richard after the first open-air dance that
what made the dancers and most of the working inhabitants
of this seaside place seem so fine was that they were doomed.
Now he himself was one of the doomed, and he recognized
the hateful falsity of his suggestion. Only a callous prig, a

sham-poetic fancier of quaintness and deformity, could have discovered anything fine about the premature ageing of beautiful girls, or Basher's pathetic sexual boasting and drunkenness, or the denunciatory madness of the man in the check suit. But worse even than being doomed was knowing that you were doomed, as most of them didn't know they were and as he now knew he was. This was a state in which he could not bear to continue, no matter what action he might have to force himself to take in order to escape from it.

He had come within sight of the edge of the cliff, and he was still walking. The edge was not much more than thirty yards ahead of him. If an act of will was required of him might it not be, he wondered, to prevent him from walking on towards the edge rather than to make him throw himself over? With ten yards of grass in front of him he came to a stop, not knowing whether he did so voluntarily or not. Perhaps the sea had surprised him out of his automatism. The bland, sunny sea, unwrinkled from the horizon inwards towards the very beach below the cliff, looking as though it had never drowned anyone. The black wooden top of a breakwater post, which the water's slow swell and lapse rhythmically covered and uncovered, did, however, for a moment resemble a human head. As he stood watching from so near the cliff-edge, he became convinced that fear had not been the only cause of his failure to throw himself over. He had been deterred also by the desire – and the sea had made him aware of it – to go on living.

He wanted to go on living, but not in the same way as now. 'What can be done to make life bearable?' he thought, as he began walking along the path that ran parallel with the cliff-edge. There was no hope in poetry, nor in love. There was even less hope, if possible, in schoolmastering. But if he went on as at present and did not kill himself he would very soon become insane. Perhaps that would solve the problem. He would take refuge in a fortress of the imagination so impregnable that the vile external world would be unable to touch him. But this idea did not attract him for long: he remembered the palpitations he had been having in the early mornings and how, when his limbs at last stopped trembling, all the feeling went out of them and became concentrated in the middle of his body, and how he then lay helpless, like a house-fly whose legs and wings have been bitten off by a wasp. Madness, if it came, would not be a refuge but an intensification and a perpetuation of his present misery. He must find some other way to escape. And now, as the cliff-path began to slope down to the seaside village from which he had begun his walk, he suddenly believed he had found it.

He would turn for help to religion. Often at the university he and Richard had been amused to imagine themselves becoming bogus rectors with country livings and plenty of literary leisure, but now for the first time he needed religion seriously. He needed a church which he could belong to not as a priest or minister but as the humblest of laymen. Oh why had he kicked against the pricks for so long? Under the shelter of religion he would find release from the dreadful struggle to be a success; and failure instead of being the end of everything would be the beginning of grace. 'In His will is our peace,' he thought. He looked down towards the roofs of the village as he walked and saw higher than most of them the slate roof of the flint-walled Congregational chapel. His grandparents had been Congregationalists, and when as a child he had spent part of his summer holidays at their house he had gone to their chapel on Sunday mornings. He would go to the chapel here next Sunday, and after the service he would ask to have a talk with the minister. He knew the minister by sight, a kind-faced man who was sometimes busy in the front garden of the manse and the skin on whose cheekbones shone no less than the skin on his almost bald and fluff-aureoled head. But Alan had no sooner visually remembered him than he remembered also what it had felt like to go to chapel, and he became aware that he would never be capable of asking to have a talk with him. He would do better to attend some church which would seem wholly strange, such as the Catholic one, visible a few miles inland, with the Italianate tower and windows. Other poets, far better poets than himself, had turned to Rome. The main difficulty would be the first step of getting himself to believe in the premisses on which the Catholic religion was based: after that – so he had read somewhere – he would find that all the rest of it followed on quite logically and reasonably. Yes, but would he ever be able to believe in the premisses? Could he bring himself to go back not only on his grandparents but on the whole progressive intellectual movement which had begun with the Renaissance and the Reformation? Could he really prefer Cardinal Newman and Manley Hopkins to Godwin and Shelley?

How much more easily he could have accepted Marxism than either Catholicism or Congregationalism – if he had not already found that it was of no help to him as a poet. But why hadn't it helped him? Perhaps because he hadn't even begun to be a Marxist yet. 'Philosophers hitherto have merely interpreted the world,' Marx had said: 'the thing is to change it.' To be a Marxist Alan would have to take action in the external world, which meant that he would have to become a Communist. Then there might be hope for him. Communism was the only force in the world which was uncompromisingly on the side of the doomed and against those who wanted to keep them doomed. It was the enemy of his enemies: it aimed at the overthrow of a society which was dominated by poshocrats and public-school snobs and which had no use for the living poets. It demanded that its converts should believe not in the supernatural nor in anti-scientific myths but in man. If he joined the Communist Party he might be able to write poetry again. After all, was there anything surprising about his present failure to write, considering the evasive 'poetic' life he had been trying to lead and his unrealistic attitude to the necessity of earning a living? His poetry had failed because it had been rooted in unreality. If he was to have any hope of writing again he must change his life. But he mustn't join the Communist Party solely in order to be able to write poetry, because if that was his purpose and it once again failed he would fall into a misery even worse than at present, with nothing at all to turn to then for help. He must join the Party for its own sake, make it his supreme interest, set all his hopes on it. Only if he lived rightly might poetry one day come back to him.

He had begun to walk faster, but just before he arrived where the descending cliff-path broadened into a sunken chalky lane a thought came which slowed him. It was that he might never have the nerve to make contact with the Communists. How could he, a bourgeois misfit, a favoured weakling who in spite of his expensive education and many other undeserved advantages had become a wretched failure, presume to ask to associate with people who, though born into sordid and hard conditions, had not succumbed but had fought back, on behalf of the whole class they belonged to, against their exploiters? He would never have the impudence to knock on the door of the Party rooms. Not that he doubted he would be let in and perhaps even welcomed, if he did knock. Other recruits had been accepted from the middle class before now. Even the founders of the movement – Marx, Engels, Lenin – had been of bourgeois origin; though these could hardly be called misfits or failures. But if he joined he would cease to be a failure, would no longer be altogether useless. If he did not join there was nothing before him except madness or death.

He was treading on the flints of the sunken lane. Downward and not very far ahead of him the chalk gave place to the greensand, and a pale brown road curved inland towards his lodgings. 'But I am not ready yet to contact the Party,' he thought. He needed time to get to know more about it and to read more of the Marxist classics. Above all he needed plenty of time to build up his courage again, to purge off the sick demoralization which had come over him during the last two months. 'But I shall never do it so long as I stay at this place,' he told himself. He would have to go home and stay with his parents for a while: he was lucky to have parents who could afford to keep him.

When he reached the brown road at sea-level he looked for a moment towards the near-by beach where a few of the holiday visitors had now arrived after finishing their breakfasts, and he noticed the tarred wickerwork of the lobster-pots which were grouped together high up on the banked shingle; then he turned and began to walk back to his lodgings. He would leave for home tomorrow. He would have to let Miss Pollock know some time this evening. It would be awkward, but he could offer to pay for an extra week or even an extra fortnight, and could explain that someone at home was ill. And soon, preferably before he left, but at any rate not later than after he'd been a fortnight at home, he must write to the agency asking to be notified of posts vacant in schools.

2

THE COMMITTEE ROOMS were in vacated shop premises not very far down a badly lit side-street. Alan had had a glimpse of them from the main road even before the tram which was carrying him came to a stop. Scratched whitewash blanked the lower half of the show windows, and above it election posters were pasted on to the glass. The mere mechanical impetus he got from stepping off the tram was enough to bring him to within a few yards of the doorway, and there was no time for misgivings. He could easily have gone straight into the rooms, but his very confidence that he would have no difficulty about going in made him decide that he could safely postpone doing so for a minute or two. 'I must be properly prepared,' he thought. He did not want to hurry in and to look flustered. He walked past the doorway as though he had not seen it. Immediately he knew that he had made a mistake, had missed an opportunity, and that now a considerable effort of will would be needed to bring himself to do what he must not fail to do.

He would at any rate turn back again before he reached the end of this street, he decided. Under the hazy light from a street-lamp he noticed on one of the large buttons of his overcoat a reflection which was like a yellow spoke in a black wheel and which moved round as he moved forward. Why had he been so stupid as to put on such a bourgeois-looking coat this evening? He had done it for the very bourgeois reason that he had been afraid that if he had worn his fairly disreputable-looking mackintosh he might have caught a cold in this end-of-October weather. And now he would be regarded, when he went into the rooms, as a middle-class interloper; or, worse, he might be suspected of being a police spy or even a runaway private mental patient. But he was thinking nonsense: the men and women inside the rooms would not be ignorant philistines who would jump to all sorts of fantastic conclusions about him – they would be intelligent, politically experienced people who would see him as he was; yes, and who would see through him, would guess the self-regarding quasi-religious motives, the sickly wish for his own salvation, which had brought him to them. This might not cause them to repulse him, but he had the duty to change his attitude towards them. From now onwards his aim must be not to help himself, save his own soul, but to help Communism.

He was passing a big warehouse, with a gamboge-coloured steel derrick fixed to and swung back against the wall high above him, and with a large nipple-shaped tie-head holding a slight bulge in the bricks of the wall. There was a smell as of ammonia or of horse-dung. He slowed his walk along the pavement in order to look at the shadowy building, and, having slowed, he turned. He began walking back towards the committee rooms. His aim must be to help the Communists: and yet what sort of help could he, reduced by failure to a state of self-distrust and timidity, give to them who – as he had read in the *Programme of the Communist International* – were the 'vanguard of the working class', and who belonged to 'a revolutionary organization, bound by an iron discipline'? But perhaps it was not for him to decide whether or not he was capable of being useful to them: it was for them to tell him what, if anything, they required of him. Once again he had been looking at the problem from a wrong, a self-centred viewpoint. The only decision he had to make was that he would go into the rooms and present

45

himself. And now for the second time he was nearing the doorway, and still he had the sense that the problem was not quite solved, that he had not found the argument which would have completely convinced him, that he was not yet fully prepared. Perhaps his best course, now that he had located the rooms, would be to go back to the hotel where he was staying the night and come here again tomorrow. Or if doing this might make him feel even less prepared tomorrow than he was this evening, surely there would be no risk in walking up and down the street once more now? He was very near the door, not knowing whether he would go in or not, and most probably he would have walked past it again, when from the main road a group of raucously singing children came marching, sighted him and seemed by the interested looks on their faces to have summed up his dilemma with precocious perspicacity, or at least to be aware that he would be well worth investigating. He turned and went quickly in through the doorway.

At a long trestle-table in the front room the voluntary helpers were folding leaflets. There was talk-noise and the clatter-kling of a typewriter. Gaslight wheezed from a bracket on the wall, alternately fading and brightening across the surface of a single mantle. Envelopes were stacked in a shabby pram near the window, and behind the table there was a cold anthracite stove stuffed with straw. One of the helpers wore a soiled white neckcloth; another was showing the young boy next to him the proper way to fold the paper; another had had a finger amputated; another, looking towards Alan, was saying, 'I expected a demonstration with a drum and fife band.' An old man sat smoking a pipe and smiling, away from the others, pleased with all this activity around him, in which, however, he took no part. The corners of his oversized overcoat touched the floor, and there was a shiny reddish growth beneath his right ear. At the typewriter a handsome fair-haired young man, whom Alan was later to get to know as Jimmy Anders, tilted his head back gracefully like a pianist. There seemed no likelihood that anyone would come forward to attend to Alan, who stood, flushed and unobtrusive, near the doorway and only just inside the room.

Several of the helpers were aware of him, and so was Ron Spalding, the builder, who continued to address envelopes at an upturned packing-case. From a back room the candidate, Joey Pearson, tough and stocky, came in to search for something. He was followed at heels by Ben Krippatch, a rapidly talking young man with crinkled black hair, and in a more leisurely way by Mike Bainton, thin, curly-headed, whose face had a withdrawn and poetic look about it. Joey Pearson rummaged among a pile of papers. Two boys, grinning slightly, their arms round each other's shoulders, strolled into the room from the street. A sound of singing followed them, but was muted as soon as they shut the door behind them. Alan began to feel that if he stood here much longer waiting for someone to approach him and ask him his business he might become an object of suspicion. Perhaps the first move ought to come from him. He brought himself to the point of looking steadily at Ron Spalding. But Spalding was watching Bainton, who had stepped to the middle of the room and was saying with controlled spite, 'Stubb must have put it away somewhere. I suppose he's gone out again.' Spalding interrupted him without excitement: 'Stubb has been working here since early this morning. He's only just gone out to get something to eat. I daresay you've had three meals today, haven't you?' Bainton sulkily evaded the accusation: 'All right, all right. That's not the point.' Jimmy Anders paused in his typing and shouted furiously, 'Oh for Christ's sake stop arguing, Bainton, you bloody fool.' At this moment Joey Pearson, who had said nothing, found the list of addresses that he and Krippatch and Bainton had been searching for. The rumpus subsided abruptly, leaving no sign that it had ever happened. Ron Spalding stood up and, as one who had had Alan in view for some time but had had other at least equally important things to deal with, came unhurriedly towards him.

'And what can we do for you?'

He spoke with a calm, catarrhal drawl, perhaps with a very slight suggestion of mockery in his tone. He was taller than Alan, formidably self-possessed, lean, wore an enamelled trade union badge in his buttonhole, had narrow dark trousers beneath which wirily strong legs could be guessed at. Alan answered in a hurry, his voice ending shakily, 'I wondered whether I could help in any way this evening.'

It was a sentence he had rehearsed several times before coming into the rooms. Now it sounded blatantly artificial.

'Of course, comrade. Let's see – do you think you could do a spot of canvassing?'

'I'd be glad to have a try at it.'

'It's what we need most at the moment. You've not done any before?'

'I'm afraid I haven't.'

Spalding undisguisedly took a good look at him, went on doubtfully, 'Well, there isn't very much to it. The main thing you want to avoid is getting drawn into long arguments on the doorstep. Of course, that doesn't mean it's sufficient to go from house to house just trying to find out which way they intend to vote – like these paid canvassers employed by some other parties I could mention. We do need to put our Party's policy across.'

Alan, hoping to raise himself a little in Spalding's opinion, dared to say, 'I suppose what matters most is not how many votes the Party collects – though I know,' he added a quick qualification, 'that that's very important too – but how many electors, I mean workers, can have it put to them, perhaps for the first time, that there's only one way out from the present capitalist crisis.'

Though Alan was confident from his recent reading of the Party press that this was the correct line, its unanticipated effect on Spalding was to make him smile a little. However, Spalding said seriously enough, 'There are now two million eight hundred and forty-three thousand unemployed, and the number's going up every week. You know what that means?' He looked hard at Alan, making him feel guilty. 'The capitalist economic system is cracking, though it won't go to pieces until it's pushed. There have been cyclical crises ever since early in the last century, but now after the 'fourteen-to-eighteen imperialist war we've reached the general crisis from which capitalism will never recover.' Alan nodded, to convey that he knew this, but Spalding went on, 'The ruling class naturally tries to solve its problems by directing its main attack against those whom it thinks least able to defend themselves – the unemployed. But it is attacking the employed too, and the only thing that's going to prevent capitalism from reducing us to general starvation will be the united working class hitting back hard and soon, as Engels foresaw in the 'nineties. That's the message we've got to get across – and not only at election times.'

'I thought the May Report recommendation about cutting the unemployment benefit by ten per cent was one of the foulest things,' Alan said, anxious still to show he was not politically ignorant. 'But the sailors' mutiny at Invergordon is a sign that the Government's economies won't be taken lying down.'

The not unfriendly smile returned, seeming to indicate that Spalding had now come to regard Alan as someone at any rate harmless.

'Perhaps as you haven't done any canvassing before we'd better not send you out on your own just yet,' Spalding said. He allowed a noise from the street to catch his attention. 'Excuse me a moment.'

He went over to the door and opened it. The children outside were singing aggressively:

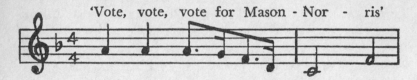

'Vote, vote, vote for Mason - Nor - ris'

They stopped, and Alan heard Spalding say to them, 'That's fine, kids – but you've got the name wrong. It ought to be "Vote, vote, vote for Joey Pearson".' He half-sang the name with a hoarseness that to Alan sounded intimidating. 'Try that. Come on, now; all together.' There was silence. He coaxed them, in a velvety drawl: 'Let's hear what you can do. Come on.' One voice, half-jeering, half-awed, weakly began, 'Vote, vote, vote for Joey . . .' then trailed off into a giggle. 'That's much better,' Spalding told them. 'Now go and sing that outside Mason-Norris's committee rooms in Drood Street. Off you go. There's good kids.'

He shut the door and returned to Alan. 'You could address some envelopes, if you like.'

Spalding made the suggestion hesitantly, as though unsatisfied with it, and he looked relieved when, from across the room, Jimmy Anders intervened: 'Wally and Elsie are going out canvassing in a minute or two. They could take him with them.'

'If you wouldn't mind waiting,' Spalding said to Alan. 'They're in the back room, I think.'

'Thanks. I'll wait for them.'

Spalding gave Alan a deliberately encouraging smile, and said, 'We can do with someone of your class, someone with a cultured voice. You understand what I mean. It'll make a good impression. Some people here have got the idea that our Party's composed of the riff-raff. When I go round they're inclined to slam the door in my face.'

He laughed. There were seborrhoeic blotches on his forehead and on the skin over his cheekbones. His lower lip protruded and exposed long yellow teeth. He looked like a bourgeois caricature of a Red. 'Now I'd better be getting on with the envelopes,' he said.

Alan was left standing by the door. He no longer felt any of the misgivings which had made him hesitate to enter the rooms. None of those things had happened which he had feared might happen. He had not been mistaken for a police spy or a runaway mental patient, he had not been repulsed or even coldly received as a bourgeois interloper. The imagined obstacles which he had unsuccessfully tried to remove by reasoning with himself in the side-street, and which might have prevented him altogether from opening the door if he hadn't been scared into hurriedly doing so by the arrival of the singing children, were decisively overcome now that he had taken the simple action of entering the rooms. He had escaped from imagination into reality; but though there was nothing here to justify the fears he had had of being rejected, neither was there the kind of impressiveness that when he had imagined it had made him regard himself as unworthy to enter. He looked at the faces of the voluntary helpers, at the physical training poster with German wording that was hanging below the gas bracket, and below this at the four disused and unusable tip-up cinema seats with mangy plush and the gilt gone cheesy on their ornamental metal-work, and he had an impression of drabness which he tried to resist. He was ashamed of having it – it seemed bourgeois and disloyal – and he was sure that it must be a false impression, not corresponding with the basic reality, and that a little thought would show him wherein its falseness lay and would enable him to dispel it.

The children were still outside the door and had begun singing as loudly as before, 'Vote, vote, vote for Mason-Norris.' Once again it was Ron Spalding who went to deal with them. He opened the door with a jerk. This time his voice was vigorously threatening: 'Clear off or if I have to get out among you I'll land you some thick ears.'

They scuttled at once, with a noise of nailed boots, and Alan had a glimpse of their disappearing legs in the lamplight. Spalding returned past him from the door to the packing-case without glancing at him.

'What did I hope to find here?' Alan asked himself. Had he imagined that the walls would be made of porphyry, or that the people here would look like some of the young men and girls he had seen in the summer who had been staying up at the big hotel on the cliff – graceful as ancient Greek athletes? But those were members of the ruling class, splendid externally like an iced celebration cake whose interior is crawling with maggots. Or had he expected to meet someone here with the sort of aphrodisiac beauty Peg had?

The thought of Peg was suggested to him by the arrival from the back room of a girl entirely unlike her who wore glasses, had a sullen-looking mouth, and whose fuzzy hair rising to a point above her forehead and jutting out sideways at her temples had the effect of a triangular frame. She was followed by a happy-faced man of about thirty-five, with sallowly chubby cheeks reminiscent of those squeezable rubber faces that used to be made as toys for children. The two of them passed Alan without curiosity and were about to go out of the door into the street when Spalding called to them, 'Just a minute, comrades.' He came over to them and, still without glancing at Alan, said, 'There's a comrade here who would like to help with some canvassing. He's not done any before. Can he go out with you?' Turning at last to Alan, he added, 'This is Comrade Elsie Hutchinson and this is Comrade Wally Ainsworth.' He did not ask what Alan's name was.

Elsie, after looking at Alan with brief friendliness, said, 'Sorry, I can't manage it. We've just come back from doing some, and I'm due to attend a fraction meeting in twenty minutes' time.'

'A fraction meeting,' Ron Spalding said with real severity. 'What business have they to call a fraction meeting now when every Party member in London ought to be giving every spare moment to helping here in the election?'

'Well, it's urgent. It's about this Tom Puttick affair.'

'What Tom Puttick affair?'

'Oh, you haven't heard? Last Saturday morning Tom went to see that old twister Sweetenham about arranging an emergency General Meeting, and while Tom was in the office Sweetenham went out for a moment to fetch a file from somewhere, and there on the table Tom spotted a sheet of paper with a complete list of all the Party members in the Union. There wasn't a single name old Sweetenham hadn't got hold of. So Tom just picked up the paper and put it in his pocket.' As Elsie described this incident the sullenness her face had shown in repose gave way to a liveliness which was almost gay and which Alan would not have supposed her capable of. 'When Sweetenham came back into the room he accused Tom of having taken the list, and Tom admitted he had, but justified himself on the grounds that it ought never to have been compiled. Then Sweetenham got very hot under his starched collar and said Tom's action was tantamount to theft, so Tom walked out of the office with the list still in his pocket; and we're holding this fraction meeting to decide what to do about it now.'

Ron Spalding was interested enough to ask, 'And what do you think your meeting will decide?'

'I don't know. Pinching the list was certainly going a bit far. Just like Tom. He may be told to give it back again.'

'I hope not,' Spalding said. He turned to Ainsworth. 'Well, Wally, it looks as though you'll be taking our comrade round without Elsie.'

Ainsworth seemed to wish he could agree, but he too –

53

though more diffidently than Elsie – had to mention another engagement: 'I promised my Old Dutch I'd be home by eight this evening.'

'Oh, come on, Wally,' Spalding jollied him, 'you can't get away with an excuse like that.'

Now it was Elsie's turn to be severe: 'If he's promised his wife he'd go home he ought to go home. After all, he's been out late every night for the last fortnight doing Party work. I think we're far too casual in the Party sometimes about comrades' domestic obligations.'

Spalding chose to accept her rebuke. 'All right, Elsie. But he oughtn't to have promised, particularly at a time like this.'

'I don't agree,' Elsie argued. 'The trouble is it's always "a time like this" in the Party, because the political situation is always urgent. As a result, some comrades who are first-rate politically behave like complete reactionaries in their own homes and don't show their wives any consideration at all.'

'Such comrades could never be first-rate politically,' Spalding said with emphasis, as though re-asserting his authority. He added rather sententiously, with an eye on Alan, 'If we don't win over the women the battle is more than half lost. It's no use a comrade complaining he can't get on with his wife because she disapproves of his political activities. It's up to him to show an interest in whatever she's interested in, and then she may begin to take a different view of his going out to meetings in the evenings and he may get her to come with him sometimes. A male comrade who sets his wife against him by neglecting her and the kids for "politics" cancels himself out politically.'

Wally Ainsworth said, smiling, 'There's no risk of me and the Old Dutch coming to blows, not over politics nor anything else. I learnt the lesson from my own mum and dad. They lived a cat and dog life together. Sunday dinner was the worst time. The Old Man had had just a little too much beer at the pub and he didn't quite appreciate her nice cooking. Then she let fly. He was slower to get really going . . .' Wally saw that Spalding was beginning to look impatient, and he came to the point. 'I think I can put it right with the Old Dutch if I'm a bit late this evening.'

'Good,' Spalding said. He stared at the wall near the door and asked loudly, 'Now where's that list showing the streets we've already canvassed? It ought to be pinned up here.' The old man in the oversized overcoat took his pipe out of his mouth and said unconvincingly, 'Stubb's got it.' Spalding, annoyed and at a loss for a moment, thought of a temporary solution: 'Perhaps as Wally doesn't want to be home too late it would be better if the two of you took round some of these handbills.' He reached towards a pile of them on the floor, and gave a thick wad to Wally and another to Alan. 'That's if our comrade here has no objection.'

'Oh no, that's quite all right,' Alan said quickly.

'I suggest you do Chadwick Mansions to begin with. After that Hemming Street, if you've any left over. Well, cheerio for now.'

He turned from them to the more important business of discovering who had so unnecessarily and inconveniently removed the marked list of voters from the wall, and of putting it back there immediately. His mere physical posture after he had stepped to the middle of the room and before he spoke – his legs apart, wirily rigid, and his torso moving slowly round from the hips carrying with it his erect head and the spotlighting glance of his serious eyes – was enough to get him the attention of everyone in the room. Alan was going towards the door which led into the street before Spalding began the investigation into the missing list, but he carried with him the impression that the person responsible would not long remain undiscovered and would be made to regret his action. And Spalding, Alan felt, was some-

55

one to be feared not only by the casual and ill-disciplined among members and helpers of the Party, but still more by the ruling class, who would never be able to daunt him; and even if they imprisoned or in the last resort killed him, others like him would rise to take his place, since the fecundity of the working class in producing leaders was inexhaustible.

Wally went out of the door first, followed by Elsie, and last by Alan, who couldn't help being conscious that the order of precedence demanded by bourgeois politeness was being violated, but who quickly told himself that he now repudiated such politeness. From the moment when the three of them stepped into the side-street, under the iron lamp which cast rays of shadow as well as of hazy light, Alan's feelings about the room he had just left were changed. The impression of drabness which he had been ashamed of having was removed, and he recognized both the greatness and the beauty of the people he had come among. He didn't idealize their outward appearance or their abilities, didn't now in the comparative darkness of the street see the gaslit room in vivid brightness – as one might see an illuminated object against the darkness of the eyelids after closing the eyes. He saw these people once again as he had imagined them before he had entered the room, and as he had temporarily been unable to see them when confronted by their actuality, and he saw them the more clearly for having been actually in their presence: they were the representatives of the future. From their eyes, bleared or bright or set in undernourished faces marked with skin disease, there looked out the life of the future, that better and beautiful life on earth which – through their efforts and the efforts of others like them – would eventually come. It was this, Alan thought, that made them even to the outward view so immeasurably more impressive than the gracefully-bodied, well-dressed young men and women he had seen in the summer (yes, or than

Peg herself), beneath whose bourgeois exterior the only future that could be detected was one of decay.

He was walking next to Elsie on the inside of the pavement, and Wally on the other side of her was telling her – so far as Alan could overhear – about a Tenants' League meeting. Wally, it seemed, was secretary of the League. Alan sensed they were not so much ignoring him, deliberately or otherwise, as trying to tide over an uncertainty they felt about what to say to him. As soon as they stopped talking to one another he said, 'Do you think Joey Pearson has a good chance of being elected?'

'Yes,' Wally said, 'if all those who've told us they'll vote for him do.'

'No,' Elsie disagreed. 'He hasn't really a hope. It's the first time the Party has put up a candidate here, and Mason-Norris has been returned as Liberal Member for the last twenty years.'

'Every Christmas he gives a sack of coals to each family where the husband's unemployed,' Wally explained. 'He must be pretty wealthy to be able to do that.'

'But the election does at least give us' – Alan dared the inclusive pronoun – 'the opportunity of doing some useful propaganda for the Party.'

'You're right there,' Wally said. 'That's the main thing. It would be good to get Joey in of course, because from the floor of the House he could publicize our policy. But winning seats in Parliament won't ever bring us Socialism, not even if we was to win a majority. The ruling class'll see to that. Parliament may look democratic – that's just what they want it to look – but after all it's only an organ of the bourgeois state, like the law courts or the civil service or the police or the armed forces.'

'If we did get a majority,' Alan said, 'the ruling class would soon use non-parliamentary methods to protect their interests.'

'Yes,' Wally said, 'and then it would be plain for all to see that what they call democracy is really disguised dictatorship, as Lenin pointed out in *State and Revolution*. What first opened my eyes was the mounted police when I was on the National Hunger March nearly ten years ago in January 'twenty-two.'

'You mean the baton charges?'

'Yes. We were treated as real "criminals of want"; and I've taken several bashings since then, and there's this to be said for them, that they've all helped to knock Lenin's lesson into my head. We've now had three National Hunger Marches – I've not been in the others, but I'm sure enough there isn't a man who's marched in them who has any illusions left about the Government's impartiality between rich and poor. It all contributes to bringing the day nearer when the workers as a whole realize that the bourgeois state machine must be got rid of.'

'The National Unemployed Workers' Movement seems to be making very good progress at present.'

'It is. And it needs to be, because now the really big battles are beginning, which will make past struggles against such things as the Blanesburgh Committee Report and the Anomalies Bill and Mondism seem minor skirmishes in comparison. This time the ruling class – we hope – is going to get a real shaking, as during the General Strike, which could have led on to the Revolution if we hadn't been betrayed.'

'I think we're farther off from the Revolution than we once seemed to be,' Elsie said. Then she asked Alan, 'You didn't come to the committee rooms yesterday did you, comrade?'

'No. I've not been before, but I'll be coming again tomorrow.'

'Are you a Party member?'

'I'm afraid not,' Alan said humbly.

'Have you ever thought of joining?'

The question made him feel much as an average middle-class young man would have felt if asked, 'Have you ever thought of trying to get yourself invited to the Garden Party at Buckingham Palace?'

'No, I haven't.'

'Why not?'

'Well, I suppose it's because I don't consider I'm' – he rejected the word 'worthy', as this might sound religious and too grovelling – 'it's because I've had no experience of the sort of work the Party does. I'm not yet fit to become a member. What I should like would be to be allowed to take part in some of the activities as a non-member for a time so that I could find my feet, as it were.'

'I think you're right. It's a good sign not to be in too much of a hurry to join. Often those comrades who are quickest in are also quickest out.'

He was aware that this was the first time she had spoken to him without asking a question. She didn't seem, however, to have been interrogating him from motives of suspicion like an intelligence officer, or from motives of personal curiosity either. Her interest in him, though friendly, was impersonal, the interest of a Party member in a possible recruit to the Party.

They had been walking along the pavement of the main road and were now passing across the entrance of a blind alley where the light came chiefly from cone-shaped tin naphtha-containers which hung on hooks above trestle-supported wooden vegetable stalls. Fallen cabbage leaves and pieces of torn blue tissue paper were littered on the cobbles beside the kerbstone. A dark-faced full-bosomed woman wearing a black skirt was helping two men to clean up. The sight of her may have had something to do with a change which at this moment took place in Alan's attitude towards Elsie, whom he began to be conscious of more as a girl and less as a Party member. He warned himself that he was in danger of sliding back into his old bourgeois habit of regarding women primarily from a sexual and romantic point of view; nevertheless, he couldn't resist a desire to confide in Elsie, to talk to her about himself in a way he mightn't have talked – at any rate not after so short an acquaintance – if she hadn't been a girl.

'I should have come along to the rooms before now,' he said, 'but I don't live in London. I travelled up this morning, because I had to go to be interviewed this afternoon for a job at a school near here.' The strict truth, however, was that he would never have had the heart, after several unsuccessful applications for jobs at other schools, to come up for this interview if his primary object hadn't been to make contact with the Party in London. 'The job won't start till after Christmas. I don't know yet whether I've got it, though I think I've a good chance, but I ought to hear tomorrow or the day after. That's partly why,' he was again not quite truthful, 'I'm staying on here for a bit.'

'So you're a teacher. I am too,' she said. 'What school is it you're applying for?'

'Condell's. It's a Secondary school.' Afraid that even though he had used the colourless word 'Secondary' he might be suspected of regarding himself as a cut above the ordinary Elementary teacher, he added satirically, 'It calls itself an Academy and likes to pose as a public school.'

'I know the place by reputation. It's certainly a bit of a snob establishment. Mine's an Elementary – Fyson's Road School.'

They had arrived at a cross-roads with traffic lights. Here Elsie was to leave them to catch a bus which would take her to her fraction meeting. At the pavement corner, where the three of them had come to a stop, it seemed that she and Wally were trying to edge away from Alan, so he moved back from them in case they might have something to say which they would prefer him not to overhear. He stood looking at the traffic lights, and he remembered the opening lines of a poem which about three weeks before, heartened by his decision that he would go up to London and make contact with the Party at election time, he had been able to begin to write:

> *'Dead slow. Stop.'*
> Who said that?
> Only the robot
> In his little tin hat
> Winking at the cross-roads.

The rest of the poem would make clear that the one-legged robot with his three eyes – menacing red and bullion golden and boom green – allegorically represented the capitalist economic system with its periodic slumps and stoppages which the capitalists wished to regard as not inherent in the system but which nevertheless recurred with iron inevitability. There were difficulties, however, about working out in detail the parallel between the lights and the system, and Alan had got stuck half-way through the third verse. But now, suddenly, with a certainty which took no account of the particulars of the problem, yet which seemed to comprehend it as a whole, he knew he would be able to go on with the poem. More than that, he knew – and in this his knowledge seemed to come from the sight not only of the traffic lights but also of the dark purple sky of London above these – that after the present poem he would be able to write many other poems.

Elsie turned to cross the road, saying goodbye to Wally very gaily but to Alan – so he thought – very curtly and coldly. Wally said, 'We go this way. Not far. Chadwick Mansions are at the bottom of the road.'

His voice suggested a shyness which hadn't been noticeable when Elsie had been with them. There was no coldness in it, but Alan, who was looking at the sky ahead over the railway viaduct that ended the street they were now walking in, did not try to start a conversation. The luminous purple was like an emanation from all the thousands of houses and flats in this district. Redness was mixed with it, as though symbolizing a revolutionary ardour prevalent among the hundreds of thousands of people living here. 'Suppose that I were suddenly to see red flags flying from all the roofs,' Alan imagined. Excitement mounted in him. The Revolution might be very near. He knew he had no real grounds for thinking so, but just because he knew this he supposed there could be no harm in not trying to check the exultation he felt. It was so strong that when they came to the Mansions the prospect of having to distribute handbills didn't make him in the least nervous.

To the right two railway viaducts intersected, and to the left were the Mansions, one side of which must – Alan thought – look directly on to the railway. Wally led him through an archway into a courtyard and then to the base of some concrete stairs.

'You do these and I'll do the next ones over there and then you'll do the next beyond mine and so on,' Wally said.

The side walls up the stairs were of dark-brown glazed brick. Alan did not meet anyone either when he was going up or when he was coming down. He had some difficulty in getting the handbills into the front-door letter-slits and he feared that he might be crumpling the paper rather badly and perhaps even tearing it. At the bottom of the stairs Wally, who was waiting for him, guessed what had been delaying him and said, 'It's best to fold them first. Here's how I do it. You see? Then when I push them in with my middle fingers they're like a kind of glove.'

The advice was fortunate for Alan, because from behind one of the doors on the next staircase as he was pushing a folded handbill through the letter-slit a dog, that had come up silently, jumped and bit fiercely at the paper and just failed to catch his finger-tips. As he proceeded to other doors and other staircases he found considerable variety in the resistance presented by the flaps covering the slits: some were quite loosely hinged, but some were held down tightly by unnecessarily strong springs, whereas others consisted of bits of felt put there to keep out the draught after the metal flap had become broken – and these caused him no difficulty at all. At one of the flats he accidentally banged the knocker below the letter-slit, then was agitated to find that the flap was one of the stiffest he had yet encountered, and before he could get rid of the handbill the door was opened by a pallid child, who, however, seemed more alarmed than Alan was and had evidently been left alone in the flat. At another flat – it was near the top of the last staircase he went up that evening – the door was opened almost as soon as he began to push the handbill through the slit, and a young working man with a handsome brick-red face stood looking at him.

'It's a handbill about the election,' Alan explained.

A girl came up from behind and stood beside the young man. The flicker from a fireplace that Alan could not see because it was round a corner, and that gave out the only light there was in the room, was reflected on her cheeks. She seemed no more than seventeen and was extremely beautiful, with loose curly brown hair which looked as though it had just been tousled and with bright eyes in which nevertheless there was a hint of languor. The couple stared mildly at Alan, who had no option but to continue, 'I am taking these round on behalf of Joey Pearson, the Communist candidate. I hope he will have your vote.'

They said nothing, and their stare had neither approval nor disapproval in it. They were half in a dream. Perhaps he had interrupted them in their love-making: they had been sitting together by the fire and then had been going towards the bedroom when they heard him at the door. Now they only wanted him to leave them by themselves. He said 'Good-night' and went on downstairs to the door of the next flat. The image of the girl was in his consciousness as he went, becoming increasingly vivid, lovelier, filling him with an admiration which was all the keener for being mixed with a regret that no girl so beautiful as she was had ever wanted to marry him. The middle class, he thought, was more restricted – by snobbery, education, convention and by its smaller numbers – in the choice of a mate than the working class was. But a time would come when there would be no more classes and no more racial barriers, and then every man and woman would be really free to choose a suitable mate. This idea made him very happy as, coming out into the courtyard after delivering a handbill at the last of the flats which Wally had allocated to him, he went over to where Wally stood waiting.

'Hemming Street next,' Wally said, smiling. 'We go along by the railway for a bit.'

When they had passed through the archway and out into the street again, Alan, wishing in his happiness to help Wally to start talking to him, said without thinking, 'It's jolly cold this evening.'

Immediately he was aware of his own overcoat and of Wally's lack of one. But to change the subject now might make Wally regard this remark as a sign of self-centred obtuseness, so Alan went on baldly, 'You must feel it without a coat.'

'I do. I'm not wearing a vest either.'

Alan could only say, 'Oh.'

Wally unconvincingly added, 'I can't wear wool next to the skin. It makes me come out in a rash all over the chest and back.'

This might be true, Alan thought. But now an incident occurred which excused him from offering any further comment. Under one of the broad arches of the railway viaduct

64

there was a cabinet-maker's workshop lit up and open to the street along which they were passing. Three men were inside, working late: one of them, youngish-looking and nearest to the pavement, was busy planing a plank of wood. Wally handed to this man, who stopped working to take it and look at it, one of the handbills, and said in a matter-of-fact way as though he knew the man and his political opinions well, 'Just to remind you, brother, to vote on Wednesday for Joey Pearson, the Communist candidate.'

Quickly from the back of the shop a middle-aged man, hot-faced, thick-necked, red-headed and with wood-shavings sticking in his hair, which was closely curled like the fleece of a Persian lamb, came forward to protect the others from contamination, saying, 'We don't have anything to do with Communists here.' He pronounced it 'Communists'. The younger man, before bending to his work again, gave Wally and Alan an amused smile. Wally did not attempt to argue with the lamb, but, looking amiable he turned and walked on and was promptly followed by Alan.

'There are a lot of these small employers round about here,' Wally said, 'and they're among the worst. This is a great district for cabinet-makers.'

'Is cabinet-making your job too?' Alan asked, not because he had any good reason for supposing so but because he wanted to know, without directly asking, whether or not Wally was unemployed.

'No, that's one of the jobs I've never done. I've worked on the railway – track maintenance. I've worked in a gas-works. I've had a year abroad in San Francisco. I've been a buck navvy. Now I'm on Public Assistance. My last job was commissionaire at the Alma Cinema.'

'In Oxford Street?'

'That's it. Yes, I wore one of them uniforms with braid on and a cap with a shiny peak and all the rest of it. While I was there I first met a young chap from Cambridge –

Symington his name was – who got me interested in philosophy. Do you know him?'

'No, I'm afraid not.'

'It was he who put me on to Feuerbach and Dietzgen.'

'You've read both those?'

'Some of both, with his help. I've tried Hegel too, but couldn't get far, not even with help. Now I'm reading Adoratsky on Dialectical Materialism. Pretty good. Have you come across it?'

'Yes, I liked it. But the book that first got me interested was Plekanov's *Fundamental Problems of Marxism.*'

'That's a grand book,' Wally eagerly agreed, 'though they say now it has its faults. But that, with Lenin's *Materialism and Empirio-Criticism* – well, you couldn't find a better introduction anywhere to Dialectical Materialism.' He suddenly remembered the handbills. 'Gor, here we are nearly half-way down Hemming Street. We'd better make a start. You do this side and I'll cross over and do the other.'

At the very first house that Alan approached he had such difficulty with the metal flap of the letter-slit that he decided to try pushing the handbill in beneath the door. A mat on the inside of the door was resilient, and before he could by-pass its resistance he noticed another folded piece of paper protruding across the doorstep. There was no light either from the hallway or from the windows of the house. He stealthily picked up the paper and saw that it also was a handbill. When he was back again on the pavement he unfolded it and was surprised to find it exactly similar to the handbills he had been distributing. Not immediately grasping the significance of this duplication, he went over and showed it to Wally, who said, 'This street's already been done.' He seemed neither annoyed nor relieved nor surprised. 'How many've you got left?'

'Just this lot,' Alan said.

'Let me have them. I'll return them to the rooms. Tomorrow, not this evening. Now I'll be able to get back in good time to the Old Dutch. Which way are you going?'

'To the main road.' Alan was unintentionally curt, scared at the thought of the impression he would make if he admitted that he was staying the night at a fairly well-known and far from cheap hotel.

'I go along Hemming Street,' Wally said, but stood still on the pavement, looking into Alan's face. 'If you don't mind me saying so, you're very like young Symington.'

'Am I?'

'Short chap, he was. I don't know what's become of him.' Wally waited, as if hoping that Alan would help him out, then went on, 'I got a lot from him – what with discussions we used to have and the books he recommended.' Again a pause. 'It was after meeting him I started my notebooks in which I copy out extracts from the books I read. He used to have a look at them now and then.'

At last Alan, who had obtusely been unable to believe that he could appear to Wally as someone capable of being useful to him, dared to ask, 'Perhaps later on – if I get this job I'm trying for in London – you would let me see them?'

'I'd be very glad to, comrade.'

Real gladness was in Wally's face, a glow beneath the skin of his sallowly plump cheeks. His dark brown eyes seemed to glisten. 'Cheerio till tomorrow, comrade,' he said.

'Yes, I'll be along in the evening,' Alan said and added with warmth after a very slight diffident hesitation, 'comrade.'

When they had separated and as Alan was walking back towards the main road he thought of Wally's parting look. It had been glad, but not simply because Wally hoped Alan would help him in his philosophic reading: it had been glad also with the gladness of sympathetic admiration, as though Wally fully understood the feelings of unworthiness that had almost prevented Alan from contacting the Party,

67

and honoured him for those feelings but still more for having in spite of his bourgeois upbringing come over to the side of the workers. A tram, lit up inside, passed over the cross-roads towards which Alan was going. He remembered his arrival earlier in the evening and the fears he had had of being rejected. Now he had not merely been accepted but had already been able to do something to help, though it had been no more than distributing handbills. Soon he would be able to do much more than that, would find a use for his intellectual training: he, the incompetent and the failure, would have something to give even to men like Wally from whom in practical organizational matters, such as running a Tenants' League, he could only be a faltering learner. He was no longer isolated, no longer worthless. He had found a place among people who wanted him and with whom, however inferior he might be to them in courage and in strength of will, he felt an affinity because they were members of the lower class to which he too, the would-be poet, in a sense belonged. He would do all he could to be worthy of them and of the great cause for which they were working. From now on he would be dedicated to the Revolution.

The word 'dedicated' had no sooner come into his thoughts than it made him regard with momentary suspicion the idea which it was representing. Because of its bogus-chivalric imperialist-religious connotations and of the sort of persons who liked using it, he and Richard could never hear it spoken or see it in print without wanting to squirm, and they would almost have preferred to lose their right hands rather than put it into their own poems. Didn't the fact that he had, in thought, used it now suggest there was a falsity about his decision to devote himself wholly to the cause? No: on the contrary, his decision gave the word a new content, purged it of its loathsomeness, renewed it. Richard would understand this. But would Richard, who had seemingly solved his own problems at present by going to live abroad, ever want to join the movement himself? Almost certainly not; and yet he would approve of Alan's joining, would see that there was no other way to get him writing poetry again. And not only would Alan recover the power to write, he would also have a new and better attitude towards teaching, when he got back to it, would seriously try to be an educator. From now on his whole life would be changed.

'A day of bliss,' he thought as he stood waiting for a tram that would take him back to the hotel. At last he had emerged from the quag of self-questioning. He knew how he must live and die. He saw now what it meant to be a Communist. A mere change of heart, a mere revolution in the soul, would not make a Communist. Only constant political action could do that. If he lived his external life rightly, kept unfailingly in touch with the Party and worked for it, there would be no need to worry about his soul or his poetry.

3

AT THE beginning of break Alan forgot as he came into
the lobby of the common-room that he had just had an
unpleasant teaching period with the Middle Fourth Form,
and he remembered that earlier in the morning he had
pinned up on the common-room notice-board – when for a
moment no one else had seemed to be about – a leaflet
announcing a coming meeting organized by the Educational
Workers' League. Now, reaching to hang his M.A. gown on
one of the hooks ranged along the dark brown Gothic-looking
panels of the lobby wall, he was glad he had after two months'
delay at last made a start on political work at this school;
but also he was apprehensive about how his colleagues might
react to the leaflet. He remained for a minute in the lobby,
facing the arched narrow window whose opaque glass was
sepia-coloured as though by the tobacco smoke of many years,
then went over and pushed open the door into the common-
room.

A cigarette-smoky brightness confronted him and in it, to
the left of the door, he saw five or six of his colleagues standing with their backs towards him and looking at the notice-
board. Among them was Brook, who would be more likely
than any other member of the common-room to comment in
a loudly hostile way on the leaflet, but who as yet was reading the notices in silence. A lean, long-armed, schoolboy-com-
plexioned former Fives Blue with an Oxford degree in
theology, he turned away from the notice-board and with

elbow held high in front of him demonstratively pinched his nose between finger and thumb. The gesture, however, had nothing to do with Alan's E.W.L. leaflet: it was directed at another colleague who had come into the room behind Alan – a middle-aged red-haired History master named Gus Chiddingfold, with whom Brook carried on a permanent semi-serious quarrel. He was reputedly related to an obscure Scottish aristocrat and had a barrel-shaped figure which was so squat as to make him seem broader almost than he was tall. Chiddingfold with feigned wonder noted Brook's nose-holding and said in a sweet-toned aside, 'He ought to have stayed longer in the lavatory.'

Brook came back at him quickly and gruffly, '*You* ought never to have *left* it.'

Laughter from those who overheard this exchange was too assertive for Chiddingfold to be able to make an audible verbal retort, so instead he pointed a forefinger at Brook and with protruding belly and thrown-back head silently shook all over in exaggerated mimicry of his mirth. Brook, conscious of a victory so decisive that he could now afford to leave Chiddingfold alone for a while, went on, 'Talking of lavatories, I've never had a good word yet to say for our Musical Director, but this morning when I was sitting in the rears as costive as a coot the orchestra suddenly started up and it went through me like a dose of salts.'

Alan saw that one of his colleagues, by name Barnet, was still facing the notice-board and was not laughing. An intelligent Jew, capable of invective that was even more colourful and certainly more wounding than Brook's, he as a rule avoided contact as far as possible with Brook, who in turn was wise enough not to try out any badinage on him; but the reason for Barnet's present silence might well be that he was reading the E.W.L. notice and was interested in it. He more than any other member of the teaching staff had seemed to Alan, judging by signs so far observable during

71

two-thirds of the school term, to hold opinions not absolutely unsympathetic to Communism and even to be a possible future recruit to the Party. However, Barnet now made no remark as he moved away from the notice-board, and his face did not indicate that he had read anything unusual there. Perhaps, Alan thought, the wording of the leaflet had been too non-sectarian, too respectable-seeming to arouse any feeling either for or against. As though casually, Alan went to have a look. The leaflet was no longer on the notice-board.

Had Brook torn it down? Fortunately there was another in Alan's locker and he would pin it up soon – or, better, would leave it lying on the common-room table – when break came to an end. The next period was a free one for him and he would be able to spend it here. Meanwhile he would read the newspapers. He went and picked up one of them from a dingy armchair, and sat down. As usual, the mere sight of the headlines and photographs was enough to nauseate and infuriate him, but before long, like someone sucked down into a bog, he was in the middle of an article that gave advice to wives on how to keep their husbands faithful to them.

At the end of break, after most of his colleagues had gone out to their classrooms, he went to his locker to find the other E.W.L. leaflet. Aldershaw, the Second Master, was still in the common-room, so Alan decided not to put the leaflet on the table just yet: instead he brought out a pile of History exercise books which he ought soon to correct, and took them back to the armchair. He had begun to glance through the first of them when Aldershaw came over and stood in front of him.

'Is this yours?'

Aldershaw held out an E.W.L. leaflet, presumably the one that had been on the board. He spoke with restrained disgust.

'Yes.' Alan, assuming that Aldershaw's disapproval was political, was a little defiant.

'Well, we have an unwritten rule here that nothing should be put up on the common-room board unless the Second Master's permission has been obtained first. It's really just a matter of avoiding congestion: we've more than enough notices already. And in no circumstances should anyone other than the Head or myself put up anything on that part of the board which is reserved for the Headmaster's notices.'

'I didn't know I'd done that.'

'There's a large oblong strip of white paper pinned above the Head's section of the board and it has the word "Headmaster" printed on it in large black letters.' Aldershaw said this with a hint of incipient jocularity, not offensively.

'Yes, I can see it all right now,' Alan said, feeling foolish. 'I'm extremely sorry.'

Aldershaw sat down in the armchair next to his. 'Luckily I removed your notice before the Head had an opportunity to read it. That word "teachers" which appears so prominently in it would have been like a red rag to him. We're all "schoolmasters", of course, in our type of school.' Aldershaw gave Alan what appeared to be a glance of collusion. 'I remember there was a chap from Cambridge who applied for a job here about a year ago, but he had the misfortune to address the Head as Mister on the envelope instead of Esquire, and, though he had a very good degree, he was turned down flat.'

Alan laughed, perhaps a little too eagerly. Aldershaw went on less genially, 'What is this Educational Workers' League of yours?'

'It's the organization which is calling the meeting,' Alan said non-committally.

'Yes, I grasped that. But who exactly are they? What are their political affiliations?'

'They're a group of teachers – women as well as men, so

they couldn't call themselves schoolmasters even if they wanted to – who are interested in the present economic situation.' Alan tried hard not to sound disingenuous.

Aldershaw gave him a wily and sceptical smile. 'I see that the subject for discussion at the meeting is advertised as being "Teachers and the Crisis".' He looked distastefully at the leaflet. 'Don't you think "crisis" is rather a big word?'

'It's rather a big thing. Nearly three million unemployed in Britain, ten million in America, five million in Germany, and so on all over the world.'

'I don't deny that large numbers of men are for various reasons out of work. What I'm objecting to is the putting about of catchwords like "the Crisis". If they're repeated often enough they can help to produce the very condition which their propagators assume to be already existing.'

'So you would say that the crisis, in so far as there is one, is psychologically caused?'

'Partly, and partly it's caused by the fact that we've been progressing too fast and have been enjoying a higher standard of living than we can as yet afford. But if by the word "crisis" you mean to suggest, as I suspect you do, that our economic system' – Aldershaw's tone here was sardonic, as though he disbelieved that the economic system was anything other than a phrase – 'is heading towards a final collapse, then I deny there's a crisis in that sense at all. Though no doubt the organizers of your meeting fervently hope for one in that sense.'

Alan ignored Aldershaw's last sentence, and said, 'I've read somewhere that business men in America are wearing badges in their buttonholes with the inscription "We don't talk Crisis". That seems to me complete superstition. Psychological factors may help to accelerate the crisis, of course; but they could never be its primary cause.'

'Why not? I think you're putting the cart before the horse. I should say that psychological factors such as loss of confi-

74

dence were primary and that economic or social factors such as Stock Exchange prices or unemployment figures were the effects and not the causes.'

'Then I don't see—' Alan hesitated before taking the risk of mentioning the name which he had had in mind almost from the beginning of this argument – 'how Marx was able to foretell in the middle of last century that the capitalist system would continually be running into crises which would get worse and worse as time went on. He didn't base his forecast on an analysis of men's psychological make-up but on a study of economic reality.'

Aldershaw was looking closely at him, through glasses which seemed exceptionally large and slightly misty. 'I rather think that your friend Marx was a little bit out in several of his prophecies. As for instance when he foretold that the Revolution would take place first in one of the industrially most advanced countries. However, we don't for some reason hear so much from Marxists about that kind of prophecy.'

Surprised that Aldershaw knew at least something about Marx, Alan didn't at once suspect him of a provocative intention. He allowed himself to be led on: 'We do hear from them about that particular anticipation. In fact' – Alan was about to mention Lenin and Stalin, but prudently refrained – 'twentieth-century Marxists have expressly said that Marx was wrong there – he could hardly help it since in his lifetime the age of imperialism hadn't really begun – and that the capitalist system must break at its weakest not its strongest point. Which explains why the Revolution came first in Tsarist Russia and not in Germany or France or England.'

Aldershaw smiled, knowingly and even pityingly rather than intolerantly, as though to convey that he had heard this sort of nonsense many times before. He gazed, saying nothing, at Alan, who, gazing back, became aware that

Aldershaw's nose was very large, triangular in shape, inquisitive, its minutely pitted skin having the texture though not the colour of a slightly shrivelled strawberry. At last, in the tone of one who was determined to help a younger and less experienced man to see reason, Aldershaw began, 'I used to hear a good deal of that kind of talk from a young chap who came into the Labour Party for a month or two and then left to join the Communist Party.'

'Are you in the Labour Party?' Alan asked, hoping that by moving to the attack he might ward off a question he felt coming about his own political allegiance.

'Oh no. At least, not now. Had to give up political work several years ago – when Sugden retired and I became Second Master in his place. I found that one job was quite enough for me. Not that I ever spent a lot of time on politics – at any rate not during term-time.' He gave Alan a sharp look. 'But to come back to what I was going to say. Marxism – it's hopelessly out of date, mid-Victorian. Life just hasn't worked out in accordance with the old man's rigid dogmas. Take for instance his assumption about the increasing pauperization of the working class. Utter bunkum. They're better off today than they've ever been.'

'Recent malnutrition statistics' – Alan was annoyed with himself for not being able to be more precise – 'hardly seem to bear that out. There must be a large number of children, not to mention their mothers, who aren't getting enough to eat.'

'Granted. And in ninety-nine cases out of a hundred who is to blame for that? The mothers. Have you ever had a look at the lunches our boys here bring with them to school every day?'

'Not yet,' Alan had to admit.

'When you do look, you'll see mostly starchy stuff, buns and cake and jam tarts. The fact is, in many working-class and lower-middle-class households the woman is just downright ignorant of dietetics, and that's the real cause of this "malnutrition" our self-styled experts are so fond of shooting their mouths off about.'

'Perhaps starchy stuff is bought because it's cheaper.'

'Most of our parents are not at all badly off, so they could well afford to give their boys a more varied diet if they wanted to. But we seem to be losing sight of the prophecies of Karl Marx. My point was that he's been proved completely wrong. Conditions were worse even in my boyhood, and certainly far worse in my grandfather's boyhood, than they are now. As a matter of fact the working man today, on the average and taking into account busy as well as slack periods, is more comfortably provided for than he's been in the whole of history hitherto. Think of the gangs of navvies digging the Duke of Bridgewater's canal and then think of Dick and Harry with their motor-cycles, their cinemas, their cigarettes, their wirelesses, yes, and their new houses on the Council housing estate.'

'Think of Jarrow and of South Wales. And in any case,' Alan added a little unsurely, 'what Marx was above all emphasizing was that the gap between rich and poor would become wider, that relatively to the ever-increasing wealth of the rich the poverty of the workers would become greater.' As soon as he had said this Alan felt that he was being dishonest, was talking like a mere debater. 'There's no need,' he thought, 'for *us* to be afraid of the truth. It can harm only those whom History has doomed.' He went on aloud, 'But even if there has been some absolute improvement in working-class conditions since the early days of the Industrial Revolution, the poverty and misery of the workers in the British Empire as a whole – and they far outnumber the workers here in Britain – has been on the increase.'

'Have you any reason to suppose that conditions in the Empire won't gradually improve as they have done here?' Aldershaw calmly asked.

77

'Every reason.' Anger, which Alan tried to keep out of his tone of voice, surged up in him. 'Even if the imperialists had philanthropic intentions – which they haven't – they just couldn't bring themselves to stop exploiting the colonial peoples. They won't begin to loosen their grip until they're forced to – and no wonder, considering the colossal profits they're making. And as for gradual improvement, well, they've already landed us in one world war to protect their colonies against other would-be grabbers. Until they're kicked out for good and all, the only prospect before the great majority of human beings will be misery and destruction.'

Aldershaw did not bother to disagree. It seemed that he had begun to see Alan as someone perversely beyond the reach of reason. He asked coldly, 'And what would you put in the place of the present social system?'

'The question really is not what I would put in its place but what new system will in fact come into being when internal stresses have finally broken up the present one. Capitalism, under which the factories and the products of labour are privately owned, although the work is done by workers co-operating with one another, will give way to Socialism, under which ownership as well as work will be collective. The mainspring that drives the whole system will no longer be profits but human needs.'

'But as a matter of fact industry is already collectively owned.'

'I don't see how you make that out.'

'The small shareholder provides a very large proportion of the capital.'

'I don't think many workers go in for buying equities on the Stock Exchange. And in any case it isn't the small shareholders but the big capitalists who *control* the capitalist system.'

'But without profits – human nature being as it is –

78

where would be the incentive that would keep industry going?'

'And this,' Alan thought, 'is the view of a man who has once been in the Labour Party.' He said, 'It has already been kept going very successfully without them.'

'Oh, where?' Aldershaw asked expectantly.

'In the Soviet Union.'

Aldershaw had the maliciously pleased smile of someone who has lured an opponent into a trap from which there can be no escape. 'The Soviet Union,' he said with open scorn. 'That proletarian paradise where if a worker so much as mutters a word of criticism against the powers that be he finds himself in a slave-labour camp for the rest of his life.'

'That isn't true. There's far more criticism by Soviet workers of powers that be, such as factory managements, than there is in England. You wouldn't find an ordinary employee of a big firm in England writing an article attacking the boss and having it published in a wall-newspaper.'

'Nor would you, I suspect, in Russia. You certainly wouldn't find him attacking Stalin with impunity, or the policy of the Communist Party.'

'The ordinary Soviet citizen realizes that Stalin and the Communist Party are on his side and that their policy is in his interests and not in the interests of financiers or imperialists. He wouldn't dream of wanting to attack those whom he regards as his own leaders.'

'I suppose you would say, then, that the population of Russia is one hundred per cent in support of the Soviet Government?'

'Ninety-five per cent. Reactionary remnants of the old régime have not all emigrated abroad. And the old harmful bourgeois ideas still linger on among the more backward sections of the people.'

'And in your view it is right that these "reactionary remnants" and "backward sections" should have no freedom at all to express their political opinions?'

'Yes, for so long as most countries in the world remain capitalist and there's a danger of intervention and counter-revolution.'

'I think it was your friend Marx who said that a people that oppresses another people cannot itself be free. He was right there, for once. The ordinary Russian citizen who votes for a government that treats even five per cent of the population as enemies is himself in danger, not from the five per cent but from the same government. However loyal he may be, the secret police can make mistakes.'

'Any kind of dictatorship, even a proletarian one, must have disadvantages. But Communists regard proletarian dictatorship as no more than a necessary phase in the advance towards a freedom far greater than any that has existed even in the freest of bourgeois democracies.'

'An illusion. Tyranny has often been violently overthrown, but it has never yet developed gradually into liberty. Dictatorship of whatever kind is an absolute evil.'

'I deny that the Soviet Government is a tyranny. It's a dictatorship, but so is our British Government, though much less frankly and openly – except of course in the Empire, where the majority of British citizens live. Behind our democratic-seeming institutions the real power is wielded by a fairly small oligarchy of rich men or of men serving the interests of the rich.' The air of superior, yet disagreeing, tolerance which hitherto in the conversation Aldershaw had never quite lost was now suddenly removed, as though the gradual accumulation of the outrageous statements that he had been listening to had at last brought about a dialectical change in him, and his eyes and his face began to have something like menace in them. But Alan, who was thoroughly worked-up, went on, 'And I don't agree that all dictatorships are equally bad. It depends upon what or whom they are directed against. If their purpose is to keep negroes in subjection to white men, for instance, or to prevent an exploited class from obtaining its rights, then they're evil. But if they aim to put a stop to the advocacy or practice of racial discrimination, or of making money out of other people's work, or of nationalistic propaganda, or of keeping women in a position of economic inferiority to men, or of any other characteristic vice of bourgeois society, then I'm heartily in favour of them. I've got no use for the kind of woolly thinking which condemns alike, and equates as one and the same thing, the suppression of reactionary anti-social tendencies and of progressive movements – of vice and virtue, in fact.'

In a tone intended no longer to be persuasive but only to emphasize the assertion of incontrovertible truth, Aldershaw said, 'You make the mistake of assuming that governments can be capable of infallibly distinguishing between vice and virtue. Whereas the fact is that under dictatorship of any kind the intelligent and honest man is the one most likely to get into trouble, while the plausible rogue who knows the right political things to say and whom it costs nothing to say them will flourish. As for Russia, forget all the political abstractions you've picked up from I wonder where and just remember that in England the ordinary working man is not only far better off in an economic and political sense but also much nearer to living in a truly socialist society than he would be in the so-called socialist Soviet Union.'

'So capitalism is really socialism and socialism is really capitalism,' Alan said with satirical emphasis.

Aldershaw got up out of his armchair, saying angrily, 'The trouble with your sort is that you always know all the answers.'

He walked to the door and went out of the room. Alan in turn got up, angry also, and went over to put back the uncorrected History exercise books into his locker. As he was stooping to open the locker-door, a colleague named Benson, who had come into the room two or three minutes before and had evidently been listening to the last part of the conversation, said, 'You know, I think Aldershaw was right about what the position of an honest intellectual must be in the Soviet Union.'

His tone seemed intended to imply that on other matters he did not always agree with Aldershaw. Alan looked up briefly at his face, which was square-jawed and earnest, then said 'Oh' and bent down to the locker again, ignoring him. Benson said nothing more. Alan behaved like this not so much deliberately or because he wanted to avoid another argument but because he was preoccupied with his own feelings about Aldershaw. Why, he wondered, did Aldershaw's outlook seem so particularly odious? Not just because it was reactionary: the views held by most other members of the staff were far more so and yet were much less repulsive. No, the really disgusting thing about Aldershaw wasn't that he was pro-capitalist and pro-imperialist but that, having at one time been some sort of socialist, he had now come to defend capitalism and imperialism not frankly and openly but by pretending that they were progressive, and so salving his conscience. But what made him want to defend them? Presumably he gained something out of them. Or if he didn't, if he lived and kept a family solely on a teacher's salary without any private income from investments, that made his defence of them even more contemptible. But most likely he had inherited some shares and lived in a newish suburban house with bay windows and a studded oak door, and an electric bulb in a sham antique lantern over the porch, and an asbestos-walled garage, and a concrete crazy-pavement, and a garden with concrete walks and regimented flowers, and forsythia in April and buddleia in August. At the thought of the concrete crazy-pavement Alan's rage rose to its climax, and after that it declined and was slowly superseded by the beginnings of another and quite different feeling – of anxiety. Alan became conscious that in talking as unconstrainedly as he had done to Aldershaw, who was the Second Master, he had been imprudent. And mingling with this anxiety there was another, quite unconnected with it in origin but now reinforcing it and being reinforced by it: before long his free period would come to an end and he would have to go and teach the Middle Fourth Form for the second time this morning.

He did not leave the common-room until some few minutes after the bell had rung at the end of the third period, and when he reached the foot of the stairs half-way along the corridor he remembered that he ought to have brought the History exercise books with him, and he hurried back to the common-room to fetch them. He had been using the Dalton method, considerably modified, with the Middle Fourth, which meant that each boy worked on his own for nearly all the time and couldn't do so properly without an exercise book. Coming out from the common-room once again, now with the books under his arm, Alan was uneasy about not having corrected them: it would have a bad effect on the boys. But even if he had corrected them, he thought, would the effect have been any better? He must recognize that his modified Dalton method, though it had gone well enough during the first one or two weeks of the term, had recently resulted at times in something not far from chaos. The idea might seem sound that 'assignments' or lists of questions long enough to keep the boys busy for a fortnight ahead should be set, so that each boy could do as much as his capabilities allowed and could bring his work up at intervals to the teacher for correction and individual advice, instead of having to sit inactively as in a formal lesson while the teacher strained to pump knowledge into the whole class all the time; but in practice some of the boys did much less than they were capable of, and others did a great deal more than

Alan was able to correct with them in class, and in both cases they tended to find themselves at a loose end and to become talkative. More than talkative – noisy and uncontrolled, Alan thought, as he came to the staircase again. Beginning to mount its worn wooden steps, he was aware that the faint smell of pine-fluid disinfectant which had been noticeable in the corridor was now superseded by a stronger and more disturbing smell, hot and dusty, confusedly reminiscent of something frightening which had happened perhaps in his own schooldays. It seemed to come from the steps he was treading on. Wooden floor-planks warmed by the friction of plimsolled feet in a gymnasium or in a boxing ring might give off just such a smell. Before he reached the top of the stairs a noise which he had been half-conscious of even in the corridor below became very loud. Boys inside one of the classrooms were shouting and roaring with laughter. He absurdly hoped that they were not members of the form which he was now five minutes overdue to take.

He had reached the top of the stairs when from the door of the Middle Fourth classroom, as though the pressure of the disturbance inside had become so great that the room could no longer contain it, three boys were ejected backwards – strangely without falling and without smashing any glass – into the corridor. They immediately saw him coming, and with wild gestures of warning directed at those inside, who evidently were mobilized to resist their return, they forced their way back, hissing loudly through their teeth as they did so. No doubt the hissing also was intended to warn the others of his approach, but he had been hearing this sound rather too often recently and had come to the conclusion that the boys reserved it specially for him, like a kind of wordless nickname. He had had difficulty in preventing himself from feeling stung by it, and now a quick anger rose in him against the three boys. He must punish them. But who were they? The speed at which the incident had hap-

84

pened and his own agitation had combined to blur his impression of them: it was as though at the moment of perception something opaque had been rapidly jerked up and down in his head behind his eyes. And his memory of the impression was even shakier than the impression itself seemed to have been. He was certain only that two of the boys were tall – louts, he thought – and that the third was very short and had messy yellow hair. However, possibly the hissing, offensive though it was in being applied particularly to him, had been meant to be heard only by the rest of the form and not by him. This thought soothed him a little as he came towards the door of the classroom, smoothed over his failure to recognize the three offenders. But as he walked in through the doorway the hissing was repeated more loudly and by more than three boys, though not by the whole form. It was a malevolent, a viciously hateful, sound, out of all proportion in its intensity of venom to any unpleasantness he might at any time unwittingly have been guilty of towards them. It suggested that they would gladly have seen him stabbed or clubbed to death on the spot. Mediaeval London apprentices out for the blood of Flemings could hardly have sounded more ill-intentioned. He came to a halt before he reached the master's desk, turned on them with open fury, said with a harshness which unfortunately he could not prevent from becoming almost hysterically shrill as he finished, 'Stop that filthy noise at once. If I ever hear it again from any of you at any time I shall have no hesitation whatsoever in keeping in the whole lot of you for two hours or more if necessary, on Saturday afternoon. Get your books out – you ought to have had them out before I came in, as I've told you often enough already. And try behaving like human beings, not animals.'

There was complete silence. Then an absurdly evil-looking boy, whose greasy face was pustule-dotted and whose short hair over his forehead had the appearance of having been unevenly nibbled by rodents, asked with blatantly insincere bewilderment, 'What noise, sir?'

He was sitting in a desk in the front row very close to Alan, who only just restrained himself from slapping him as hard as possible across the face.

'You, Dibble, will do an hour's detention on Saturday. Evidently you didn't understand that I meant what I said.'

'But what for, sir?'

'For impertinence. And you'll do two hours, not one. And if you say another word without being asked I shall have to find a more drastic way of dealing with you.'

Alan would not have been surprised if after this Dibble had sat back with a look of sulky enmity on his face, but, instead, the boy seemed, now that punishment was clearly unavoidable, to accept it with a good grace and even to find some sort of satisfaction in having brought it upon himself. The devil-like ugliness which Alan had seen in him a moment before had gone and in its place was something that asked almost for sympathy – a mere ugliness, a juvenile spottiness, and perhaps in the background a poor home and inferior food. A change appeared to have come also over the rest of the form, who had got out their text-books and were quietly beginning to read them. But Alan himself could not so easily switch over from one kind of behaviour to another. Rage could not simply give place to a comfortable mildness and be immediately forgotten. It could and did change, but only into a feeling of degradation, of self-loathing, of disgust that he had permitted himself to be so deeply stung by the boys' rudeness and, worse, that he had exhibited his inner reactions so plainly. He had befouled his true nature, and quite unnecessarily: he could have brought the boys to order just as effectively – perhaps more so – if he had dealt with them on a purely professional level without feelings of any kind, like an ambulance man dealing with a nasty street accident.

They were orderly enough now. They were reading, and they had not even asked him to return the exercise books which he had brought into the room with him. He called out the Form Captain, Chiverton, a boy of divided loyalties who, though he liked bossing the form, did not like appearing to them to be at all subservient to the master.

'Give these back, with the minimum of disturbance, will you?'

Chiverton distributed the books rather casually, dropping them on the desks rather than placing them there, and this gave rise to some protesting and consequent conversation, though not loud. After Chiverton had gone round to all the desks no one risked asking Alan why the work in the books had not yet been corrected. Alan sat down at the master's desk, and, leaning forward with his elbows on its surface and his shoes contacting the wicker wastepaper-basket underneath, he stared steadily at the form. What had made them behave towards him as they had done, so offensively, when he had given them no cause? It was their petit bourgeois origin, he momentarily and spitefully thought: real working-class boys wouldn't behave like that. But this was nonsense, because anyway some of them were working class; and suppose they had all been working class, would they have been any better? Mightn't they have been far worse, and wasn't he letting himself be deluded by inverted snobbery? Perhaps the truth was that their venomous hissing expressed resentment not so much against him individually as against the school whose authority he willy-nilly represented, and the reason why they chose him in particular as a victim was just that he was a weaker disciplinarian than some other masters who had given them a good deal more cause for resentment. Yet if they really disliked the school, why did so many of them voluntarily dawdle about the building and grounds after school-hours every day? Wasn't he making the mistake of assuming that they must have the same attitude towards their school as he at their age had had towards his? Perhaps a more likely explanation of their hostility was that they detected something alien in him, a strangeness which nothing in their experience could enable them to understand, the kind of streak which was to be found in poets and which had so often got poets into trouble with the communities they lived among. The boys were impelled to attack him rather in the same way that hens attack another hen which has something 'different' about it. They hated him with the same kind of intense hatred with which public-school boys at his own school had hated any boy among them who wore boots instead of shoes. But this explanation wasn't satisfactory either. One of Alan's colleagues, Oliphant by name, a real eccentric and ludicrous to look at, almost dwarfishly short, with a small round mouth and straggly moustache and protruding teeth (which Gus Chiddingfold, who detested him, had once compared to a pingpong ball stuck in a mare's behind), was unquestionably liked by the boys, whom he was able to control quite adequately and without severity. 'No,' Alan thought, 'the true reason for my failure is simply that I haven't so far discovered – and haven't tried hard enough to discover – the right approach to boys in the mass.'

He had been slacking off lately, he told himself, aware now that the boys in front of him were beginning to talk among themselves and would do so less quietly when he had to call individuals out from among them, as he soon must, to mark their work. He had been losing the desire to succeed as a teacher which he had felt four months ago at the time of his first contact with the Party. Why? Not only because his pupils were hostile to him, but above all because he had neglected the one essential thing – which was that he should keep in constant touch with the Party and be politically active among and for the working class. His work with the Party during the election had changed his whole outlook from misery to hope and had enabled him afterwards to write poetry again, and he had tended to be content merely with writing poetry, excusing himself from political activity on the grounds that in the small town where his parents lived and where he must stay for as long as he was jobless no Party members were to be found. Then, when he had started teaching here at the beginning of this term, he had persuaded himself that he must first get thoroughly settled into his new job; and except for writing a letter to the secretary of the E.W.L. – who in return had sent him the leaflet he had put up on the common-room notice-board this morning – his only attempt to contact the Party had been at a public meeting where Elsie had spoken and he had admired her but she hadn't recognized him afterwards at the door when she had been handing out leaflets to people leaving. Remembering the meeting now, and remembering the bliss after his first visit to the committee rooms in October, and recognizing that his failure to keep in touch with the Party would, if prolonged, injure his poetry just as it had already injured his teaching, he decided that he must write as soon as possible to the Centre and ask where the local secretary lived. He must write this evening.

The chatter was getting louder, and it would infallibly before long develop to the point where at least some of the boys would give the impression – not only to Alan but also to anyone who happened to be passing in the corridor – that they were shouting rather than talking. With apprehension he glanced through the glass panes of the classroom door, but saw no one. At least twice recently – on occasions when there had been considerable disturbance in the room – he had noticed a plump figure, which he had recognized as Gus Chiddingfold's, moving with unnecessary slowness along the corridor. Chiddingfold would be quite capable of mentioning to the Headmaster, with whom he was on terms of personal friendship, that Alan seemed to be finding the boys difficult. 'The fat snake,' Alan thought. Certainly at this moment the noise in the room was too loud for him to be able to quell it by speaking to the boys in an ordinary voice: he himself would have to shout, and perhaps without immediate effect, and that would make an even worse impression on a passer-by than if the noise had seemed to be due to a deliberate free-discipline policy on Alan's part. He was standing up and staring threateningly at the form, but with a quarter of an eye still on the door; and inwardly, and with a much greater nervous effort than actual shouting would have cost him, he soundlessly bawled at them, as though he hoped against hope thereby to bring some sort of telekinetic pressure to bear upon them which would force those who were standing to sit down and all of them to bend their heads to their books. But even his inner exertion was deprived of some of its vigour by the persisting fear that at any moment someone would come along the corridor. At last, in a voice which had to be strident but which he tried to make as mechanical and devoid of emotion as possible, he spoke to them aloud:

'In a moment I am going to call you out one by one to go over your written work with you. I should like you to reduce talking to a minimum and get on with your assignments while I have boys up here at my desk. You can understand that the kind of individual work I'm trying to do with each of you will be made quite impossible if those I'm not immediately attending to decide to talk at the tops of their voices all the time. If you *can't* understand this I'd better remind you now of what I've already said about detention on Saturday afternoon.'

After this there was quiet once again. He wondered how long it would last.

4

CLOSE TO THE pavements and beneath the high walls
of warehouses along the sides of the not very large square
the eight-hundred-strong contingent of demonstrators was
already lined up in fours on the roadway when Alan arrived.
He saw banners not yet raised high, their poles resting on
the ground and loosely held by the bearers; and above the
banners the reflected light of street-lamps glinted from the
dull, blank, dusty glass of warehouse windows. Out in the
roadway two men wearing red arm-bands on which the word
'Marshal' was lettered in white stood facing a stout police
sergeant and appeared to be arguing with him. A dark group
of policemen waited near the demonstrators on the side of
the square farthest from Alan. Someone suddenly shouted,
'One – two – three – four. Who – are – we – for?' He was
answered by shouters in chorus, 'We are for the *working*
class. *Down* with the *ruling* class.' It was not very loud, Alan
noticed, nor was it taken up by the demonstrators in general.
Perhaps this slogan had not been one of the slogans recommended by the organizers as specially appropriate for this
particular demonstration, which was in support of the unemployed Hunger Marchers now in London from all over
Britain; or perhaps the demonstrators did not want to prejudice their marshals' chances of persuading the sergeant;
or, more likely, eagerness to get moving preoccupied them,
Alan thought, as he walked along the pavement looking for
his own local group.

Wally saw him before he saw Wally.

'Hullo, comrade stranger. You're only just in time.'

Wally made room for him, causing one of the fours to become a five; but it would sort itself out on the march, and, if it didn't, well, this wasn't a military procession.

'Why stranger?' Alan asked.

'Because you've missed the last two cell meetings.'

'I couldn't come,' Alan said lamely, having no real excuse.

Elsie, who was in the four behind him and who had Mike Bainton next to her, said without severity but not altogether jokingly, 'It's beginning to look as though he's somewhat unreliable.'

She laughed; but the word 'unreliable', which up to the present Alan had heard applied to Party members who were regarded with strong disfavour and as potential renegades, alarmed him deeply, even though he was not yet a Party member, but only on probation. He could find nothing to say in reply.

'If you had been at our last meeting,' Wally said kindly, 'you would have heard that the time for the start of this demo has been changed. From seven p.m. to half past six.'

'But the time is now ten to seven already,' Alan was able to say.

'We've been held up,' Wally explained. 'It's the police. They don't like the route we're going to take, and they want to divert us. They won't succeed, but we shan't mind losing a little time in trying to persuade them peacefully. We don't want to start the march with a battle.'

'There'll be plenty of battles before the evening's out,' Mike Bainton said.

His tone, which had something of an apprehensive eagerness in it, gave clear expression to the tension that Alan had been aware of hitherto only as an unusual quality in the sound of the other's voices, as though they were speaking in

92

a place with peculiar acoustics – a tension that he now knew he had himself been feeling even before he had come into the square.

'The police'll agree to let us through, most likely,' Wally said; 'they know there aren't enough of them here to turn us back. But later on they're going to do their damnedest to stop us getting anywhere near the approaches to Parliament. That's when we'll see them in force, masses and masses of them.'

'There's not a single regular copper left in the suburbs this evening,' Bainton said. 'I was noticing from the bus window as I came along, and everywhere was lousy with Specials.'

'My guess is they'll try to block us when we get to the Strand,' Wally said. 'Or perhaps before that, at Holborn. But what with big contingents marching from north, south, east and west they're going to have their work cut out.'

'I suppose they'll try to stop the southern contingent from getting as far as Westminster Bridge,' Bainton said.

'There are plenty of other bridges,' Elsie said.

'And there are boats,' Wally said, laughing.

'Think of a mounted police charge across Tower Bridge,' Bainton suggested.

Wally corrected him. 'The bridge would be raised before the marchers got there – like in the *October* film.'

'And a white police horse would get caught in the middle of the bridge as the roadway began to split in two,' Alan imagined. But immediately, even before he noticed the unappreciative looks on his hearers' faces, he wished he had not come out with this idea.

Wally said to him in a matter-of-fact way, 'If we are stopped at the Strand or at Holborn, and can't march any further, then we're to break up and make our way individually or in very small groups to Parliament Square – and if we can board buses and do some slogan-shouting from the top deck so much the better. But it's likely the police will stop all public transport that goes near the Houses of Parliament.'

'We discussed these details at our last cell meeting,' Elsie said, implying 'which you did not attend'.

'Never mind about our last cell meeting,' Bainton surprisingly said. 'When's our march going to start from here? We've been kept waiting for more than half a ruddy hour.'

At this moment Alan, looking about him at comrades standing in near-by fours, noticed that Ron Spalding, the secretary of the cell, did not seem to be here yet.

'Where's Comrade Spalding?' he asked.

It was obvious from the faces, not only of the three comrades he had been talking with but of several others near by, that his question had been audible, yet no one seemed prepared to answer it. Wally at last said gravely, 'There's been some trouble. He's in prison.'

'Good God!' Alan said. 'When did that happen?'

'Four days ago.'

'Have you been able to see him yet?'

'Party members aren't allowed to. He's not there for any political reason. He's been arrested for burglary.'

'Burglary? Surely it must be a frame-up? Hasn't anyone heard what he has to say about it?'

'I'm afraid there's no doubt. He was caught with three others, loading timber from a builder's-merchants' yard on to a lorry — also stolen.'

'And he mustn't be visited?'

'Party members must have nothing more to do with him. He's been expelled from the Party. We can't have it put about that we tolerate burglars among us.'

A shiny-faced, dumpy comrade named Turton, who was a member of the local cell and who had been listening, said, 'I don't see why anyone should want to visit him. He's been deceiving us and doing the dirty on the Party for years. But I admit I was always a bit suspicious of him – that voice of his whenever he took the Chair, so oily.'

Mike Bainton said, 'He did a lot of good work for the Party.' Then with indignation, 'It's all bloody nonsense, this respectable line we're taking about Ron. What's wrong with burglary anyway? Isn't it a form of rebellion against the capitalist system, even though it's not the most effective form in the long run? Joseph Stalin himself was a burglar once. He robbed the bank at Tiflis.'

Alan, to whom it often happened that he was more inter-ested in a speaker's manner and appearance than in what was said, now for the first time became sharply conscious that Bainton was not of working-class origin, nor of quite the same middle-class origin as Alan himself, but could perhaps be regarded as upper petit bourgeois.

A bitter voice said, 'You're talking tripe, Bainton. Stalin was carrying out a Party decision when he raided the bank, and the money went to the Party and not into his own pocket. Besides, political conditions in Tsarist Russia were totally different from what they are here and now.'

It was Jimmy Anders, standing in the four behind Elsie's, who was speaking. But the argument went no further, because at this point someone said, 'We're off,' and all saw that the marchers at the head of the contingent had begun to move out of the square. Those who were moving started slogan-shouting – a shouting as of release, far more vigorous than the shouts Alan had heard earlier on – but those who were stationary remained silent mostly, until the gradual back-ward ripple of the forward movement reached and included them, then they too shouted, though between their getting moving and their shouting there was a lag of a moment or two. Different slogans came from different sections of the procession. 'Support the Hunger Marchers' Petition', 'Down with the Means Test', 'Against Hunger and War' and others

95

mingled and reverberated in the square and their sound was magnified by the comparative narrowness of the street into which the marchers came after leaving the square. Alan's group chose 'Down with the Means Test' and he joined in as loud as he could. Everyone was shouting, except the police, who had now spread out all along the column so that individual policemen marched at intervals of about ten yards from one another beside the demonstrators.

Alan, who was on the outside of the column, had Wally next to him at his left side and a policeman almost as close to him at his right. There was nothing menacing about this policeman's expression of face. On the contrary there was something that was not unbenevolent and that seemed to suggest he had attached himself by choice to Alan as a person less repellent or less likely to give trouble than the others in the group. This made Alan more uneasy than hostility would have done. He tried to put a harshness into his shouting which would show that he wasn't open to ingratiation and that he associated himself entirely with the others. After a time the contingent as a whole no longer shouted continuously, though nearly always slogans were still to be heard coming from one section or other of the marchers, and Alan's group were quiet for periods at first short but lengthening later. When the contingent passed under a big main-line railway bridge, each of the sections in turn, as they came directly beneath the bridge, yelled at the tops of their voices, taking full advantage of the echo, even though few members of the general public were there to hear them. The marchers shouted loudly also whenever there were more people than usual on the pavements as they passed. Gradually from among these people a second, irregular procession was spontaneously formed, which hurried along the pavements on both sides of the road in the same direction as the contingent. During a lull in the slogan-shouting a woman comrade named Mrs Grindel marching in Alan's group – a powerfully-

built housewife – began singing to the tune of the chorus of
'John Brown's Body':

> 'We will bolshevize the police force
> We will bolshevize the police force
> We will bolshevize the police force
> When the Rev – o – lu – tion comes.'

One or two other members of the group began to join in
the song. Alan became aware of a reluctance in himself to
do so, but just because he was reluctant and knew he ought
not to be, and also because he didn't want to appear to be
cowed by the presence of the policeman beside him, he too
joined in. His singing took evident effect on the policeman,
who had shown no sign of being annoyed when Mrs Grindel
started the song and had even seemed to have a very faint
grin on his face, but who now looked sullen. Alan caught
himself feeling a slight regret, but soon remembered that,
however personally inoffensive this man might have been if
he had never joined the police force, he was in fact a policeman and therefore an instrument of the capitalist class, whose
will he must do.

The buildings were becoming larger on both sides of the
street as the contingent advanced. The very centre of British
capitalism, with its heavy banks and its Portland stone offices,
was not far off now. Soon the slogans of the demonstrators
would be echoing down the streets of the inmost stronghold
of the ruling class: slogans of protest and revolt. And one
day not so far distant, Alan thought, Revolution itself would
come. The working class would overthrow the capitalist class,
which admittedly in its earlier phase had led the human race
forward, had achieved technical and industrial wonders, had
shaken the world out of feudal sluggardliness, but which at
this present date was holding humanity back, was hampering
the far more rapid advance that was now scientifically pos-

sible. It was throwing millions of men out of work just because to keep them in work would have been unprofitable to it. It would stop at nothing in its dreadful senile determination to preserve its own power. It had killed millions in one world war and, unless it could itself be destroyed first, it would sooner or later kill millions more in another. And it made life so slavish and wretched that many of its victims didn't care much whether they were killed or not. Alan himself did care now after he'd become politically awake, but in one sense he was still – though his plight was not to be even remotely compared with that of the unemployed or of colonial workers – a slave under capitalism, was forced into a job he did not want, was prevented from being himself and from living the life of a poet.

The thought of his slavery caused him, just at that moment when his part of the procession was passing a traffic island on which several people, including a sad-faced old man, were standing, to shout on his own with passionate intensity, 'Down with the Means Test.' The old man, though startled, remained sad. But from the four behind Alan there came a laugh. It was Elsie's, and she seemed to be jeering at him. He recognized immediately that he deserved something worse than to be jeered at. He had made use of a political slogan as a mere cover under which to vent his personal discontent. No, perhaps not quite that – he had also felt a genuine indignation against the Means Test when he had shouted – but the point was that, even if his shout had been an expression purely of his feeling about the Government's treatment of the unemployed and not at all about his own personal situation, it would still have been wrong. The political struggle required not that he should express his emotions, however noble, but that he should help to get a message across to the masses. Propaganda was a serious art, and had to be learnt. Mortification at his silliness remained with him for some time after he had heard Elsie's laugh.

Between then and when the contingent came to a stop twenty minutes later he did not shout again.

The front part of the contingent was round a corner and hidden by buildings from the other marchers, who did not know what had halted it. But a very slow forward-pushing movement seemed to be going on among those who were grouped just at the bend and who presumably could see something of what was happening right at the front. The halt had evidently not been called by the leaders, because, if it had been, the forward-pushing group would be standing still in a disciplined way. There was a sudden brief clattering sound from round the corner. A slight undulatory heaving became visible among the corner group, as though they were uncertain about the direction in which they meant to move. Then the rest of the demonstrators, including Alan's group, began to move forward.

'It's those bastards, the police,' Mike Bainton said. 'They're trying to stop us.' He spoke just loudly enough for the policeman near Alan to hear, though not loudly enough for him to be sure that he had been intended to hear. The man took no notice.

A contrary, backward movement had started among the corner group, but the others pressed on, breaking ranks and spreading out across the roadway as soon as they found themselves held up by the backward pressure of the retreaters. Alan thought fleetingly of Macaulay's lines – and without the disrespect he would normally have felt for them: 'Then those behind cried "Forward". And those before cried "Back".' Mike Bainton, tall and having an aggressive look on his thin face, was conspicuous among those who seemed the most impatient to get forward. He did not succeed, even though the retreating movement from in front soon came to a stop. Then there was a call, which may or may not have come from one of the marshals and which was repeated by individual demonstrators here and there, to get back into the column, and someone shouted, 'Don't let yourselves be provoked, comrades.' The demonstrators, like people remembering something they had only for a moment forgotten, began to collect themselves again at the left side of the road and gradually re-formed their fours.

Bainton, unwillingly back in his group, objected: 'What's the point? Any fool ought to see we aren't going to be able to march any farther, or if we do it'll only be a few hundred yards and then the police will block us again. Why shouldn't we break up into groups now as arranged, and make our own way to Parliament Square?'

'Because there's such a thing as not behaving like a rabble of individualists,' Jimmy Anders said coldly. 'We shall break up into groups when we get the word from the leaders, and not before.'

After they had stood waiting there in the column for a time that might have been as long as twenty minutes – though to Alan, whose almost static emotion of expectancy made the passage of external time seem comparatively rapid, it was more like five – one of the marshals came walking quickly down the roadway from the direction of the front of the column, and Bainton called out to him, 'What's up, comrade marshal?'

'Tell you in a minute, comrade,' the marshal answered, turning his head but not slowing his pace. Alan watched him walk on towards the rear of the column, saw him stop and speak briefly to the comrades there, who then broke ranks in a leisurely way and began moving off, individually or in groups of two or three, back down the street by which they had arrived. Bainton, too, saw what was happening.

'They've started,' he said. 'Come on, let's get going.' There was no response. 'We aren't doing any good here.' No one contradicted him. He moved out into the middle of the roadway. 'Oh, come on,' he repeated to the near-by comrades in general, then fixed on Alan in particular: 'You'll come, at any rate.'

'But hadn't we better wait till we've been given the word?'

'It's been given already. You can see for yourself.'

Not even Jimmy Anders made the objection that, though the comrades at the rear of the procession might have had the word, this group certainly hadn't yet. Alan couldn't find the assurance to make it himself. And no one said anything to dissuade him from going with Bainton, whose evident confidence that he would come had an absoluteness which caused Alan to doubt whether his own misgivings were reasonable. Bainton, stepping in from the middle of the roadway towards Alan, stretched out a hand to his elbow but did not actually catch hold of it. There was no need for that. Without physical persuasion Alan followed him across the road. They came, after walking about twenty yards, to a side-street and turned into it, unprevented by two policemen at the corner, who stared nastily at them.

Nobody else from the group came with them. Even after they had turned into another side-street at right angles to the first one Alan several times looked back, hoping for evidence that the contingent as a whole had been given the word to break up, but not a single demonstrator was visible behind him. He began to think of himself as a deserter, and the hurried pace which Bainton set him helped to intensify his guilty uneasiness. At last, however much it might annoy Bainton, he had to say, 'Let's go back. I don't think we ought to leave the others in the lurch like this. They might be having trouble with the police.'

'Who's leaving who in the lurch?' Bainton asked with vigour. 'If anyone's being left in the lurch it's all those comrades who are already in Parliament Square facing the mounted police and without half the support they should be getting.' His tone became milder. 'But don't you worry.

The others are coming on behind us. You're not really in any doubt about that, are you? You saw the rear of the column starting to go off, didn't you?'

Alan, not answering, walked on beside him. The guilty misgiving was still there, but together with it and in opposition to it was the desire not to be thought uneager to get to Parliament Square. And in fact, as they hurried on, turning into yet another side-street, he did feel an eagerness to get there, and not only because he needed to justify himself after absconding from the contingent. A little to his surprise he found that he wanted to be in the battle if there was one. To take part with the workers in resisting an attack by the capitalist police would be dialectically different from shouting slogans or attending meetings, would be on a higher level, nearer to effective revolutionary action against the evil power under which the workers, and to a lesser extent he himself, suffered. It wouldn't matter if he were injured – or if he were arrested and as a result lost his job. The workers weren't afraid to face such risks; and why should he be when all he had to lose was the slow misery of his day-to-day slavery at school? He was glad that he had come with Bainton, and he knew now that it wasn't just Bainton's persuasiveness that had made him come. It was his own wish, at first unconscious, and he was grateful to Bainton for having helped him to act upon it.

They were in a street not far from Trafalgar Square when Alan, once again looking back, though now hardly at all guiltily, saw a group of ten or twelve workers walking up quickly from behind. He asked Bainton, 'Do you think they're some of our lot?'

Bainton slowed, but only for a moment, to have a look. 'Don't recognize any of them. There's no one there from our cell. But you needn't worry,' he added understandingly, 'the whole contingent will be with us in the end. Then our little bit of individualist indiscipline' – he laughed – 'will be forgiven and forgotten. There's nothing succeeds like a *fait accompli.*'

Alan felt almost but not quite able to adopt the same attitude as Bainton. The slight uneasiness that remained in him, however, was removed when a few minutes later they arrived in Trafalgar Square, across which large numbers of workers were moving purposefully towards Whitehall.

Bainton said, 'Now we're going to see some life.'

There was in his voice a happy note that Alan had never heard from him before, and a freedom, as though now at last he found himself in a situation where his nature could truly come to flower.

They crossed Trafalgar Square and began to walk along Whitehall on the road towards Parliament Square. They did not get far. In front of them a big crowd, stationary at the moment, covered the roadway and the pavements on either side. Beyond this crowd and a little higher than their heads appeared the blunt vestigial spikes of many police helmets, like obstacles placed at the top of a low wall. Beyond the spikes, which belonged to foot police, it seemed there might be another section of the crowd, which the police had perhaps cordoned off from the rest, and beyond this other section – or gap it might be – Alan could see the helmets and shoulders of the mounted police. These were moving slowly from left to right across the road. A ludicrous memory came incongruously into his head as he watched them; it was of blue-jerseyed longshoremen seen in his boyhood, astride horses which used to draw bathing-machines up or down the beach according to the state of the tide. But he was shocked out of his associative fancies by the abrupt arrival, on the pavement quite near to him and Bainton, of a solitary mounted policeman who had ridden up from behind them. This man's object seemed to be to pursue and drive off the pavement a short-legged middle-aged woman demonstrator who was hurrying away from him just in front of his horse's head. Bainton directed a brief jeering laugh at him. The policeman was dead-white in the face and had a conspicuous mole on the skin of his neck just below his ear. He ignored the laugh. Having driven the woman off the pavement he turned, causing Alan and Bainton to jump back away from him, and headed his horse towards Trafalgar Square again. A long brown shiny narrow leather holster containing his baton – so different from the fat batons of the foot police, though both types were believed by some Party members to be similarly loaded with lead – hung down against his horse's left shoulder. Perhaps he had somehow gone astray from the other mounted police and, seeing the size of the crowd, had decided to take no further action on his own. Alan and Bainton were staring round to watch his departure when Bainton said, 'Oh good, there's Paddy Mullins over there just behind us. I must go and have a word with him.'

As Alan did not know Paddy Mullins, he stayed where he was while Bainton pushed a way back into the new crowd, which had already become quite deep behind them since their arrival here from Trafalgar Square. A noise made him turn to look in the direction of Parliament Square again. The crowd between him and the foot police were excitedly straining to see what was happening farther up the road. Somewhere near the entrance to Downing Street a mounted police charge seemed to have begun. Nothing of it was visible to Alan except the movement of the helmets and shoulders of the mounted police, though once he thought he saw a long thin baton swiftly lifted in the lamplight. The charge was quite soon over, but its ceasing did not have the effect of relaxing tension among the crowd, who on the contrary began to press slowly forward against the foot police.

A man near to Alan shouted shrilly, 'Get out your knives.'

'A provocateur,' Alan at once thought, looking at him with detestation. But members of the crowd near enough to have heard the shout were seemingly quite uninfluenced by it: they did not increase their forward pressure against the foot police nor did they turn – as Alan half-expected they might – and deal violently with the shouter. This provocateur, if he was one, did not shout again, possibly because he was aware of Alan's deliberately suspicious stare. He was a short, round-shouldered, sag-kneed man of at least fifty, who had watery eyes in an off-white face that was sporadically tufted with unshaved hair. A homburg hat with a very narrow brim was pulled down almost on to the bridge of his nose, and the forward tilt of the upper part of his body caused his trousered rump – which was overhung by the tails of a loose herringbone-tweed jacket – to jut out behind him. He had the look, Alan thought, of a many-times-magnified flea. A miserable, perhaps even a pitiable, little man who had got into the clutches of the police and was being paid a few shillings a year by them, or possibly just being blackmailed, to act against the working-class movement from within. Alan continued to watch him, on and off, for a time that might have been as long as a quarter of an hour but seemed shorter, then forgot about him and merely stood still, filled with the same steady expectancy that held the rest of the crowd there even after they had failed to make further headway in the direction of Parliament Square. Suddenly a tremendous roar of shouting and of cheers started up behind him. It came from Trafalgar Square, and the whole crowd turned and most of them began to move towards it.

Another mounted police charge had begun, more clearly visible this time because the roadway where it was happening was on a higher level. Alan saw a horse stumble and go down, flinging off its rider. Exultation arose in him. The crowd began to move faster. A man at his side said, 'Marbles, that's what done it. They should a' used them before. A few of them scattered in front of the 'orses'll soon put a stop to those mounted police.'

The fact that the crowd was continuing to move forward without meeting any resistance made Alan think that the battle might be going unfavourably for the police. The impression that the workers had won a victory was strengthened when, just as he came into Trafalgar Square, he saw a helmetless policeman standing on the pavement and holding two riderless horses by their bridles. He went forward with the crowd into the Square, now more slowly because of the other crowds already gathered there, but the deceleration of his physical movement was compensated for by an acceleration of emotional and imaginative activity within him. If the workers had got the better of the police in Trafalgar Square, what might that not lead to? The police would bring up reinforcements, though not without weakening themselves elsewhere perhaps, and then the workers might break through in force into Parliament Square. Suppose the soldiers had to be called out, and they opened fire and unarmed people were killed? It would not be the beginning of the Revolution, but it would never be forgotten and later on might make the starting of an organized revolt more possible. Alan's imaginings got no further. There was a flurry and a backward movement among the crowd just ahead of him. A foot policeman came, as it seemed, straight towards him, walking very rapidly, and then passed within a yard of him and was followed by a long line of other policemen in single file. After the last one had passed Alan turned and watched them make across the roadway towards the entrance of Northumberland Avenue. The leading ones broke into a run, and the others – not all at the same moment but successively – did the same. They drew their batons. Alan could not clearly see who it was they were attacking, nor whether there was any retaliation, but he saw with the utmost vividness the body postures and limb-movements of individual policemen as one by one they went in to strike at members of the crowd. The style of their hitting had a uniformity which suggested that this was the way they had all been trained to do it. As they raised their batons they half-crouched, with their knees forward and apart and their buttocks stuck out behind; and they advanced in a series of vigorous hops, both feet seeming to spring off the ground simultaneously. They held the batons at right angles to the forearm as they struck downwards, and they extended their free left arms stiffly in front of them with the palm of the hand raised as if signalling to bring traffic to a halt – though the real purpose of this gesture was no doubt to give protection against a possible kick in the crotch. Hatred for the police filled Alan as he watched, but like the rest of the crowd around him he made no move to help those who were being assaulted. It was as though the details of the hitting had fascinated him and the others into immobility. And in what seemed a very short time the charge was over and the policemen who had made it had disappeared, presumably down Northumberland Avenue. A woman near to him in the crowd said tensely to two men companions with whom she was standing, 'If I was a *man* I wouldn't stand by and see that happen without doing something about it. I'd get a brick or a bit of paving stone and I'd let them have it.'

The men looked sheepish, and even a little ashamed, but made no move. Alan all at once remembered Mike Bainton and, wondering whether the police might have injured him, he decided to walk round among the crowd and try to find him.

It seemed as he walked that the crowd was gradually becoming thinner. There was no general movement towards any one of the streets leading out of the Square, but from time to time people were drifting out in various directions and were not being replaced by others entering. He could not see either Bainton or Paddy Mullins. They were almost certainly not among one of the many stationary groups which remained waiting in different parts of the Square and which Alan had a good look at as he walked round. He came to a stop near one of these groups, and he overheard what two men in it were quite loudly saying:

'. . . smashed all the plate glass windows at Gamage's.'

'There was a woman batoned and knocked down on the pavement, just outside the National Gallery, and she was lying there groaning and couldn't get up and she asked wasn't there anyone who would finish her off and put her out of her agony.'

'There was a child crushed to death against a wall by a police horse near Charing Cross.'

Alan did not believe it. He was less impressed by what was said, which he guessed to be the kind of rumour that might get about during any big demonstration, than by the tone of the speakers. They spoke not as though they were urging one another to immediate action but as though they were summing up and drawing lessons for the future from a demonstration which was already over. They would have started to go home by now, Alan thought, if they hadn't happened to get talking. There was nothing else to keep them here. The crowd was dispersing. There was nothing to keep him here either. He felt suddenly depressed. The hopes he had had earlier this evening that something of historic importance might at any moment happen had been disappointed. And his depression was deepened by the recognition of how unrealistic, how naïve he had been to allow himself to indulge so excitedly in these hopes. The best thing for him to do now would be to take a bus and get back to his lodgings.

Traffic was moving almost normally through the Square again. There was a short queue at the bus-stop and after he had been standing in it for a minute or two he noticed Elsie near the head of it. He managed to get on to the same bus as she did, and, seeing her go up the stairs to the top deck, he went up too. She sat in a seat at the front next to a man, and Alan sat in the only other vacant place, which was four seats behind her. The man looked as though he might have been one of the demonstrators, but he and Elsie did not speak to one another during the whole of the twenty minutes or more they were together, so it was probable they did not know each other. When at last the man got up and left the bus Alan hesitated to go and sit next to her. He was afraid she might be annoyed that he had deserted the contingent. But if he remained where he was and she stood up to leave the bus before he did and saw him sitting here, that would add to the bad impression he must already have made on her this evening. He got out of his seat and went forward to the front of the bus. He was surprised that she seemed very pleased to see him.

'Where are the others?' he asked.

'Wally and Jimmy have gone off to a coffee-stall run by a friend of theirs. But I wanted to get home. And we lost track of the rest of the cell long ago. '

'I've been feeling rather guilty about the way I hurried off with Bainton.'

She was significantly silent, seeming to imply that that was just how he ought to feel. She did not ask what had happened to Bainton. He changed the subject.

'It's been a jolly good demonstration.'

He was aware that his enthusiasm sounded as factitious as it truly was.

'Fairly good,' she said. 'We don't know yet whether the comrades carrying the petition have been able to get through to the House of Commons.' Then she added, 'Why weren't you at our last two cell meetings?'

'I've got no excuse. I just spent the time reading' – the truth was that he had been working on a poem – 'at my lodgings. But I'm going to take myself in hand and attend regularly in future.'

'You might find that easier to do if you joined the Party.'

'I would rather become a regular attender at cell meetings first, then I might be a little more fit to join than I am now.'

'This probationary period you've decided on for yourself could be dragged out too long. I know there's a lot to be said for not joining in a hurry – though that's how I joined, and I learnt what the Party stood for as I went along – but when anyone becomes a member and accepts the discipline he begins to see things in proportion. He finds that what really counts is not so much the more spectacular events such as demonstrations but the steady everyday political grind.'

It was clear to Alan that she understood him very well. Just as earlier on she had detected the personal overtones in his shout of 'Down with the Means Test', so now she had guessed that behind his expressed enthusiasm for the demonstration there was an excessive disappointment. But she was not blaming him, only advising him how to avoid disillusionment of this kind in the future. He felt a warmth towards her which he risked trying to put into his voice as he asked, 'When is our next cell meeting? I know I ought to know, but I don't.'

'On Thursday, usual place and time.'

He looked down at her gloveless hands, which were resting well forward on her lap with the finger-tips close to her knees. The sleeves of her coat were drawn back, showing wrists that had a suggestion of plumpness about them. A small watch, apparently a gold one, was attached to her left wrist by a narrow black watered-silk ribbon. He was incongruously reminded of a painting which his grandparents had owned and which had portrayed an eighteenth-century lady with piled-up powdered hair and with black velvet ribbons round her wrists instead of bracelets. He had an impulse, which at first he resisted, to say something very slightly humorous to Elsie about her gold watch. After a time, noticing out of the window that they were now not far from where he would have to get off the bus, he did say, 'That's an impressive watch you're wearing.'

She was surprised, but then seriously explained, as if to exculpate herself, 'It was given me by my mother for my twenty-first birthday.'

A moment later – in spite of his not having had any encouragement from her, and perhaps just because of it and because, whatever the risk of making her annoyed with him might be, he needed to be sure she understood that he wanted encouragement – he was impelled to say, 'Can I call at your house on Thursday before the cell meeting?'

'What for?'

It seemed she genuinely did not know, or if she did was unwilling to believe he could be so silly. He did not answer. She suddenly stood up, saying, 'I get off the bus here.' He did not dare to go with her, though this stop was not much farther from his lodgings than the next, which was his usual one on this route. She frigidly avoided looking at him as she went.

Soon after he had got back to his lodgings he remembered that she had not told him he wasn't to call at her house on Thursday before the cell meeting.

5

AT A MINUTE or less past nine o'clock Alan was looking
out into the corridor from the open doorway of his form-
room, having sent the boys down to Assembly in the so-called
Great Hall rather more punctually than usual but wanting
to make sure that none of them had chosen to linger on the
way, and he was thinking with relief that his first period this
morning would be a free one, when he saw Hotchkiss, the
school porter, coming towards him. 'For you, sir,' Hotchkiss
said, handing him a small square piece of paper on which
Alan quickly read that the Headmaster wished to see Mr
Sebrill at 9.30. The message was a printed one, only the
time and his name being handwritten, and it was of the kind
customarily delivered to boys who had offended against
school rules. He was on the point of asking what this was
all about, but Hotchkiss – who anyway would have been
unlikely to know – had turned and was already walking off
down the corridor, a stiff figure uniformed in a blue frock-
coat-length tunic which on previous occasions had made
Alan think of the Crimean war but which now did not seem
comic.

Alan tried to guess what particular offence the Head might
want to reprimand him for, and he supposed it might be the
habit he had recently developed of staying in his form-room
during Assembly instead of appearing with other members
of the staff on the platform in the Great Hall. However, there
was the possibility that the Head mightn't be going to repri-

mand him at all, though what else he might want to see him for Alan couldn't easily imagine, unless it might be to tell him about a salary adjustment. The fact that the message was a printed one might be due merely to a pompous intention on the Head's part to hold himself at a distance from a younger assistant master who had been on the staff for only two and a half terms. Such an intention would be typical of him, and quite in keeping with the spirit in which the school as a whole was run. Presumably he believed he was behaving like Thring of Uppingham, whom he so much admired. Almost everything that was done here was modelled on what was usual at the great public schools of England. 'We're a cheap petty-bourgeois snob-imitation,' Alan thought, and in an instant he was filled with a soaring anger that lifted him entirely clear of the anxiety which the Head's note had been making him feel.

He went striding from the doorway back into his form-room, swinging his fists as though to strike out at someone, and when he arrived where the windowed outer wall prevented him from striding farther his knees rose in a rapid prancing movement which was like marking time at the double. Then, becoming aware that his antics might be seen from the corridor, he abruptly stood still, blindly facing the window. Rage, cut off from venting itself physically, at once found expression inwardly, however, in a violent activity of mind. What was so infuriating, he thought, was that if this school had been allowed to develop along the lines natural to a day school it could have been far superior educationally to the public schools which it grovellingly and unsuccessfully aimed to resemble. It could have been the friend, not the despiser, of the local community from which it drew its pupils; it could have co-operated with the parents instead of trying to insulate itself from them; it could have based its educational theory and practice on the principle of family kindness and not on the diseased ideal of a discipline half-military, half-monastic. But it had spurned its opportunities, had snobbishly strained to reproduce in detail a reactionary pattern even where the detail was manifestly inapplicable to a day school. It had mystically insisted that on the first morning of every term each boy should bring with him a health certificate stating that he had not been in contact with infection during the holidays – a precaution which could be logical only in a boarding school, where the boys would be segregated from the normal life of the community during all the remaining days of the term. It had tried its futile best to convince boys who went home every evening that they ought not to have during term-time any life outside the life of the school. Instead of the self-discipline which in their circumstances they above all needed, it had given them – from nine o'clock till four or five every day during term – authoritarianism. It had placed over them from among themselves prefects who were allowed to use the cane; it had uniformed and drilled them in the cadet corps; it had subjected them to a would-be boarding school 'house' system, which included fagging. Instead of making scientific humanism the basis of its teaching, it had exalted the Greek and Latin classics above all other studies, had compelled every boy on the scientific side to learn Latin, but had allowed the boys on the classical side to remain complacently ignorant of science. Instead of trying in its teaching to relate every subject on the curriculum to ordinary life, it had made even science seem an abstract academic puzzle remote from common experience, and it had done this deliberately in the obstinate belief that the value of any subject as a means of 'training the mind' varied inversely with the degree to which that subject might be of practical use in the twentieth-century world. It had regarded with extreme suspicion the 'modernist' view – held also in the sixteenth century by Montaigne – that boys work better when they are interested than when they are not, and had preferred to think that no work could be truly beneficial to the worker unless performed against his inclinations and under external compulsion. Its favourite morning prayer – read out at least once every week by the Headmaster in Assembly – was the one which went, 'Teach us, good Lord . . . to give and not to count the cost; to fight and not to heed the wounds; to toil and not to seek for rest; to labour and not to ask for any reward save the joy of knowing that we do Thy will.' The real aim of this school was to train its pupils to be good hard-working unquestioning servants of modern British imperialism. What it above all feared was that these pupils might grow up to follow the 'devices and desires of their own hearts', might be ruled by natural human feelings and might become unwilling to accept the wars and the wounds and the restless toil that the imperialists were preparing for them.

Fortunately natural human feelings and desires could not so easily be suppressed – though the attempt to suppress them might cause them to express themselves in a distorted and ugly way. This thought was suggested to Alan by the sound of the hymn that the boys were now loudly singing in the Great Hall. Only the tune penetrated to him up in his form-room, but he had come to know the words very well since he had been at this school. What motives the person in authority who chose the hymn each morning might have for choosing this one so often he couldn't confidently guess, nor why it was as popular with the boys as the noisiness of their singing indicated: very possibly the tune was the attraction. 'Lift up your hearts' were the harmless opening words, but soon the writer was moving into the attack with 'Above the level of the former years, The mire of sin, the slough of guilty fears,' and then, still more accusingly, he continued with 'Above the swamps of subterfuge and shame, The deeds, the thoughts that honour may not name'; but rebellious human nature, although or because so vehemently denounced, got its own back at last in a homophone and a double-entendre – 'the halting tongue that dare not tell the whole'. Most of Sigmund Freud's generalizations, Alan thought, were rightly rejected by Marxists as emptily speculative, but surely the theory was correct that slips of the tongue and unconscious puns have their origin, no matter how accidental they may seem to be, in feelings that we have been trying to repress. And at the beginning of the final verse of the hymn came the grand phallic climax – 'Lift every gift that Thou Thyself has given.' Sex had won. The 'public' school had proved and would always prove to be as powerless against it as against, for instance, the natural desire of the boys to do work that interested them. Sex took its revenge in obscenities, and the desire for interesting work took revenge in disorder and ragging. Unfortunately, however, the boys directed their main counter-attack not against their oppressors but against their would-be liberator, regarding him perhaps as the weakest link in the chain that bound them.

But mightn't the boys be right in repulsing his efforts to interest them? Alan thought. He stood looking out of the form-room window. There was a narrow lawn below, and beyond this a line of evergreen shrubs with the earth freshly dug around them, and beyond these were three autumnal, though not yet entirely leafless, chestnut-trees and a big copper beech still covered in leaves. For a moment the trees appeared to him as if they had no connection with the school but were miles away in the country, and, although he soon saw them again as standing in the school grounds with a suburban railway embankment just beyond them, they did not become defiled for him by their real situation; on the contrary, the school seemed by contrast with them even more vile, unfree and unnatural than before. And he with his soft-soapy 'progressive' methods had been aiming to persuade the boys to enjoy working in this prison. How completely justified they had been in their contempt for him. He had behaved like a smarmy reformist, hoping to make acceptable to them a system which was fit only for abolition. His aim should be to work for its overthrow. But that could not be brought about from within, because even if he were miraculously to convert the Headmaster and the rest of the staff to a belief in scientific humanism, and if as a result the teaching here were revolutionized, there would still be the capitalist State with its inspectorate and all its other means of bringing pressure to bear. Anyone who genuinely wanted to reform education must work politically outside the school for the destruction of capitalism. To try to be an educator under the present system, as Alan had been trying, was fraudulent and shameful. He would try no longer. He would cleanse himself of educationism, would from henceforward be as nearly as possible an automaton while in school, and all the energy he thereby saved should go into the political fight outside. An excitement such as comes to a man who at last liberates himself from a stock idea that has been hampering him made Alan turn from the window and stride out across the form-room. Once again his fists were swinging and he was beginning to prance. He checked himself abruptly. Footsteps were approaching along the corridor. Benson, wearing a gown and big glasses and seeming to stare straight ahead, went past the open doorway. His chin was stuck forward and the muscle at the corner of his jaw was bunched beneath the skin and had a groove in it like the fluting on a tumbler, suggesting that he was clenching his teeth hard. He carried a steep pile of exercise books under his arm. Dead keen on his work, he no doubt made a point of getting to his classroom immediately after Assembly and before the boys arrived. But his coming now meant that Assembly must be over and that Alan would have to go downstairs at once or risk meeting the full horde on their way up.

Alan got through to the common-room just as the Sixth Formers were being let out of the Great Hall by the prefects, and he still had a quarter of an hour to wait before he was due to see the Head. The anxiety which his angry meditations in the form-room had enabled him to overcome began to return as he waited. Very punctually he made his way to the Head's study and knocked on the door, which was opened after a pause by Sidney Bantick, the Head's secretary. The severity of Bantick's black jacket and striped city trousers was contradicted by a look of melancholy friendliness in his large eyes.

'The Headmaster is not quite ready for you yet, Mr Sebrill. Would you kindly wait out here just a moment?'

The last two syllables of the word 'Headmaster' were pronounced more softly than the first syllable, as if to mitigate the effect of formality produced by his using the full word instead of the more usual and colloquial 'Head'; and the word 'kindly' was softly spoken too, though warmly, as if Bantick did not want it to be heard inside the study. Then he gently shut the door.

Alan had not been standing outside for long when Brook, who also had a free period, came walking past in a leisured and almost lounging way suggestive of an athlete relaxing between races. His unbuttoned Harris tweed jacket was wide open, exposing the protrusion of a chocolate-brown woollen pullover, and his fists in his pockets made the upper part of his trousers stick out on both sides. Not pausing in his walk, he asked gloatingly, 'Getting the sack, dearie?'

'Probably.'

His head, crested with fair undulating hair, swivelled back as it went by and directed a sadistic grin towards Alan over the tweed shoulder; then, before it turned to face forwards again, it changed its grin to a serious look which seemed meant to convey that if Brook had had his way Alan would have been sacked long ago. Alone once more, Alan had time to wonder how it was that so often insensitive persons were able much more effectively than others to detect and to hit at the most vulnerable spots in the sensitive. But perhaps there was nothing very subtle about Brook's present attack; perhaps, even, it had been based not on any shrewd guess at what Alan's feelings might be but on general talk that might have been going on for some time in the common-room concerning Alan's efficiency.

The door of the Head's study opened again. Bantick came out into the corridor, saying very quietly indeed, 'The Old Man's fully prepared for you now.'

Giving Alan a restrained sympathetic smile in which there was a hint of mock-heroic encouragement, he went off along the corridor in the direction of his office. Alan pushed open the door more widely and stepped forward on to the dark red carpet inside the study.

The Head shifted a wire tray on his desk, making a show of not being quite ready for Alan even yet, then colourlessly asked him to sit down. A chair, which the Head indicated to him by nodding towards it, had been placed in the middle of the room, facing not the desk but the fireplace, and as soon as Alan sat down on it the Head pushed back his own chair, got up and walked thoughtfully over to stand on the hearth-rug. In a clerical-grey suit and a secular, minutely-white-spotted blue tie, the corner of a blue handkerchief sticking out of his breast pocket, he stood tall, with neatly-shoed feet apart and hands behind his back, the skin of his big face slightly brown, unwrinkled, not even lined, giving – especially as seen now against the framed engraving which hung above the mantelpiece and which pictured the caryatids of the Erectheum – the impression that he lived a life of Mediterranean ease. His voice, when he at last began to speak again, was very smooth: 'I have asked you here this morning, Mr Sebrill, because I think the time has come when I should have your views on your work at this school.'

He waited, plainly not for any immediate statement from

Alan but so that the significance of these words should sink deeply in. Alan recognized that something much more serious was coming than he had foreseen when Hotchkiss had handed him the printed note. He had a sensation as of a sudden but protracted pause in the circulation of the blood in his arms and body, then immediately afterwards he felt his face flush hot.

'It has become evident that the relations between you and the boys you teach are, shall we say, not as happy as could be wished.'

Again the Head waited. In the interval of several seconds before he continued speaking Alan was able, thinking at a speed which emotion caused to be far above normal but which seemed quite leisurely to him, to decide that if he got the sack it would enable him to give himself wholly to the poetry he was now once more writing and that he would leave London and would go again to the seaside village where he and Richard had been eighteen months before.

'At the end of this term you will have had a year with us here – your probationary year.'

Though the Head's tone was polite there was behind it, and in his eyes, an unartificial resentment – as though he considered himself to have been let down capriciously by a man from whom he had had sound reason to expect better things. Alan looked away from him and towards the tall glass-fronted bookcase which was to the right of the door. Three large leather-bound books with Gothic-lettered backs stood on the lowest shelf next to a copy of *Who's Who*. Alan, before the Head spoke again, had leisure to note the titles, which were *Sermons of Bishop Jewel*, *Works of Bishop Latimer*, and *Remains of Archbishop Grindal*.

The Head said, 'The question is –and I hope you'll appreciate that if I seem to be speaking rather frankly I'm doing so at least as much in what I believe to be your interests as in the interests of the school – the question really is whether you intend to make schoolmastering your permanent job in life.'

Alan continued looking at the bookcase, and now he saw not the books behind the glass but the reflection in the glass of a strip of sky and of the trees outside the study window. The trees were the same that he had seen from his form-room, with coppery or pale brown or lemon-yellow leaves, and their reflection inside the study had the double effect of bringing them very near to him as appearances on the surface of the glass and of making them seem at the same time less substantial, more remote from the school, closer to the countryside, more than ever desirable. A sudden involuntary change of eye-focus caused him to see once again the books behind the glass, and the reflection began to appear as filmy as an almost invisible vapour. He tried to bring the trees back in their former definiteness, and he was partly successful: as the reflection became more distinct the books became less so, though they remained visible, and at last they and the trees reached much the same degree of apparent substantiality. However, the books seemed to be a little way beyond and behind the trees, and shadowy, recessed, as in a grotto whose entrance was fringed by dipping leaves. No other life, he thought, could compare with a life of poetic leisure in the country. As he looked, the books vanished again and the reflection grew more vivid. He began in imagination to move forward among the trees, and then to move beyond them where there were open fields and downs. Aware that the Head's pause now was different from the earlier pauses and was probably meant to allow Alan to speak at last, he nevertheless felt he had ample time to continue his imaginings. As though he had drunk from a phial containing H. G. Wells' New Accelerator drug, all his processes seemed to have been superhumanly speeded up and he was able to move beyond the trees and the fields and to reach the seashore while the Head was in the uncompleted act of slightly flexing both knees beneath the clerical-grey trousers. And yet Alan did not feel at all hurried: moving along a path below the downs he could notice a dead thistle with its rayed sepals having the colour and sheen of slightly tarnished silver and with its central disk pale yellow like the fluff of a new-hatched chick; he could observe that the grey-bearded purplish seeds of the wild clematis resembled frogspawn when they were viewed against the sky; and, arriving at the almost calm sea, he watched how the wind hachured its surface with criss-crossing dark lines, and how in the minute parallelograms formed by these intersecting lines the water seemed to rise in blips which immediately burst into sparkles and spangles. Suddenly in his mind's ear he heard a calm voice speak the word 'freedom'. He had only to admit aloud that he did not consider himself really suited to be a schoolmaster, and he could be free. He could walk in actuality among trees, reach the seashore, live the poetic life. And the exquisiteness of that possibility was intensified for him by the thought now of the slavish unhappy half-life he had been living at this school. He could cleanse himself utterly of the muck that covered him here. He could leave at the end of this term, perhaps even before the end. But instead of giving notice to the Head, he found himself saying, 'I would rather be in schoolmastering than in any other job.'

And this seemed truthful, unless writing poetry could be counted as a job. Having said it, he knew how foolish he would have been to have given notice. The poetic life was an illusion, as he had finally discovered a year before. Another attempt to live that life, even though at present he was able to write poetry again, would lead only to suicide or madness. If he got the sack this morning he must go all out at once to find another job, and he must say nothing now which might help the Head to give him the sack. However the Head's next remark suggested that his intention from the start of this interview might have been no more than to give

Alan a healthy shock: 'I'm glad to hear you say that. There remains now the question whether we still have a reasonable chance of putting right what has gone wrong.'

The poetic life, Alan thought, had never been anything better than the sentimental dream of a young bourgeois. Necessity required that he should rid himself for ever of the irresponsible longing for months of love and poetry in the sun by the sea. There was only one way for him to live and to extricate himself from the effects of a daily drudgery into which economic need had forced him but for which he was temperamentally unfit, and that was by giving himself more and more in his free time to the service of the working-class movement. His next goal must be to join the Party, perhaps not immediately but after a month or two when he had shown by uninterrupted hard work and regular attendance at meetings that he was worthy to become a member.

The Head said, 'It seems that a possible cause of the trouble is that you don't really know the boys in the forms you take and that you couldn't for instance speak to them by their individual surnames.'

Though this was untrue, and though in fact Alan was keenly aware of the individualities and names of all of them, except perhaps one or two who had never called attention to themselves by misbehaving, he was not going to bother to deny it; but the angering thought suddenly came to him that the Head's criticism was likely to be based much less on personal observation than on the reports of some tale-bearer, and he said, 'I think I know them pretty well.'

'They are restless,' the Head incontrovertibly said. 'More so, to be frank with you, than they would be if there were no master in the room. There must be something about your approach that rubs them up the wrong way.'

Alan had nothing to say, was uncomfortably caught in the straight gaze directed at him by the Head, whose neck seemed to have become elongated and whose face jutted out with a severe look on it such as it might usually reserve for a prevaricating boy whom he'd driven at last into a dialectical corner.

'The secret of good discipline in the classroom,' the Head went on, 'is to get the boys working and to keep them at it. Boys in general *like* being *made* to work. As for those few who don't – there are ways of persuading them.'

Alan managed slowly to disengage his own gaze from the Head's and to strengthen himself by looking up at the wall to the right of the mantelpiece, where there was a framed architect's plan of the not-yet-built school chapel, by the future building of which the Head dreamed to raise the status of this school to an incontestably public-school level.

Abruptly and briskly the Head asked, 'Have you tried beating any of them recently?'

'No.'

Alan couldn't help sounding a little apologetic, though the idea of beating was repulsive to him. The Head's silence retroactively made clear that, though his words had taken the form of a question, they were intended as an injunction. At last, releasing into his tone a little of the exasperation he had probably been feeling all the time, the Head said, 'Really you ought not to be having this trouble with discipline. After all, you yourself as a boy were educated at Reptile' – he quickly corrected this – 'I mean at Repton.'

He had to allow himself to smile slightly at his slip of the tongue, though no doubt he was just as unaware as most other contemporary headmasters would have been that it was a perfect example of the Freudian error. It revealed not only his sense that in appointing to the staff an ex-public-school man who hadn't behaved like one he had been made the victim of an almost satanic kind of trickery, but also probably his discovery via Aldershaw of Alan's political views. And yet the distinction of having been a boy at a well-known English public school was evidently going to be sufficient to save Alan, no matter how serpent-like he might seem, from the sack. But he had better say something now to consolidate his advantage.

'I will do what I can to improve in future.'

'Good.'

There was no return of the brief naturalness shown by the Head when he had smiled at his own error, but there was a relaxing of tension. He became again the smooth head-masterly personage that by years of deliberate effort he had succeeded in making himself. Alan, waiting respectfully for what he would say next, took inward revenge by thinking satirically about him: clergymanlike without ever having been ordained, capable at times of heavy humour, a fanatical upholder of the Classics not so much for their own sakes as for the social cachet he believed they conferred, a hobnobber with bishops on Hellenic tours, a detester – for what he claimed to be solely aesthetic reasons – of lower-class polite-nesses such as the use of the word 'pardon' instead of the words 'excuse me', a personage who could be further mollified now if Alan would call him 'sir'.

'Well, that's all, Mr Sebrill,' the Head said.

Alan got up and, saying 'Thank you', moved sideways towards the door. He couldn't bring himself to add 'sir', even though there would have been no one but himself and the Head to hear that sycophantic word. As he opened the door he thought of Brook, who fortunately was not coming along the corridor now to make inquisitive remarks about the inter-view. Shutting the door behind him carefully in order to avoid all risk of seeming to slam it, he felt doubly relieved. But by the time he had walked back to the common-room he was fully aware of the unpleasantness of the experience he had just had in the Head's study. What had happened there could not be contemptuously or cheerfully forgotten, but must grimly influence everything he did at this school in future. His decision reached during Assembly to take no more interest in education would have to be rescinded. Instead of aiming at becoming an automaton during school hours and of conserving his nervous energy for political work, he would have to try to be aggressively wide-awake all the time here. Abandoning 'progressive' methods didn't mean freeing himself from every kind of educational method: it meant becoming educationally a reactionary. He was prepared to be that. There seemed no other way of keeping his job. He would redeem himself by the work he would do for the Party in the evenings.

6

ALAN ARRIVED EARLY for the meeting at which he was to be made a member of the Party. Crossing the cobbled stableyard, he reached the coach-house whose upper room or loft had for the past six weeks been very cheaply rented and regularly used by the local Party cell, and found that the outer door was locked. He stepped slowly backwards on the down-sloped cobbles, avoiding an iron grating that covered a drain in the middle of the yard, and stood waiting for someone to come with the key. The summer evening sunlight was on the yellow brick of the coach-house and on the ivy that bifurcated up the wall-faces from the corner of the building. The adhesive roots of the ivy had the colour of dry string that has once been soaked for a long time in water. Pollarded lime-trees ineffectively screened the yard from a large house, also of yellow brick but turreted and with stained glass in some of its windows, where lived the old man from whom the cell rented the room in the coach-house. There was an appropriateness, Alan thought, in the Party's having taken over this decayed outbuilding, which belonged to a bourgeois urban mansion, once imposing but now outfaced and down-valued by a tall block of flats on the opposite side of the road. He stood looking at the coach-house, at its ivy and at the gilded wind-vane topping a small square-shaped louvred tower on its roof, and he allowed himself to feel its period charm – as he might not have allowed himself if it had not been rented by the Party. This evening the room upstairs would become his, he told himself. No freehold house that he might one day own and live in with a wife and perhaps children could ever more truly belong to him than this rented loft which, when he had been accepted into the Party at this evening's meeting, he would fully share as an equal partner with his comrades in the cell.

There were brisk steps along the pavement and Wally came into the yard, alone.

'Door locked?' he guessed cheerfully. 'Anders'll have the key. He's not usually late – like some – but perhaps we're early. And I was just longing for a good sit-down in one of those canvas chairs you've helped to provide up there. I'm fair worn out.'

'You don't look it,' Alan said, pleased to be reminded of the five pounds which he had lent – without expecting or wishing to get them back – to the group as a contribution towards buying second-hand chairs for the loft.

'I am. Three hours' travelling every day – that's what I have to do now. And on top of that the new job isn't a rest cure.'

There was no suggestion of complaint in his voice: on the contrary he sounded almost proud of himself.

'What's the new job?'

'Buck navvy. On a building site over at Barking. Carrying timber and ironwork about all day.'

'It must be pretty wearing.'

'You get used to it. It's worst at the start. There's a bone in the shoulder which hurts when you carry planks – till you find the proper way. Everyone has his own way of carrying them. But there's one thing I shan't ever really get used to.'

'What's that?'

'Having to run across a six-inch girder high up in the air. It makes me shiver.'

'It would do more than that to me,' Alan said sympathetically. 'It would paralyse me before I even started.'

'It wouldn't, not if you had to do it for a living.' Wally smiled. 'But the job has its lighter side. We've just got a new carpenter who has a liking for the bottle. You should have heard him yesterday. He was well and truly drunk and he was shouting up from the ground at the other carpenter, who's deaf, and he couldn't even attract his attention, so at last he bawled out, "Who is that monkey up there in the rigging?" You can imagine how all the brickies looked down at him.'

Listening to Wally, Alan felt a warmth towards him and at the same time was gladdened suddenly by the thought that after this evening's meeting there would no longer be between them the class barrier which he had seldom been able altogether to forget, though Wally on the other hand had never seemed aware of it. However little hope there might be of his eventually becoming Wally's equal as a human being, Alan would no longer need to regard his bourgeois origin as putting him in a position of social inferiority to Wally. Membership of the Party transcended class differences between the members. After this evening he and Wally would more truly be able to be friends than before.

Three other comrades were approaching along the pavement: they were Jimmy Anders, Harry Temley and Eddie Freans. Anders, with a mildness unusual for him, said as they came into the yard, 'Sorry to have kept you hanging about, comrades. Pity we have to leave the place locked, but the Old Boy's very particular about it: afraid that if burglars got into our room upstairs they'd also get into the garage below – though how they'd do that short of knocking a hole down through the ceiling I don't know.'

'His old Chevrolet isn't worth pinching anyway, Harry Temley said, giving Alan a very friendly look. He worked as a mechanic in a garage. He was twenty-two, thick-set and handsome-faced, and he had bright yellow hair which rose

129

in high floppy curves above his broad forehead on both sides of his parting.

'Wonder how the Old Boy would react if he knew that the Acme Sports Club he believes he's letting his room to is really the Party,' Eddie Freans said to Alan with a warm smile. He stood at Harry's side, physically very different from him, slim and having a thin face that was dark with subcuticular hair along the jaws and the sides of the chin. He seemed like a Spaniard, though he wasn't one. He had a job in a small workshop where lampshades were made.

'The Old Boy would shut himself in one of those cylindrical rooms inside a turret and never come out again,' Alan suggested, moving beside Eddie behind the others, who were beginning to follow Anders up the wooden steps to the loft.

Alan asked Eddie, 'How's your invention going?'

'Which one?'

'The slotted brick you were telling me about after the last cell meeting.'

'Oh *that*, that's all right. The Patent Office have been giving a bit of trouble, trying to make out that something similar to my brick has been thought of before. It hasn't. The trouble was they didn't bother to look carefully at my drawings. I've written, pointing out to them what makes my brick different from the others, and I've just had an answer. They admit I'm in the right.' He was starting to go up the rather narrow steps in front of Alan. He stopped, turned round to face Alan and said with frank enthusiasm, 'But now I've got something far better than that.' He went on up the steps.

At the top Alan asked him, 'Another invention?'

'Yes, to do with lighting. It's a new kind of reflector. Not like the ordinary ones made with mercury and glass – which tend to separate when heated. Mine's made with glass, pure tin and copper – a sheet of tin and then a sheet of copper behind that. It's angular, and ribbed.'

They picked out two upright canvas chairs in the second

row back from the chairman's table, and sat down. Eddie, like Alan and like most other Party members, for some reason preferred not to sit in the front row at meetings. Eddie continued, 'I'm starting business with another man. We shall go round to various firms, showing them how they can save money on lighting by using my reflector.'

'In fact you're about to become a small capitalist,' Alan said, smiling. 'You may even become a big one before you've finished.'

'Some hopes.' Eddie grinned, then added, 'But if I do you needn't worry; because the money'll go to the Party.'

Other comrades were coming into the room: Jock Finlayson, Sam Cowan, and Jean Pritchet (who was Anders' girl). They made their way to the chairs just behind Alan and Eddie, with whom they exchanged gay and friendly hullos. Eddie turned to Alan again for a moment and said, 'Of course, I have to look out nowadays when going round corners. The big electricity people don't like me.'

Whether this was meant at all seriously Alan wasn't able to discover, because Jean Pritchet then tapped Eddie on the shoulder and began to talk to him about some pamphlets which she as 'lit. sec.' had given him to sell during the week. 'And suppose it was meant seriously,' Alan thought, 'what would that matter?' Eddie might have his moments of naïveté, but about things that were really important he had a far better understanding than was to be found in the university-educated intellectual chatterers of whom Alan had met too many. For those, and for members of the middle class generally, Alan could never have the respect that he had for Eddie; and in spite of the things Alan had in common with them – education, accent, manners – he felt much closer to Eddie than to them. He was happier and more at home with Eddie, just as he was happier and more at home with the other comrades here, even with those whose experiences had been most different from his and whose usefulness to the Party was so much greater than his: Jock Finlayson, who was a branch secretary in the A.E.U. and was likely to go far in the trade union movement; Sam Cowan, also a very active trade unionist, an orator with a real gift for words whom Wally called 'our poet'; red-haired Jean Pritchet, who seemed indifferent to her own beauty and of whom Alan had once overheard a politically hostile young man say when she was speaking in Hyde Park, 'I understand now why men join the Communist Party.' He was at ease with them, at one with them, and with every comrade here. They were, in the profoundest sense, his friends.

The speaker who was going to lead the discussion this evening – Willie Dean Ayres – had now come into the room, accompanied by Beatrix Farrell, the woman comrade to whom he was married, and by Lily Pentelow, who had recently been elected to an important position in the Co-operative movement, and by Mike Bainton, who was talking without pause to Willie. Alan couldn't help reflecting that Bainton seemed to have a fondness for associating with comrades who were in any way prominent in the Party. Then he thought, 'Elsie doesn't usually arrive late for meetings.' However as soon as he had thought this, or perhaps simultaneously with or even previously to his thinking it, footsteps which sounded as though they might be hers were audible on the stairs. She appeared in the doorway, her face a little flushed and her hair straying; but, instead of coming to sit next to him as he hoped and expected she would, she chose a chair at the far end of the front row.

Perhaps she was displeased because he had not turned up at her house as usual this evening to go with her to the meeting. But she would forgive him afterwards when she knew that he had been suddenly asked just after lunch to umpire an under-fifteen cricket match and that he hadn't been able to let her know he'd be kept too late at the school to call for her. Her displeasure with him – if in fact she was displeased and hadn't chosen that distant chair merely because she was late and it was near to the door – could easily be dispelled. It didn't worry him or prevent him from looking with interest at Willie Dean Ayres, who had just sat down next to Jimmy Anders, the chairman, at the table.

Dean Ayres wore a dark blue shirt and a dark red tie and a rather small proletarian-looking cap whose colour might originally have been grey-green. His head seemed round as a ball and his face was pleasant and mild. Alan had heard him lecture several times before but had been unable to decide whether he was a proletarian turned intellectual or an intellectual turned proletarian. There could be no doubt, however, that his plainly-dressed wife Beatrix, who was sitting in a chair in the front row facing him, was not of working-class origin and might even have been born into the kind of family whose daughters are presented at Court. Willie's very surname had a class ambiguity about it: being a double name, it might have belonged to someone who was or wished to be regarded as on the fringes of aristocracy, but, being unhyphenated, it gave a suggestion of American vulgarity which democratized it. He was a very capable lecturer, clear, and always in sympathetic rapport with his audience. The group was lucky to get him here this evening: as a rule he was booked up for larger meetings – at branch level, or above. He did not take off his cap.

Jimmy Anders, without standing up from the chair, opened the meeting: 'It's time we started, comrades. . . . In accordance with the decision taken when we last met I suggest we get through the business part of our meeting as quickly as possible and move on to discussion. There's no doubt that for some time we've been tending to allow political discussion to be crowded out by items of immediate practical importance. This won't do, comrades. We all know that theory without practice is barren, but we seem to have been forgetting that practice without theory is just as bad or perhaps worse – is blind, in fact. The difference between a genuinely Marxist party, comrades, and all other socialist parties is that a Marxist party is scientific, that's to say it is guided by Marxism and it draws theoretical conclusions from its practical experience and uses them as an aid to further practice. If we find we've more and more business to get through at group meetings, this doesn't mean that political discussion must be cut down to nothing but that we must hold extra meetings for discussion. That's why we've called this meeting here this evening. But before I ask Comrade Dean Ayres to lead off on the present political situation there is one item of business we must deal with.' Alan wasn't sure whether or not Anders smiled very slightly before adding, 'We have had to postpone it at our last two meetings. I mean the application of Comrade Sebrill to join the Party. I think you were going to propose him, Comrade Elsie Hutchinson, weren't you?'

Elsie stood up and, looking not at the chairman but straight in front of her at the semicircular window which was based diametrically on the floor of the loft, she began speaking in a voice that gave no hint of any personal feeling towards Alan:

'Comrade Sebrill has been working with us now for more than a year. He has attended cell meetings regularly during the last few months, it being understood that he wished to be regarded as on probation for eventual Party membership. He has taken his full share in Party activities. He has helped in selling the *Daily Worker* outside the bus garage; he has been useful in door-to-door canvassing; he has turned out on slogan-chalking expeditions; he has become active in his union and I believe there is a chance of his being co-opted on to its branch committee. Comrade Sebrill has hesitated for a long time about joining the Party, but I think this has been to his credit. He has a high conception – and quite rightly – of what Party membership means, and he wanted

134

time to prepare himself properly for it. I think comrades will agree that if we decide to accept him he will make a satisfactory member.' Elsie sat down, and Jimmy Anders asked from the chair, 'Has any other comrade anything to say on this?'

There was a noticeable pause, surprising to Alan because usually comrades were ready enough to speak when asked. Wally at last said, 'Would Comrade Sebrill like to give us an idea of what first made him want to get in touch with the Party?'

Alan had expected that someone would ask this question and he had roughly prepared an answer to it. He had intended to say that in the conditions of modern monopoly capitalism the independence of the middle class was being increasingly undermined and would soon cease to exist and that the only hope for individual members of his class was to go over to the side of the workers against the monopoly capitalists, and that therefore he had decided to contact the Party. But now, with everyone expecting him to speak, he became aware that he would not be able to say any of this. The occasion seemed much too serious for such abstractions. He needed to be absolutely sincere. The most important event of his life so far was happening now, and he must tell them the truth, not mouth out convenient generalities picked up from books and pamphlets. But what was the truth? What were the actual personal motives which had made him turn towards Communism? He could not, for the moment, remember. Or, rather, he could remember only one motive, but it had been one that might sound ridiculous if he told them of it. Yet it had been real; and they were waiting for him to speak, were even seeming to become a little embarrassed on his behalf because of his silence, and Jimmy Anders – who had been looking down at the table – now looked straight at him.

So Alan said, 'I suppose the very first time the idea crossed my mind that I'd like to get in touch with the Party was while I was reading a prayer aloud to the boys when I was on duty one evening at a boarding school where I used to teach. I was suddenly filled with disgust at the dishonesty which I, an atheist, had been forced into in order to keep my job. Then I realized that not merely this school but the social and economic system as a whole was to blame for the compulsion put upon me, and before I'd finished reading the prayer I knew I was in sympathy with the Communist aim of social revolution. However, I'm ashamed to say I made no attempt – until several years afterwards – to contact the Party, and I hardly gave another thought to Communism while I was at that school.'

Alan became aware that he couldn't possibly go on and tell them how his final and effectual decision to contact the Party had been reached during a walk which he had taken along the top of a cliff with the intention of committing suicide. But even though it was now obvious that he was not going to say anything more, no one else spoke. Then a brief slight noise resembling an incipient laugh came from Jean Pritchet behind him. There was nothing of ridicule in it, but it did suggest an indulgent attitude towards him, as though she saw him as someone rather less adult than the others. Soon everyone in the room, including Jimmy Anders, was faintly smiling. Alan did not feel foolish, because he was aware of their friendliness and their approval, but he was pleasantly puzzled about what their amusement meant. The least improbable interpretation of it seemed to be that they had responded to his brief speech rather in the same way that he would have responded to a strange, though effective, conceit in a seventeenth-century Metaphysical poem, finding him slightly funny as well as admirable. But he was still doubting whether this interpretation was right when Anders asked, 'Those in favour of accepting Comrade Sebrill?'

They put their hands up, and there was no one against and no abstainer. (There never seemed to be abstentions at Party meetings, Alan reflected.) Anders addressed Alan: 'You are now a member of the Party, comrade. If you'll see me at the end of the meeting I'll give you a card, and you may as well get it stamped up for a week or so ahead. That's better than having to get it stamped up for a month or so back.' His face showed a minatory smile that seemed to be aimed not so much at Alan as at some other already guilty comrade or comrades in the audience. 'Consistent failure to pay dues punctually may – and should, according to the rules – result in the offending comrade being lapsed from the Party. And now we come to the main purpose of this meeting. I call on Comrade Dean Ayres to open the discussion on the political situation.'

Dean Ayres, after standing up, walked slowly away from the table and – at first facing neither the chairman nor the audience but the door in the right-hand back corner of the room – began meditatively and intimately, yet very distinctly, to speak. His hands were in his pockets and he still wore his cap. When he turned his face to the comrades its look suggested not that he was recalling himself from abstract cogitation but rather that he had been happily aware of them all the time and had for a moment out of necessity turned away from them in order to be able to collect his thoughts on the subject he was due to speak about. Alan, though admiringly observing Dean Ayres' tactics and briefly wondering how far they were consciously adopted and how far natural to the man, paid no more than a superficial attention to the earlier part of the speech. He heard the sound of the words and understood their meaning, but at the same time he was deeply occupied with his own feelings about having been accepted as a member of the Party.

Once when he had been with Richard in the country they had come to the top of a hill from which the sea had been brilliantly visible and seemed very near, but they had reached the sea only after walking on for miles and miles across low fields from which it had again been invisible.

Alan's journey towards Party membership, he now felt, resembled his walk then. More than a year ago he had seemed to be within sight of becoming a member, but there had been days since when he had doubted whether he would ever be capable of it. 'Now I have arrived at the seen sea at last,' he thought. He stared at the semi-circular window whose panes were held in place by narrow spokes of wood like the spokes of a wheel, or like rays in a conventionalized representation of the setting sun, and beyond the glass of the panes the varicoloured light of a real sunset could be seen. He had become a member of an organization which intended to and would bring into actual existence a world such as had been dreamed of by the best minds and hearts in all the ages, by prophets and poets whom the ruling classes of their day had been able to regard as ineffectual cranks. The poet of today, if only he would turn to the Party, need no longer be ineffectual. Already over one sixth of the earth the Party had led the workers to victory against the enemies of poetry, and it would do the same in England. It might seem insignificant now, it might be unable to afford a better meeting place than this dusty stable loft which even the pettiest and crankiest religious sect would have scorned to congregate in, but the time would come when it would have buildings at its disposal more magnificent than any cathedral. It would become far more important than even the greatest religious organizations had ever been, because unlike them it would be world-wide and without rivals. Though it might have its heretics and its persecutions, it could never find itself faced by a totally different faith in the way that Buddhism for instance had found itself faced by Hinduism and by Christianity. There could only be one Communism, just as there could only be one body of scientific knowledge. However, Communism was distinguished from most of the great religions not merely by its coming universality but by its rejection of the doctrine that man is naturally sinful and by its confidence that heaven can be established on earth. Also Communism was not – except in the eyes of the more ignorant of its opponents – dogmatic, as the religions were; it was a method, not a set of unalterable rules. But suppose eventually, after thousands of years, when man had colonized the planets and discovered the limits beyond which it would be impossible for him ever to travel, the Marxist method were to be superseded by a new ideology very different from present religions yet having in common with them a belief in the ultimate helplessness of humanity? At this point Alan pulled his thoughts up sharply, blaming himself for indulging in empty speculation and for not attending to the speaker.

His inattention, however, had not been absolute: he had heard certain phrases which enabled him now to infer what Dean Ayres' speech must have been mainly about so far. It had begun, he guessed, by stating that since the imperialist war capitalism had entered upon a new and final phase, a general crisis which was qualitatively quite distinct from former periodic crises. The only way out from this present crises was by proletarian revolution and by the abolition of the capitalist system, which was strangling the forces of production, and this way could and should have been taken all over Europe during the period following the 1917 Revolution in Russia. What had prevented it from being taken? Mainly the political attitude of the Social-Democrats, who instead of co-operating with the Communists had preferred to try to help capitalism to its feet again and had even been responsible for the suppression by violence of workers' risings. The Social-Democrats had acted as the faithful backers of senile capitalism, but later, when the crisis deepened and disillusionment began to spread among those sections of the working class who had hitherto trusted them, they were no longer useful to the capitalists. 'Capitalism in extreme decay,' Dean Ayres was at the moment saying, 'is forced to use other means, more openly dictatorial and more crudely demagogic, to maintain itself in power. The Social-Democratic hostility to revolution brings not a gradual progress towards Socialism but – as we have seen in Italy and recently in Germany – the temporary victory of Fascism.'

Dean Ayres went on to say that Fascism meant war. Monopoly capitalism everywhere must of its very nature tend towards war, but under German Fascism the conditions of a country at war were already present in a pre-war period. Nevertheless Communists must not allow themselves to adopt a fatalistic attitude towards war, and certainly not to feel that it mightn't be altogether a bad thing for Communism. True, another imperialist war would lead to the victory of Communism in a number of countries where capitalism at present ruled, but the devastation that such a war would cause would make the building up of socialism a far more difficult and lengthy process than if the workers could take power now. The struggle for the overthrow of the bourgeois State was also a struggle for international peace, just as the Party's propaganda against war preparations was also a means of undermining capitalism – which could not maintain the profits that were its life-blood except by periodically destroying the goods it had 'overproduced' and by violently eliminating its capitalist rivals.

Alan knew that what Dean Ayres was saying was in all essentials true to political and economic reality, and he knew too that large-scale fighting had in fact already been started by the Japanese imperialists in China, and he was convinced that before long, unless the working class were able to prevent it, there would be a war involving millions all over the world; but his awareness of the danger ahead was merely intellectual, not yet emotional. 'I must feel it,' he told himself, and his attention to what Dean Ayres was immediately saying became once again superficial. 'I must realize what might happen in this very room.' He looked at the semicircular window, trying in imagination to see it explode inwards towards him, its glittering splinters, sharp as darts, sticking into the back wall and some of them stopped by human obstructions, by the flesh of a cheek or a nose, by an eyeball – his own for instance. Yet injuries just as gruesome might be caused by a car accident: thinking of physical horrors would not help him to realize emotionally the true or the whole vileness of war. He was right to try to imagine it concretely instead of merely considering it in the abstract, but he must try to imagine it in its totality, to feel what it would mean to everyday life all over the world. And he must do this constantly, each day. Only so would his work in the Party against the Government's war preparations be consistently vigorous.

After Dean Ayres had finished Wally was the first of the other comrades to speak. He elaborated on Dean Ayres' point that the struggle against capitalism was also a struggle for peace, emphasizing that this was true of whatever Party work a comrade might do – selling the *Daily Worker,* for instance, or organizing a Tenants' League – but he added that comrades must also use every opportunity to carry on direct propaganda calling attention to the Government's ever-increasing expenditure on armaments and its anti-Soviet foreign policy. Jean Pritchet, who followed him, stressed how important it was that every comrade should take a hand in ensuring as wide a sale as possible for a first-rate pamphlet just out, which exposed in a way any worker could understand what Fascism meant. After her both Jock Finlayson and Sam Cowan reminded all comrades how essential it was, particularly in this present phase when reaction had begun to go on to the counter-offensive, for them not merely to join but to play an active and a leading part in working-class organizations such as trade unions – no matter how right-wing the leadership of these might be at present. Then Lily Pentelow said much the same thing about Co-operative Societies. Mike Bainton made a speech whose *enfant terrible* manner half amused and whose content half irritated the other comrades: he suggested that the British working class, because the monopoly capitalists had been able to hand over to it as a sop some of the gains extorted from colonial peoples, might be more susceptible to Fascist propaganda than many comrades supposed. Beatrix Farrell stood up to state in the calmest tones that Comrade Bainton had posed the problem wrongly and that the small share which British imperialism out of its super-profits chose to hand over to the workers in this country as an insurance against revolution did not benefit the workers but prevented them from obtaining their due, and that they could not obtain this until they had brought about the imperialists' overthrow, which in turn would be possible only when the subject peoples of the Empire were freed. Alan, who had been feeling that he ought to contribute something to the discussion and who might have been able to do so if he had stood up immediately after the finish of Dean Ayres' introductory speech, had become increasingly conscious while listening to these other comrades of the difficulty he would have in finding anything worth-while to say. All he would be capable of would be repeating in slightly different words what he had read in Party publications, or what Dean Ayres had just said. He would sound unnatural and ungenuine, whereas the others spoke with ease and each had something new to contribute from personal experience. If, however, he tried to be natural and to speak his own thoughts – those, for example, that had passed through his head at this meeting – he would give an impression of eccentricity that might make his comrades distrust him. He therefore continued to sit silent, in an unease which would have intensified if he hadn't been aware that none of the others seemed to take his silence amiss or even to notice it. As the discussion went on he became less apprehensive that Jimmy Anders from the chair might suddenly eye him and ask, 'Well, Comrade Sebrill, what are your views on this?' And when at length Dean Ayres was asked to begin summing up the discussion Alan's discomfort had so far diminished that he felt no relief. He was ashamed of his diffidence and he decided that next week without fail he would force himself to speak.

After Jimmy Anders had declared the meeting closed Alan went over at once towards Elsie. Moving hastily between two rows of chairs, he said rather too loudly, almost blurtingly, while he was still several yards away from her, 'Sorry I couldn't come to your house this evening.' His foot collided with a chair-leg, jerking the chair out across his path. He grinned briefly, replaced the chair, added as he came up to her, 'I was kept late at the school because they asked me to look after a cricket match.'

'I didn't wait very long for you,' she said.

He couldn't tell whether she had been at all offended by his not turning up, or if so whether she now forgave him. There was nothing of wariness, however, in the way she looked at him. Her face was by nature unrevealing, but it was a genuine face. Its expressions were never histrionic, though they might sometimes understate her feelings. She did not use lipstick or rouge. The high and at present disordered curls which rose to an apex above her forehead were, he was certain, natural. A tenderness keener than he had felt for her at any time before quickened in him as he looked at her. He would have liked to quote to her, semi-jocosely, Tennyson's lines – 'Shine out, little head, sunning over with curls/To the flowers and be their sun,' but instead he said again, 'I'm sorry I couldn't come along.'

She didn't answer. They went towards the door, following and followed by other comrades. From the bottom of the steps they moved off across the stableyard in a group with the others, who then, however, separated out, mainly into threes, along the pavement and let Alan and Elsie bring up the rear as an unaccompanied pair. He wondered, with pleasure, whether this meant that the others already sensed the beginnings of a special relationship between him and her.

She commented on Dean Ayres' speech, 'He was in good form again this evening.'

'Yes.' Alan was careful to pause before changing the subject. 'Well, I've done it at last.'

'Done what?'

He was sure that really she had understood his meaning, and that her question was intended to show disapproval of the unclear and irrelevant way in which he had expressed it. She disliked anything that savoured at all of the illogical or the intuitive, and perhaps also she disliked the suggestion of intimacy conveyed by his making a remark that assumed she knew what must be going on in his mind. He explained, 'I meant that I've joined the Party at last.'

'You certainly haven't done it in a hurry.'

'The thought of my middle-class origin was what delayed me. I needed time to get myself fit for membership.'

'Let's hope you're fit for it now,' she said, partly making fun of him.

Honesty, combined with a wish to reveal himself more deeply to her, caused him to add, 'But there was another reason why I hesitated for so long. I was afraid that if I became a member I should be involved in so much political work that I should have no leisure or energy left for writing poetry.'

'Have you found in fact that you've been able to write it since you've been working with the Party?'

'Yes, I'm glad to say. Though, what with meetings and other political activities nearly every night on top of the work I do for a living every day at school, I don't know how I've managed to write as much poetry as I actually have. Whether I shall be able to go on writing it is another matter.'

'You mustn't blame the Party for getting in the way of your poetry; you must blame the school, or capitalism, which made you become a teacher when you would have preferred to be a poet.'

'You're right. And yet I wish my poetry could be regarded as Party work, and I don't see why it shouldn't if I succeed in purging it of bourgeois preciousness and in making it express a Marxist attitude towards life.'

'I think poetry could do a lot to help the Party, but a poet can't confine himself to it if he wants to be a Marxist. He must get out and be politically active among the workers – otherwise his writing is not likely to be much good anyway.'

'I agree. Though the thing that worries me is that compared with direct propaganda – factual prose pamphlets, for example – poetry seems a very weak aid to the cause. At times I wonder whether it's worth going on with at all.'

He spoke with melancholy, hoping that she would contradict him or perhaps even positively urge him to go on writing. She was silent, however, and he couldn't guess whether this was because she was carefully considering what he had said, or because she didn't think much of such poems of his as she might have read in literary magazines, or because she felt unqualified to advise him. He would have tried to find out by putting a direct question to her, but Wally, who was walking just in front of them with Eddie Freans and Harry Temley, suddenly turned and, shouting 'Cheerio' to all the comrades, went off down a side-street. After this Elsie began talking admiringly about the work that Wally was doing in his Tenants' League. For the next five minutes she and Alan gossiped pleasantly about him and about various other Party members.

They came to where a narrow passage between houses led off from the street along whose pavement they had been walking. A gas lantern, which seemed to give a dimmer light than had been given by the lamps along the street, was fixed to the wall of one of the houses above the passage entrance. Alan, without premeditation, said, 'Let's go this way.'

'Why?'

'Because it's a short cut.'

'It isn't.'

'Well, it's nicer.'

She was surprised, and perhaps amused; and as she didn't immediately make a further retort he took the opportunity of calling out goodnight to the comrades walking on in front, and when these answered she too called out goodnight to them.

He touched her elbow lightly with his fingers and said, 'Come on.' She did not resent his touch and she moved with him towards the passage entrance. He remembered how once, when on an impulse he had placed the back of his hand against her bare arm, she had shaken her arm free of his touch and had looked at him as though she suspected there might be something abnormal about him. Because of that incident and of one or two other similar rebuffs, he had never yet tried putting his arm through hers when they had been walking together. But he tried it now, as soon as they had passed beneath the lantern above the entrance. She did not resist his action, nor, however, did her arm press his in response. They came round a house corner, and from here the passage broadened out into an asphalted path which stretched ahead of them for about a hundred yards. He had the sudden thought that the contemptuousness she had shown in the past towards his physical advances might have been due not to his being too forward but too backward. After all, she was a Party member, and she could hardly be so inconsistent as to hold prudish views about sex. He looked ahead along the path and saw that fifty yards in front of them there was another gas-lamp, seemingly rather brighter than the one beneath which they had just passed. He slowed in his walk and, finding that she made no attempt to free her arm from his retarding hold, he brought her to a stop. A creosoted wooden fence on their left divided the path from a shallow railway cutting, and on their right a six-foot-high brick wall concealed the backyards of a row of houses. He brought her closer to the wall. No one else was in sight up or down the path. She said nothing. He thought of speaking poetic endearments to her but was deterred by a fear that she might find them, and be justified in finding them, sentimentally silly. Instead he put his arm round her back. She stood half-facing the wall, and he was at her side, his shoulder behind her shoulder. He thought of pulling her round to him and kissing her, but he suspected that this might even now seem too abrupt. Instead he leant over from behind her and softly touched her cheek with his. She did not turn her face away, nor did she press it against his. The need came upon him to force some kind of reaction from her, whether favourable or not. He slid his arm farther round her back beneath her shoulder. She wore no coat or woolly over her cotton summer frock and he briefly wondered whether she found these evenings cold. His hand felt the firmness of her ribs beneath her arm, and then soon after the gentle outswelling of the side of her breast. She remained passive under his handling. A minor desperation urged him on to search with his fingers over the cotton surface for the outline of the nipple beneath, but at first he could not locate any protuberance, and finally he was not certain that what he tweaked between forefinger and thumb might not be merely part of her clothing. At any rate she continued to give no sign of pleasure or displeasure. He, disheartened and feeling a fool, withdrew his hand. She made a movement – the first of any kind she had made since they had stopped here by the wall – as if she was about to begin walking again. He took this as a pretext for actually beginning to walk on, himself. She followed and caught up with him. Her face showed no disappointment. He was angry with her and would not be the first to speak. She did not seem to become aware of his mood until they reached the lamp at the far end of the asphalt path. Then he saw in her side-face a clear resentment such as nothing else he had been guilty of that evening had been able to evoke.

When they arrived where the path led out again along a passage between houses to the pavement of a street, she said, 'There's not much point in your coming all the way home with me, is there?'

'Perhaps there isn't.'

She brusquely said good-night and walked off.

Afterwards on the bus back to his lodgings he tried to think out what could have been the meaning of her unresponsiveness. He compared her behaviour towards him with Peg's voluptuous provocativeness, and the idea crossed his mind that Elsie might be not quite normal, might be afflicted with some form of infantilism. He decided that, in any case, he would make no more advances to her at any time in the future.

7

SOME BOY unidentifiable among a group near the iron
railings made an insulting noise as Alan was walking across
the quad at the beginning of break. A coarsely suggestive
variation on the kind of hissing that he had quite often heard
during his earlier terms, it began with a strongly plosive '*p*'
sound. The distance and the moment had been slyly chosen:
the offender was just too far off for Alan to observe the
facial contortion that must surely have accompanied a noise
so violently spiteful; and now already the whistle had blown
for Physical Training, the boys had hung their brown blazers
on the railings, the suspect group quickly dispersed and its
units were mingled with others all hurrying across the
asphalt. Childers and the younger Marston, either of whom
was quite capable of an offence of this type, had seemed to
be standing where the noise had come from; but Alan could
not be certain. Could he even be entirely certain that it
hadn't been accidental, an automatic boy-noise as unconscious and unintentional as a locomotive's letting-off of
steam, or, if intentional, might it not have been aimed at
another boy rather than at him? Such doubts, Alan quickly
recognized, were nothing but wishful thinking. He must
cope with what had happened, not try to believe that it
hadn't. Since his crucial interview with the Headmaster a
year ago he had at four different times caned four boys, and
had put a stop to the hissing at least inside the classrooms.
Suppressed there, it had today burst out in a new and a more
cunning manifestation, more difficult to deal with. But he
could and must suppress it again, and by the same methods.
If he didn't it could become very nasty indeed. It might

before long begin to assume the dimensions of a persecution.

He watched the boys form up into squads on the asphalt, stared at the nearer faces but could detect none of the signs he looked for – no smirks, no side-glances of collusion. The farther squads were less easy to examine. From the iron railings and from the crenellated brickwork of the lavatories in the background an encroaching indistinctness defeated him as he tried to extend his investigation to other faces, an emotional blur, a dimness which was caused by the agitation of his feelings and which was suddenly reminiscent of a dream he had had one or two nights before. In the middle of a badly-lit assembly hall he had stood surrounded by boys, two of whom had come very close to him and had calmly and in unison spoken an outrageous word. He had tried to raise both hands to strike at them, but his arms had been bound with invisible elastic whose resistance had strengthened with every new effort he had made. Now for a moment the movements on the quad in front of him had the quality of movements in an unpleasant and uncontrollable dream. But the moment passed, and he was able to take warning from it against allowing his feelings to get the better of him. Complete calm would be necessary if he was to stand any chance of discovering who had made the noise. To let the offence get deeply beneath his skin would not only cause him misery, which was what it was intended to do, but might also lead him into some furiously ineffectual action which would be seen and relished by the undiscovered offender.

A colleague wearing a gown was coming towards him round the outside of the quad from the direction of the railings. It was Benson, pale-faced and strongly built, moving with large strides, his big glasses calling attention to his pale eyes which had no expression in them. Alan, although there could have been few of the younger members of the staff to whom he would less willingly have appealed for help, stopped him and spoke to him, and the soul behind Benson's eyes looked sharply out like two synchronized toy dogs coming to the doors of their kennels.

'I wonder if you spotted the boy who made that noise just now when you were over by the railings?' Alan asked.

'What noise?'

Alan was forced to go into details. 'A sort of hissing. Rather like this.' He gave a subdued imitation: 'Pssss.'

'I don't remember hearing it.' Benson hardly bothered to seem concerned. With no change of tone, he contradicted himself, 'Yes, I believe I did hear it.' Then with some amiability, 'What about it?'

'It was meant to be offensive.'

'Oh, did you think so?' But, having said this, Benson seemed to become aware that an offence might in fact have been meant and that if so he ought to be showing support for his colleague. 'Perhaps you're right. Though a noise can be unpleasant without being directed against anyone in particular.'

Again Alan had to say more than he wanted to: 'I happen to know from past experience that this noise – or one very like it – is reserved specially for me.'

Benson was momentarily incredulous, then thought he understood. 'I suppose it might be some kind of an attempt at an imitation.'

'I don't see how.'

'Unrecognizability is no proof that an imitation isn't intended.' Benson couldn't help smiling. 'A noise which would mean nothing to most members of the staff might be regarded as exquisitely apt by the boys themselves.'

Alan, a little surprised to find that Benson could be observant and humorous, said, 'No, this noise is only imitative in the sense that it probably derives from the first letter of my surname.'

He did not know whether Benson answered him. He suddenly saw – what Benson wasn't facing the right way to be able to see and mightn't have noticed anyhow – that a boy in one of the near-by squads was watching them. The boy was Childers, and his look unmistakably expressed an insolent triumphing which was tempered perhaps by a suspicious curiosity about what they might be discussing. Alan said, not caring how irrelevant he might sound, 'Well, thanks very much,' and without even glancing again at Benson walked off immediately towards Spriggs, the gym instructor.

A short, broad man, standing on a low oblong stool to view and be viewed by all the squads, Spriggs was aware of Alan's approach but took no visible notice of him until he spoke: 'Would you mind if I had a word with that boy Childers? I'm sorry to interrupt, but he's been impertinent and I should like to get hold of him at once before he has time to think up an alibi.'

Spriggs gave Alan a displeased look – unwilling perhaps to turn his eyes from the boys here in such numbers, and perhaps wondering whether Alan would have taken the liberty of interrupting any other man on the staff in this way – the look of an ex-naval petty officer who suspected, not without reason, that certain members of the common-room had snobbish though not openly expressed objections to his being admitted there as one of them. Nevertheless he asked Alan, 'Which boy did you say?'

'Childers. He's in that squad over there.'

Spriggs, whose expression of face did not thank Alan for this information, stared successively at two or three other squads and ignored the squad in which Childers was. Evidently he meant to emphasize, just as he had when he'd pretended not to hear the boy's name, the trouble he was being given by Alan's request. At last however he fixed his stare on the squad Alan had indicated, and called out, 'Childers.'

He had a peculiarly unresonant voice for so large-chested a man. The boy heard, and only for a moment pretended or hoped he had not; then stepped from the squad and came forward. Alan, not wishing Spriggs to overhear what he was going to say, went to meet Childers.

Alan said, 'As I was crossing the quad just before P.T. started you made a hissing noise, like this –pssss.'

Alan had found by experience that it was best to be precise about the sound, otherwise an accused boy would ask with affected puzzlement, 'What noise, sir?' and would gain the initiative. Preciseness also had the effect of shocking the boy slightly and of taking him off his guard. It took Childers off his guard now.

'Yes, sir,' he admitted.

'I happen to be aware that that sort of noise is meant particularly for me,' Alan said, and Childers did not try to dispute this. 'Why did you make it?'

'I don't know, sir. I'm sorry. I just wasn't thinking what I was doing.'

'I doubt whether that comes very convincingly from you, Childers, but in any case you *should* be thinking what you are doing. How old are you?'

'Sixteen, sir.

'Your behaviour gives the impression that you might be at least two years younger. And Marston was with you at the time, wasn't he?'

'Yes, sir, but honestly, sir, he didn't do anything. He was talking to Anderson. You can ask Anderson.'

'All right, all right. I don't require *you* or Anderson to give him a certificate of virtue.' Having said this, Alan was ashamed of its near-facetiousness, and he added quickly and angrily, 'I'll hear him speak for himself.'

Childers stood almost at military attention. He was tall for his age, athletic, with wide shoulders and narrow hips like an ancient Egyptian. His face however had no gipsy look about it: its colouring was mainly a warm red, though the paler parts of it seemed faintly dusked with yellow like the paler parts of the skin of a not-quite-ripe peach. He waited expressionlessly for what he guessed must be coming next.

Alan said, 'You will go to the masters' changing-room immediately after P.T. and wait for me there outside the door. Return to your squad now.'

Childers went off at a slow run, and Alan walked after him. Marston, who was in the same squad and who had watched the interview and guessed its purport, put an extra vigour into the jumping exercise he was doing. Alan looked back towards Spriggs, and, not unexpectedly failing to catch his eye, decided to dispense with his permission and to give Marston a direct order to leave the squad.

'Come out here, Marston.'

Marston, who unlike Childers was short and rather child-ish-looking, obeyed at once.

'Did you make a hissing noise just before P.T. as I was crossing the quad?'

'No, sir. I was talking to Anderson.'

The boy seemed to expect not to be believed. Alan looked closely at him, summed him up as probably mischievous and an admiring hanger-on who had come under the influence of his hero Childers, but was telling the truth at present.

'I'll take your word for it. Get back to your squad.'

Soon Marston was jumping again with the others, flinging his arms up rigidly and kicking out sideways stiffly with his legs. Alan walked on towards the main school building. He felt calm, much calmer than he had felt before any of the four previous beatings that he had performed. Those, in spite of his telling himself then that the Party's education policy avoided condemning corporal punishment and that he was performing them only because he could not other-wise survive as a teacher, had filled him with anticipatory misery; and one of them, which he had had to postpone for a day, had kept him apprehensively awake for a long while in the early hours of the morning. But now, as he went up the steps into the school building, he had no worry except the thought that he would have to get some other member of the staff to be a witness – because of the Head's precautionary rule that there must always be two men present at a caning – and he was in doubt about whom to ask.

He came into the common-room. Brook, standing in front of the fireplace, called out aggressively, 'Enter the Red Menace.'

Alan grinned; then he remembered that Brook was Childers' form-master, and, taking a chance, he went up to him and said seriously, though he hoped not loudly enough for all the others in the room to hear, 'I want to beat someone in your form. Would you witness it?'

'Of course, old boy.'

An immediate change came over Brook's manner. It was almost the sort of change that could have been expected in him if he had suddenly discovered an unprepossessing stranger to be good at fives. He looked at Alan with approval. There was quite a long pause before he thought of adding, 'Who is he?'

'Childers.'

'You couldn't have picked a riper one.'

'I've told him to be outside the masters' changing-room when P.T.'s finished.'

'Good. I'll be with you.'

'I'd better go and get a cane.'

Alan turned rather quickly, a little afraid that Brook might even now aim some loud gibe at him, and went to the door. In the common-room lobby he brushed past raincoats and academic gowns that were hung from hooks against the Gothic-arched wooden panels and he reached a corner where, behind dusty rolled-up maps and a black first-aid box, a cane was usually kept. He fumbled for it and could not find it. He was beginning to feel agitated, when the common-room door was opened behind him and Brook's voice asked, 'Not there?'

'No.'

'You'd better use mine. I'll get it from my form-room.'

'Oh, thanks very much,' Alan said. 'But don't you bother, I'll fetch it for you' – an absurd offer, since he had no idea of the cane's whereabouts in the form-room and anyway Brook would be bound to keep it locked up.

'That's all right,' Brook said, opening the lobby door and moving out into the corridor.

Alan caught up with him. The presence of boys moving across where this corridor joined the main one showed that P.T. must already be finished. Brook's form-room was round the corner. Arriving there, he took out a form-room key from his sports-coat pocket, unlocked the door, entered in front of Alan, who followed hesitatingly, took out from his trouser-pocket a ring of smaller keys which was attached to him by a thin gilt chain, went over and unlocked a cupboard beneath a glass-fronted bookcase. He produced a thick-looking three-foot cane, gripped an end of it and with his wrist stiff shook it to test its whippiness. He re-locked the cupboard and after that he re-locked the form-room door. When he was once again in the corridor with Alan beside him, he walked very upright, with emphatic strides, exhibiting the cane as conspicuously as he could and giving the impression that he would be happy to strike out at any boy who might pass too close. All of a sudden, as though realizing with compunction that he had been arrogating to himself a privilege that should have belonged to Alan, he handed over the cane to him. Alan took it, and as they walked on he tried to conceal it from passing boys by pressing it against a fold in his trouser-leg.

They went down the stairs that led to the masters' changing-room. Childers was waiting tall outside the door, startlingly immobile as though he had been made of wood like the varnished planks of the wall against which he stood. Brook, ignoring him, pushed open the door, and politely – because the boy was watching – signed to Alan to go in first. Childers moved to follow them in, but Brook turned on him and said gruffly, 'Stay where you are till you're told you're wanted.'

Inside the changing-room a smell of linseed oil and sweat and football leather impressed itself irrelevantly and unpleasantly upon Alan. For the first time since he had stared at the faces of the boys on the quad he felt an apprehensive uneasiness. It passed, but he stood confused about what he ought to do next, now that Brook had told Childers to stay outside. Brook, however, was obviously in control and with his head cocked sideways was ocularly measuring the distance between the shower-bath and a long table which occupied the middle of the room. Dissatisfied, he reached out for the cane that Alan was holding, took it and experimentally swung it backwards and upwards from the table towards the shower-bath. He laid the cane with a slap on the surface of the table, which he then pushed a couple of feet farther forward. He gauged the interval between table and shower-bath again with his eyes, was satisfied, said to Alan, 'Ready?'

'Yes.'

Brook called to Childers, who had had a clear view of these preparations through the open doorway, 'You can come in now.'

Childers came in. His face showed no fear, had a look of unhurried concentration such as it might have had if he had been about to take part in an athletic event at the school sports. He went towards the table with a directness which suggested that previous experiences had familiarized him with the procedure in here, and Alan was only just able in a clumsy hurry to remove the cane before Childers could get between it and him. Brook went over to the door, shut it, and stood with his back to it, demonstratively leaving Alan in charge of the proceedings from now on.

Alan said, as tonelessly as he could, to Childers, 'I shall give you six. Bend over there.'

Childers had already bent over the table even before being

157

told – well over, making no attempt to arrange himself otherwise than conveniently for Alan. There was no sign of padding beneath the flannel trousers that tightly covered his buttocks. However, the back hem of his brown school blazer, which looked a new one and was rather large even for him, projected above his buttocks like the protective edge of a roof above a wall. Alan, squeamishly unwilling to lift the hem out of the way with his hand, might have left it where it was in spite of the risk that it would impede the cane, but remembering just in time an expedient used by an older colleague – for whom he had once acted as a witness – he now used the tip of the cane to lift the hem and to push it forward up the flat of Childers' back. As he did this he remembered also how that colleague had unashamedly transgressed the unwritten rule about not raising the cane above the shoulder. Alan would keep the cane low; but in order to avoid loss of power he would swing it backwards as far as possible, pivoting his body from the hips like the golfer he had in his bourgeois days occasionally been, though unlike a golfer he would try to make the cane move in a plane parallel with the ground throughout the stroke. He would thus have a better chance of achieving what all who claimed to be expert caners recommended – hitting the same spot each time. He raised the cane and, bringing it slowly forward, sighted it against Childers' buttocks to determine the level at which it should be swung, then he brought it not too quickly backward – like a golfer careful to avoid spoiling his rhythm by jerking – and, with a rigid arm and a wrist springily tensed, he struck forward almost as hard as he could, not forgetting that at the moment of impact he mustn't relax but must try to follow through as it were after the ball. The impact made less noise than Alan expected, perhaps because the follow-through had a muffling effect. His second stroke was as careful as his first, and he seemed to succeed in landing it on the same spot, but Childers did not wince yet. Alan's third and fourth strokes were more confident, less careful and delivered with all the strength he had. After the fifth stroke, which was inaccurate and came much too near to the base of the spine, Childers turned his head slightly as though about to look back from the surface of the table towards Alan. The sixth stroke was weaker. Childers remained bending over the table. Alan could hardly believe that the boy hadn't been counting the strokes, but at length had to say to him, 'All right. Get up now.'

Childers stood up, but did not move from the table. He seemed to expect something more, perhaps a verbal admonishment that would emphasize the purpose and the justice of the beating. Alan however was unable to bring himself to say anything at all. He would have liked to apologize for the beating, to shake Childers by the hand and confess, 'I admired the way you took that.'

Eventually Brook spoke for him: 'You can go now.'

'Thank you, sir.'

Childers addressed this not to Brook alone but to Alan also, and there was in his tone a disturbing suggestion that he was genuinely grateful for his punishment. As he went out through the changing-room doorway, Brook, who had opened the door for him, looked closely into his face, suspecting that an impertinence might have been intended but deciding to give him the benefit of the doubt. Almost before – or perhaps actually before – Childers was out of hearing, Brook said to Alan with an admiring grin, 'Well, you touched him up all right. I fancy that our Master Childers won't give you much trouble now for a long time to come. You landed him some real beauties.' Alan was ashamed, but in order not to seem unthankful for Brook's aid he attempted to grin back at him. Casually Brook added, 'By the way, what was his crime this time?'

'He was offensive,' Alan said vaguely.

Brook was not interested enough to press for details. Alan

made a movement to hand him back the cane. Brook said, 'Would you mind taking it along to the common-room for me, old boy? I've got to go and rout out Pringle about some fives balls.'

'All right.'

Saying this, Alan became conscious of the feel of the cane in his hand and would have liked to drop it, to throw it across the floor, get rid of it somehow. He followed Brook through the doorway. In the passage he parted from him and turned towards the stairs. He absurdly tried to hide the cane by pushing it up the sleeve of his jacket, but, finding it too long, he removed it and carried it pressed against his trousers. As he mounted the stairs he heard in his mind Childers' voice saying, 'Thank you, sir.' Its tone held no resentment, was respectful without sycophancy, seemed to imply that Childers regarded his punishment as being all in the day's work, yet also that he was leaving the room with a sense of achievement as though he had just had a success at the high jump or the hundred yards. 'If he gets the opportunity,' Alan thought, 'he will do to others what I have done to him.' But would that be so very terrible? After all, a caning on the buttocks was something very different from a beating on the kidneys or genitals with a steel-cored rubber truncheon in the cellar of a Nazi Brown House, was different even from a British police birching administered on the bare flesh of a juvenile delinquent till blood trickled and faeces exuded. Canings had been going on for years past, for generations, for centuries, and the boys who had had to submit to them had not all grown up to be brutish reactionaries. Milton as a boy at Christ's College, Cambridge, had been beaten. 'Yes,' Alan thought, as he arrived at the top of the stairs, 'but history has moved on.' What might have been harmless in an earlier setting, what might at the hands of a Renaissance schoolmaster have even been excusable, had now come to have a new and sinister meaning. By using the cane Alan had aligned himself with those in the modern world who placed authority above reason. He, a Communist, had behaved like a Fascist.

Turning the corner into the short passage that led to the common-room, he recognized how sophistical he had been in his interpretation of the Party's line on corporal punishment. Though the Party did not include the abolition of caning as one of the items in its published educational policy, this wasn't because it approved of corporal punishment — which had been made illegal in the Soviet Union — but because its overriding aim was to obtain unity between Communist and non-Communist teachers in the fight for better educational conditions, and it didn't want to raise controversial matters of secondary importance which might make unity harder to get. He opened the door into the lobby of the common-room. He went quickly to put the cane up against the wall in a corner where hanging gowns would partly hide it. He was not quick enough. The church-vestry-like shadowiness of the lobby was abruptly penetrated by bright daylight as someone swung back the door leading out from the common-room. Gus Chiddingfold appeared, and was just in time to see Alan start furtively backwards after putting the cane down. Chiddingfold came to a halt in the doorway, keeping the door behind him half-open with his shoulder, no doubt in order that colleagues inside the room should be able to overhear what he was going to say.

'An execution, eh? You brutal man. Didn't you think of the injury you might be doing to the boy's soul?'

Grinning suggestively, he pronounced 'boy's soul' as one word. Then the grin faded and a crafty and almost serious expression came over his pallid and tough-skinned face as he added, 'I'm surprised that one so up-to-date as yourself in the very latest theories should descend to such primitive practices.'

His tone was enigmatic: while evidently satirical of Alan,

it did not make clear whether or not Chiddingfold approved of corporal punishment. Quite possibly he disapproved, since so far as Alan knew he never used the cane himself. Uncertainty about Chiddingfold's real point of view caused Alan to feel more uneasy than he would have felt even if he had known him to be a sincere opponent of caning. Alan did not attempt to retort, but pushed past Chiddingfold into the common-room. He was soon made aware, by the turning towards him of the faces of several colleagues, that Chiddingfold's comments had been overheard.

Hefford, the head of the English Department, asked, 'Just beaten someone?'

'Yes.'

Moberley, the Handicraft man, asked, 'Who was it?'

'Childers.'

Langton, one of the Maths men, said, 'Good. He's a nasty bit of work. I hope you gave it him hot and strong.'

There were smiles all round. There was a feeling of festival in the room. Suddenly Alan lost control of himself and burst out with, 'The whole thing's loathsome. Messing about with boys' posteriors – that's what caning amounts to. No wonder the status of the teaching profession's no higher than it is. I feel as though I'd just buried my face in excrement.'

There was a silence, during which his colleagues appeared to be considering not so much the substance of what he had said as the excitable manner in which he had said it, and finally he got the impression that, though puzzled, they were not unsympathetic. Moberley, with an air of intending to smooth over an embarrassment rather than of wanting to express a strongly-held opinion, said very calmly, 'A beating is soon over and done with. There are worse forms of punishment.'

Hefford, more assertively, said, 'It's far better than moral bullying – the sort of thing that goes on in some girls' schools, I mean.'

Langton, and after him Ransome, a Classics man, joined in with, 'It saves a lot of time and, unlike lines, it doesn't ruin their handwriting.'

'It's the only thing that some boys understand.'

Then Barnet, who had been looking out of one of the windows and had not been noticed hitherto by Alan, turned and said aggressively, jerking his head up and forwards in a way that was reminiscent of the head-movements of a cock or hen, 'Sebrill's right. And he might have added that a large percentage of the enthusiasts for child-beating are unconscious sexual perverts. At best it's the refuge of the teacher who's lazy or incompetent. Personally I've never caned a boy in my life. I prefer more rational methods. For instance the other day I found the word "twat" chalked on the blackboard in my form-room. No one owned up, but the form captain and vice-captain were both pretty certain who was the culprit. So we had a trial – spent the whole period on it – with myself as judge, and the boys as counsels for prosecution and defence, and so on. Very instructive for them all.'

The silence after this had nothing sympathetic in it, was pregnant with hostility. Not only had Barnet's tone been provocative in the extreme but he had admitted to holding a mock trial for an offence of exceptional gravity and to doing so during a period when the boys should have been seriously working. Alan felt grateful to him and would have liked to express approval of the trial but, ashamed now of having been so intemperate and undiplomatic in his own outburst against caning, decided to involve himself no further on the subject. He went over towards a window other than the one near which Barnet was standing, and pretended to look out of it. He told himself that in future he must cultivate Barnet more, must not fail to ask him along to meetings organized by the Party. After all, on the one occasion when Alan had had the nerve to ask him Barnet had come readily enough. If Alan had not been remiss in following up that first success Barnet might by now have become a Party member.

The silence was ended by Hefford, who asked Langton if he knew whether the team had been picked yet for the first eleven match to be played on Saturday against Ridley Upper. Alan at the window thought, 'I shall never again, whatever the provocation, cane a boy.' He must find other methods of keeping discipline, progressive methods, even if they might mean much harder work for him and even if they might prove to be not very successful. He must try once again to become an educator. It would be grim, a perpetual struggle, not the pleasure which he had at one time deluded himself into hoping it might be. And he would be able to achieve little. But to give up the attempt to educate on the grounds that education was reformist and that nothing of value could be done in schools under capitalism was the worst kind of leftish idiocy, and like all leftism had led to reaction, had made him a beater. No doubt real education could flourish only after the Revolution, when its importance would be generally recognized and when educators would be honoured and respected by the community in which they lived, but something could be honourably achieved even now. He must try to do his job as effectively as the existing educational conditions and his own limitations allowed. Though he could not without inviting the sack introduce revolutionary politics directly into his teaching, he could aim at propagating humane ideas and getting his pupils to think. And only by becoming an efficient teacher could he hope to gain the confidence of his colleagues and eventually to win some of them over to the side of the working class.

When the school bell was rung for the end of break, Alan, moving across to his locker to fetch out a book he would need for his next period, felt unusually free of apprehensiveness at the prospect of having to go into his form-room and teach.

8

ALAN DID NOT EXPECT, as he passed Woolworth's at
the corner on his way along the High Street, to see Elsie
coming towards him up a side-road from the left – since
neither her home nor her school lay in that direction – but
an irrational hope made him turn his head to look down the
road for her, and there she was about a hundred yards away
from him. During the past few months he had become increasingly regretful of his decision not to call for her any more
at her home before Party meetings, and the sudden sight now
of her characteristically bobbing walk caused him to think,
as he had thought on several earlier occasions, 'That is the
sort of girl I ought to marry.' She did not see him yet. The
very inelegance of her walk increased her attractiveness for
him, because it helped to assure him – just as did her avoid-
ance of standardized female allurements like high heels and
rouge – that the appeal she had for him must arise from her
real worth. She was not physically ugly, however: her face
at its best had the look of the face of the 'Maja Clothed' in
the painting by Goya. But as she approached him he remembered the unpleasant failure of his former advances to her,
and the idea abruptly left him that he might be able to
marry her. She did not seem displeased when she saw him
waiting for her at the corner. Nevertheless he had difficulty
in trying to prevent glumness from showing in his face. He
made himself say, as lightly as he could, 'How do you happen
to be arriving from that direction?'

'I've been to see an E.W.L. contact. He talked for three

quarters of an hour but couldn't make up his mind to join.'

'Rather a rush for you immediately after school, with this evening's meeting to follow.'

She didn't deny it. Then surprisingly she said, as they began to walk on together, 'You look tired.'

This was the first time, as far as he could remember, that she had shown so personal a concern for him.

'Do I? Well, it can't be due to school, because I'm finding teaching positively a rest cure nowadays.'

He became conscious that he had reproduced a saying often used by Party teachers who wished to call attention to the amount of political work they did when they were out of school. In revulsion from the platitude he tried to be more precise: 'What exhausts me is attempting after a day's teaching and an evening's Party activity to settle down at half past ten or even at eleven to write a few lines of poetry.'

Instead of telling him, as he half expected and as the tone of his remark almost invited her to tell him, that he ought to drop the poetry, she said, 'Why don't you mention at the next cell meeting that you're finding you haven't enough time for writing poetry and that you would like to be relieved of some of your ordinary Party activities?'

The suggestion shocked him a little. 'I couldn't do that.'

'But why not? The comrades in the cell would regard it as a perfectly reasonable thing to ask, and I'm sure they'd agree to your having at least two evenings in the week free.'

'It would make me feel that I was specially privileged, not a proper member of the Party.'

She said nothing. Perhaps in the hope of making her argue him into changing his mind he added with exaggerated conviction, 'Any poem I might write in such a situation would be bad even as poetry.'

She appeared to accept this. He, though the idea of asking his comrades for time off for writing was beginning to seem much less outrageous and more practicable than he had at first thought it, was not prepared without further persuasion from her to contradict what he had just said against it. He asked, 'Do you know what the meeting's going to be about this evening?'

'No, I don't.'

'I'm surprised. And reassured.'

'Why?'

'Well, usually I'm alone in not knowing what I should know about such things, and it's comforting to discover that you, whom I've always looked up to for efficiency, are for once not much better than me.'

She took it more than half seriously. 'I hadn't heard anything about this meeting till yesterday morning when the typed slip arrived by post, giving hardly any details except that Ben Curtis will be coming from the Centre to speak to us.'

'I wonder why he's coming.'

'Probably to talk about the international situation.'

They themselves, as they continued walking, began a discussion, which was at first on the Soviet Union's recent joining of the League of Nations and then on the establishment in the previous year of diplomatic relations between the Soviet Union and the U.S.A. What interested them most about the agreement signed by Litvinov at the White House was the first clause, which pledged each country to refrain from interfering in the internal affairs of the other. Did this mean that the Comintern would have to cease being active altogether in America, or was it merely a form of words included to placate the Americans but not really referring to the Comintern, which the Russians had always stated to be an organization quite independent of the Soviet Government? For both Elsie and Alan the question was not an abstract one about a remote political event; it was as immediate to them as the street in which they walked and incomparably more important. It was more important than the personal relationship between them or than either of their individual selves. They did not become aware of themselves again until they arrived at the tailor's shop above which the meeting was to be held, and were under the necessity of turning from the High Street down the passage which led to the side entrance.

In the backyard just beyond the side entrance Mike Bainton had leant his bicycle against the wall and was removing the metal clips from the bottoms of his trouser-legs. The bicycle had drop-handlebars around which adhesive tape had been wound. Alan thought of the duplicated notice which Bainton, when acting temporarily as cell secretary, had once sent out to members and which contained the facetious question, 'What did Charlie Marx say in 1848?' Bainton's acquisition of a bicycle of this type – so obtrusively unmiddle-class – seemed too to have been made with a humorous intention. He looked at them, appearing for a moment not to recognize them, his face bonier than ever, then gave them a smile which lifted his eyebrows and ascended his forehead in wrinkles till it reached the curls on his scalp. Alan became aware of not having seen him at Party meetings for some time, and remembered that he was supposed to have gone away to some town on the south coast, and was glad to see him again. Elsie sounded glad also as she said, 'What have you been doing with yourself all these months?'

'Oh, various jobs. Selling peanuts at the seaside, for instance.'

Elsie laughed in what seemed to Alan a jeering, though not unpleasant, way, and Bainton laughed too. After a moment his face turned serious and he said, 'I'd better tell you what I'm here for this evening. You evidently haven't heard. The fact is I'm in trouble with the Party. That's why this meeting has been called.'

'What sort of trouble?' Elsie asked.

'You'll get to know all about it at the meeting.'

He spoke with a gravity which Alan, believing him to be something of a self-dramatizer, assumed to be more than the occasion called for. Bainton, without giving them another look, moved towards the back door of the building. They followed him. As they went up the stairs after him to the room above the shop Elsie smiled at Alan in a way which showed that she too, though puzzled, supposed that Bainton had exaggerated the seriousness of whatever trouble it was he had got into. When they entered the room and began to move towards three unoccupied chairs at the end of the middle row Bainton pointedly detached himself from them and went to sit at the front. Ben Curtis had already arrived and was sitting next to the chairman, Jimmy Anders, at the table. These two tried but were not altogether able to mask their awareness that Bainton, for whom perhaps they had waited with uncertainty as well as with eagerness, had come to face the meeting.

Though Alan and Elsie were not late the room was already almost full. Comrades, some of whom Alan had not seen before, were there from several other cells. With seeming casualness, but punctually at the time which had been stated on the typed slip, Anders opened the meeting by saying, 'Comrade Curtis, would you begin now.'

Ben Curtis stood up, but his tone when he started speaking was informal and mild. He did not tell his audience what he was going to talk about. At first he gave the impression that his main theme would be more or less what Alan and Elsie had expected from him before their brief conversation with Bainton – the policy of the Soviet Union in the existing international situation. He said nothing that Alan hadn't already been told in approximately the same words by the *Daily Worker* or the *Labour Monthly* or by other Party speakers. He wore a noticeably good double-breasted grey flannel suit and an open-necked khaki shirt, and out of one of his side-pockets the top of a paper bag – containing perhaps sandwiches – protruded. His face was pleasant, was not conceivably the face of a man capable of malice. Alan might have paid closer attention to the speech – the familiarity of whose phraseology and theme would no more have lessened its momentousness for him than the repetition of ritual phrases would have lessened the significance of a religious service for him if he had been a believer listening in a church – but for the fact that he was wondering at what point in the meeting Bainton's affair would be dealt with. He was, however, aware that Curtis, after going over at some length the main events in the history of past relations between the Soviet Union and the capitalist powers, drew the moral that the first socialist country in the world needed, if it was to survive, to take advantage of any differences those powers might have among themselves – such as the differences arising since the Nazis, with their *revanchiste* anti-Versailles policy, had gained control in Germany – and must even be prepared in certain circumstances to go so far as to make an alliance with one group of imperialists against another. To criticize the Soviet Union for joining the League of Nations, on the grounds that the Soviet leaders had previously condemned this organization as imperialist, was sheer leftism. Soviet policy was guided not by rigid preconceived notions but by a Marxist-Leninist-Stalinist understanding of the world situation and by the determination to ensure at all costs the survival of the Soviet Union. That survival was of vital interest not only to the Soviet people but to the working class of the whole world. 'It is not for us,' Curtis said with a sudden sharpness that alerted Alan's attention to the full, 'to spend our time criticizing the Soviet leaders: let us leave that to the capitalist gutter press, and let us not forget the job which we still have to do here and which has already been done in the Soviet Union, the job of winning working-class power.' Then, his voice lapsing back into mildness, he referred to charges that had been made against Comrade

Bainton of having on several occasions criticized the Soviet Union in public. He emphasized 'in public', and added, 'But before I say anything more on this I think we had better hear Comrade Bainton's reply to these charges.'

Bainton stood up as Curtis was sitting down. It became clear soon after he started speaking that far from intending to recant what he was accused of having said against the Soviet Union he was going to repeat and to amplify it. He stood sideways to the chairman as though wishing to address not him or Curtis but the other assembled comrades. His rather narrow shoulders were rounded just below his neck, which was inclined so as to cause his sharp face and bony temples to jut forward. There was nothing aggressive or passionate about his manner, however. He seemed to be trying calmly to proselytize among the comrades present, and he had an air of optimism as though he expected, if not to convince them, at least to sow the seeds of future conviction in some of them. His main contention was that over the past fifteen years the Soviet Union had been moving at an accelerating rate away from Communism as Lenin had conceived it. Without referring to notes, and with a fluency which suggested that he must have been constantly going over such details in his mind, he mentioned the dates – year and month – of each of the six Comintern Congresses which had been so far held: the first in March 1919, the second in July 1920, the third in June 1921, the fourth in November 1922, the fifth – after a slightly longer interval – in June 1924, the sixth – after a longer interval still – in July 1928, and since then six years had elapsed without a Congress at all. Didn't this, together with such significant acts as the signing of an agreement binding the Soviet Union not to interfere in the internal affairs of America, show that the present Soviet leaders were in process of abandoning international revolutionary Communism? And even at home, in the Soviet Union itself, Communist Party Congresses had, after the period from 1917 to 1925 when they were held annually, been held with ever-increasing gaps between them. Communism of its very nature couldn't be expected to flourish nationally if it was neglected internationally. 'The Petrograd Bolsheviks who died fighting for the revolution in 1917,' Bainton said with emphasis, 'would turn in their Brotherhood Grave on Mars Field if they knew what is going on in the Soviet Union today.'

The words 'Brotherhood Grave' and 'Mars Field' were much more effective than the facts about Congresses had been in modifying the antipathy which Bainton's speech had from the start aroused in Alan. There came into Alan's consciousness an emotional picture of revolutionary Petrograd. He thought of snow and of the noon cannon booming from the fortress of Peter-Paul, of Smolny's lights shining throughout the night, of the battleship *Aurora* with its guns trained on the Winter Palace. He thought of what the revolutionaries must have felt at the time of their victory. Partakers in the greatest event that had occurred in the history of the world, they must have believed that external political reality had at last matched the highest emotions that human beings are capable of. How was it possible for anyone who had lived through the events of that time, even if only in sympathy and at a distance, to be content with the hard everyday work of construction which followed and with the gradual subsiding everywhere of the revolutionary upsurge? Yet very many had adapted themselves to the change. If revolutionary romantics like Bainton hadn't, Alan thought, then the Party must not hesitate to discipline them.

No one interrupted Bainton's speech at any point, but the fact that as soon as he had finished three comrades stood up simultaneously suggested that indignation had been accumulating among the listeners.

Wally was one of the three, and he began, 'Comrade Chairman, it's a good thing at least that now we all know where

172

Comrade' – he still gave him the title, out of habit – 'Bainton stands. But what he's said this evening is purest Marxism compared with what he's been putting across to whoever would listen on the sands at Bognor. I was down there myself one week-end and I heard him. It was out-and-out Trotskyism.' Here Bainton said, 'No,' but Wally went on, 'It was Trotskyite filth. The sort of lies about the Soviet Union that even the capitalist press might find too smelly to serve up. No Party member who'd heard it could have had any doubts that Bainton' – this time Wally remembered to omit the 'Comrade' – 'had gone right over to the other side. But perhaps that's nothing to be surprised at, considering Bainton's petit-bourgeois origin.'

Wally spoke with an intensity which Alan at first regarded as out of character but which on second thoughts he recognized as arising from the very essence of the man, from the central principle without which Wally's other and gentler characteristics could not have continued to exist. And Alan wholeheartedly agreed with his condemnation of Bainton's point of view, agreed too with everything – no matter how bitterly expressed – that subsequent speakers said against Bainton. He might himself have joined in the attack if he hadn't felt deficient in first-hand knowledge of Bainton's recent activities, and perhaps it was a scruple similar to his own that made Elsie too abstain from speaking. But what deterred Alan even more was that the particular aspect of Bainton's conduct which seemed to him most noteworthy and most odious was one which he would have had difficulty in describing intelligibly to the comrades, and if he had described it he might have planted in them a suspicion that he himself was a potential Bainton. Alan saw in Bainton's deviation the act of a typically flighty ex-bourgeois intellectual, who being at the same time non-creative – and therefore essentially different from Alan, whose modesty however would have prevented him from pointing this out to the

173

comrades – could not rest content as a poet could, or as an ordinary worker could, with the great and simple basic truths of Communism, but must always be pseudo-creatively hankering after some novel way of expressing himself politically. And yet Alan, deeply though he loathed what he regarded as Bainton's shallow volatility and irresponsible inconstancy, couldn't help being impressed by the courage that had brought him here to be attacked by Party members who, he must have foreseen, would, from the moment they understood he was opposing the Party line, be stone-deaf to his arguments and would abuse him with all the greater relish when they found him resolved to persist in his error.

Ben Curtis, in summing up after the other comrades had spoken, was less harsh than any of them had been, but his voice conveyed a frigidity instead of the mildness noticeable during his opening speech. Sometimes it had happened, he told them, that members had been expelled from the Party because of political differences which at the time had seemed almost trifling, though in the end these ex-members had with hardly an exception developed a political line absolutely opposed on all important issues to that of the Party. But the case of Bainton was different: he had *begun* by disagreeing with the Party on an issue that was more vital perhaps than any other, the issue of the Soviet Union's role in the worldwide struggle for working-class power. A pointer to how Bainton was likely to end up had been given in his speech when he had mentioned with approval the French renegade Doriot, who was little better than a Fascist. Bainton had claimed not to be a Trotskyite, and maybe he genuinely believed he wasn't or maybe he meant to deceive them about this, but the Party couldn't be interested in Bainton's subjective processes: the important thing was that objectively he had behaved like a Trotskyite and that he had made it clear he intended to go on behaving like one. The Party could no longer tolerate him in its ranks. Curtis finally moved a resolution, to be sent up from this meeting to the Central Committee, recommending that Bainton should be expelled from the Party. Everyone voted in favour, including Alan, who experienced an irrational uneasiness as he put up his hand however, and including Bainton himself, whose un-ironic expression of face gave no clue as to whether or not he was clowning.

As Alan and Elsie were following other comrades out of the room after the finish of the meeting they saw Bainton waiting, perhaps for them, at the door. Alan, momentarily forgetting the significance of what had happened since he and Elsie had talked briefly with Bainton in the backyard, felt an impulse to speak jocularly to him about his having voted for his own expulsion, but became conscious that badinage on such a subject would be a disloyalty to the Party. Badinage of any kind with him now, or even perhaps speaking to him at all, would be disloyal. Bainton stood looking steadily at them, seeming to expect them to speak, and his look suggested that he was equally prepared to hear them call him 'you rat' or say something friendly. They hesitated in the doorway and were held silent partly by inability to think of any appropriately noncommittal remark to make and partly by awareness that they ought not to be noncommittal. Then, without having spoken to him, they went down the stairs.

On their way out of the side passage to the pavement of the High Street neither Alan nor Elsie glanced back to see whether he was behind them. But as they walked along the pavement he grew closer upon them in their thoughts.

Elsie said, 'I can't get used to what's happened. Of course he always liked to be different and to disagree, but I never guessed he'd go to these lengths.'

'I half believe he intended the whole thing as a subtle practical joke. Though it's no joke of course.'

175

'It certainly isn't. And he was really quite serious, I'm sure.'

'Yes. The fact is he's a complete individualist. What's astonishing isn't that he's turned against the Party but that he ever wanted to join it.'

'No doubt he was one of those who are brought to it by a genuine but woolly social idealism.'

'I suppose Lenin would have said of him that he conforms to the classic type of the unstable petit-bourgeois intellectual.' A slight sense of guilt made Alan add, 'But there, but for the grace of . . . Marx, go I, if not you.'

'Oh, I'm at least half petit-bourgeois – my father was a clerk, though my mother's father worked as a chair-maker. Perhaps that's why I felt uncomfortable when we cut Bainton dead at the top of the stairs.'

'I felt bad about it too. It seemed so mean and crude. We were forced to behave rather like two petit-bourgeois snobs pretending not to know a neighbour who'd become an atheist or done something else unconventional.'

'Yet we could hardly have spoken to him after the meeting had voted for his expulsion.'

'And after we'd voted for it.'

'Whether we'd voted for it or not,' Elsie said a little sharply, 'we should have been bound by the majority decision. And anyway the decision was a right one.'

'Yes. So why are we uncomfortable about it?'

'Probably because only an hour and a half ago we felt friendly to him, and we can't easily adapt ourselves so soon to seeing him as an enemy.'

'The fact is that people of his sort would quickly wreck the Party if they weren't expelled from it.'

'That's the thing to remember.'

As Elsie said this, Alan's uneasiness was removed. His sense that their behaviour towards Bainton had been deficient in ordinary human kindness gave place to a recognition that if the Party were to disappear from the world there would be no hope for humanity. The showing of kindness to a few deviationist human individuals could lead to disaster for human beings in general. At a time when decaying capitalism had taken the form of Fascism in Germany and Italy and was preparing for an all-destructive war, and when only the Soviet Union stood unequivocally for international peace, anyone who like Bainton spread propaganda against the Soviet Union was objectively helping Fascism and working to bring violent death to millions of men, women and children. He was a traitor not only to the Party but to humanity. Alan, in arriving at this view of Bainton, felt an exaltation not altogether different perhaps from what might have been felt by a religious person in the act of subordinating natural human desires to the supposed will of God. It was an exaltation that arose from the very suppression of his natural kindly feeling towards Bainton.

He told Elsie most of what he had been thinking, but made no mention of the exaltation or of the brief and vague speculation which had passed through his mind about its meaning. There seemed to be no more they could say to each other about Bainton; and because any other topic would have been an anti-climax they walked on without speaking.

After a while Elsie said, 'I'm fed up.'

'Why?'

'I don't know.'

'Because of Bainton?'

'No. I suppose it's because of the amount of Party work I've been doing lately. I haven't had a free evening for over a fortnight.'

'No wonder they call us slaves of Moscow,' Alan said, repeating a stock Party joke.

Elsie, without changing her tone but speaking a little more quickly, said, 'Can I come back to your lodgings with you?'

'Yes, do.'

He spoke with a suggestion of politeness, unready at first to risk believing that her question could mean what it seemed to, but soon he felt certain that it could not mean anything else, and a joy warmed inside him. He did not ask himself yet why her former apparently asexual attitude towards him had now changed. He put his arm through hers and pressed it. She gave his arm only a slight responding pressure, but he guessed that this was because she did not want to seem more forward than she had already dared to be.

They took a bus, even though the distance to Alan's lodgings wasn't such that they would have got there much less quickly if they'd walked, and on the bus they talked very easily not about themselves or Bainton but about a ramble in the country which the Teachers' Anti-War Movement had arranged for next Sunday and which Elsie was to lead.

When they were on the pavement again and within a hundred yards of Alan's lodgings, he said gaily, 'I don't know what my landlady's reactions might be to my bringing you in at this hour, so we'd better try to creep in unobserved.'

'Is she very prim?'

'Not really. Though she didn't like it when the young bank clerk who also lodges here – he's very nice – was visited three evenings running by a peachy platinum blonde. But you,' Alan said, and he could have kicked himself for the archness of it even before he'd finished saying it, 'aren't that type of girl at all, of course.'

Elsie, however, laughed – in a way that indicated that she did not discover anything crude in what he had said.

They walked up the short tiled path to the front door, whose upper half was leaded and glazed with stained glass in fleur-de-lys patterns, and Alan got out his key and very carefully turned it in the Yale lock. He had closed the door quietly behind them and they were going towards the stairs when – just because he was moving on semi-tiptoe – he staggered a little and pushed lightly against a shaky hall table and caused a papier-mâché plate containing artificial apples and pears to fall to the floor. As he was picking up the wax fruit Mrs White, his landlady, came out from the back room.

'I'm so sorry, Mrs White,' Alan said. 'I'm afraid I've knocked these over.'

'Oh, that's quite all right, Mr Sebrill. Don't worry about them.'

She smiled. Alan wondered whether it might not be best for him to introduce Elsie to her, but Mrs White, still looking amiable, turned and withdrew into her room.

When Alan and Elsie had reached the top of the stairs he said, 'Evidently you're not the sort of girl that landladies disapprove of.'

Elsie this time did not laugh. He opened the door of his bed-sitting-room for her. Inside she at once went towards the armchair, not the divan, and sat down. Respect for her obvious shyness caused him to sit on the divan, at a distance of three quarters of the room's length away from her, instead of following her and sitting on the arm of her chair as he very soon realized he ought to have done. She began talking again about next Sunday's ramble, asking if he could suggest a route to take that would avoid roads altogether – because last time she'd led a ramble two elderly comrades had been very annoyed at having to walk on roads for part of the way. She clearly did not intend to say or do anything that would help him to begin to make love to her. And yet he could hardly doubt that in inviting herself to his lodgings she had hoped that he would make advances to her there. Probably her unencouraging manner now was due not to her having changed her mind but to virginal inexperience and to the fear of making herself seem too cheap. And he ought, like a proper male wooer, to overcome her fear. But as they continued talking he felt an increasing disinclination towards her. He became aware too that this disinclination was not new, that he had felt it almost as strongly when he

179

had tried long before on the path by the railway to arouse her sexually. Perhaps the explanation why she had been unresponsive then wasn't that she was in any way abnormal but that she had sensed the repugnance in him contradicting the outward love-making movements of his hands. And what had caused this repugnance, and what was causing it now? Simply an unregenerate and contemptible bourgeois hankering after romantic beauty, after a woman with honey-coloured hair and Greek features who would admire his poetry and would have limbs like a goddess's or like Peg's. Or was the repugnance caused by something far more disgraceful, by a deeply surviving class snobbery in him, which shrank back from every sign, whether in her speech or dress or manners, that she was ignorant of upper-class customs? At this thought an indignation against himself came over Alan, and he remembered how much better a person Elsie was than Peg, for example, or than any other bourgeois girl he had met.

But he was no nearer to being able to begin to make love to her. Words of endearment would sound altogether artificial if he tried them out now after discussing the ramble, and he couldn't just baldly get up and walk over to her chair. Some sort of introductory gesture was necessary. He suddenly thought of one, an absurd one. Talk between them had come to a stop. He picked up the nearer of two pillows, disguised in oatmeal-coloured covers as cushions during the daytime, which were lying on the divan, and he threw it quite hard across the room at her. She just had time to put up a hand to fend it off from her face. He hurried over to her while she was still in the act of lifting the cushion away from her and was hesitating where to get rid of it. Her sitting position deep in the chair prevented him from closing with her and embracing her frontally, which was what he would have preferred from the point of view of avoiding too many mechanical preliminaries; and, since he couldn't acrobatically bend his legs backwards from the hips and sit on her knee in reverse, as it were, with his chest against her bosom, he had to go round to the side of the chair. He leant over her and, placing his hands on both sides of her face, he stroked her cheeks with a rotary movement of his palms. She let the cushion fall to the floor. His knees pressed into the outer side of the chair-arm. She moved her face against his palms in response to their movement. He was encouraged to expect that this time at last his advances would not be met with an enigmatic passivity, though he could not yet be sure whether her response arose from pleasure or whether it was willed. He sat on the rounded corner of the chair-arm, turning his body halfway over towards hers, pushing his legs alongside hers at the front of the chair. She moved her legs to make room for his. He felt no desire, was driven mainly by his will, though partly also by a fear that even now he might achieve nothing. Having stroked her cheeks, he stroked her neck; and then, after far too perfunctorily hand-ling her breasts beneath her vest, he quickly, as if in panic, pushed his hand beneath her skirt. They remained in the chair for ten minutes, and he did not know whether the activity of his hand excited her at all: he was certain only that in her acceptance of what he was doing there was some-thing more positive than a mere absence of disapproval.

He removed his hand, and she raised herself in the chair so as to bring her face close to his and said, 'Kiss me.' He kissed her, half on the lips and half on the cheek. Up to now he had deliberately not kissed her, believing that to have done so would have been hardly less insincere than to have used words of endearment, and that a purely animal approach was the only genuine one for him. To be genuine with her was, more even than he was yet aware, a necessity for him. She got up from the chair soon after he had kissed her, and stood a short way away from him to adjust her underclothes.

She then asked, 'Have you a mirror here?'

'Yes. It's fixed to the inside of the door of my wardrobe.'

She went over and opened the door of the wardrobe and began to tidy her hair. There came upon him, as he watched her and thought of what he had just done to her, the feeling that he had committed an obscene act. He experienced foreboding, as though he were a pagan expecting punishment for having scamped the rites of the Goddess of Love. But his apprehensiveness was lightened a little when he saw in her side-face, and in her full-face which looked at him out of the mirror, that she herself felt no disgust or regrets about what had happened. On the contrary she seemed unambiguously glad. There was a flush on her cheeks and her whole expression indicated triumph. Though he felt less guilty now that he saw her happiness, he was puzzled by it. Sensual satisfaction had, he was sure, hardly any part in it, nor could his mechanical love-making have made her believe he loved her. Perhaps the explanation might be that she had always been aware, from the day when he had first made physical advances to her, of a factitiousness or an uncertainty in his desire for her, and that her awareness of the ambivalence in his attitude had been the cause of her earlier unresponsiveness to him; and that during the time since he had stopped making advances to her she had found she wanted him as a lover and had decided not to be discouraged any more by the revulsion she had detected in him but to try to lead him on.

She turned from the mirror and asked, 'Is my hair more or less tidy now?'

'I don't know. It seems much the same as usual – somewhat wild, in fact. But that's just what I like. Your curls are natural, not faked up by a hairdresser.'

'How do you know they aren't faked? Perhaps I wear curl-papers every night.'

'I know you don't. Not only because you're not that sort of person but because I can see you don't.'

'You're right. I've had them since I was a baby and I've got photographs to prove it. But if you think that just by looking at a girl's curls you're capable of telling whether they're artificial or not – well, you're in for another think, as Comrade Finlayson would say.'

She gave him a smile which had little to do with their talk about curls. It was calm and happy, a smile of gratitude and of kindness, and, strangely, of trust. It was a smile as for a best friend, the closest and dearest of friends. And seeing it he immediately knew the impossibility of his intention – already half-formed when he had been in the chair with her – that this occasion should be the last on which he would have sexual contact with her. He had committed himself to her now. To try to go back on what he had done would be a treachery not very different – though why he felt this about a Communist girl was unclear to him – from the treachery of an eighteenth-century gentleman abandoning the cottager's young and only daughter whom he'd seduced. He knew he would have to go through with what he had begun, would have in the end to marry her. He could not make the general good of humanity a pretext now, as he had made it when breaking with Bainton, for being unkind to a human individual. And the certainty that there could be no escape had the effect of abolishing in him utterly the feeling he had had earlier in the evening that she was the sort of girl he would like to marry. A misery grew upon him as he looked at her, but with it came the recognition that it was disgraceful, that it was rotten with bourgeois romanticism, and that basically what he had allowed to repel him in her was her having been born into another and lower class than his own.

He compelled himself to say to her, 'We must go away together for a week-end soon.'

'Yes, we must.'

She went and sat on the divan, and he sat in the armchair. He asked when her half-term holiday would be and found that his would coincide with hers. They discussed where they would go and decided that somewhere in the country south rather than north of London would be better from the point of view of avoiding people who might recognize them. They discussed what name he should sign in the hotel visitors' book. She suggested buying a cheap wedding ring through the N.U.T. trading scheme. She mentioned that her next menstrual period would just be over by the beginning of the holiday. She said she had better be going home now or what would Mrs White think? They stood up, and he kissed her.

He went downstairs to the front door with her to see her out, though she said he needn't. This time Mrs White did not emerge from the back room.

9

AFTER LUNCH Alan walked across the quad towards the masters' billiard-room, which was secluded just behind the armoury in a corrugated outbuilding known as the 'A.B.' – short for Asbestos Bethel. He carried his gown under his arm, and his gown hid a large dry electric battery entrusted to him by the committee of the Teachers' Anti-War Movement. He was expected to raise money among his colleagues by means of this battery, which had rows of numbers in gold print on its dark-blue glossy paper-covered surface, each number having a small metal socket concealed underneath; and attached to the battery by a piece of flex there was a small plug that could be pushed through the paper surface into any of the sockets, and if it was pushed into the correct socket a red-tinted bulb that was connected with the plug would light up. He was to ask fourpence for each attempt and to pay out one-and-six whenever the bulb lit up, and he had been told that the proportion of lucky numbers was generous. The first person he had asked had been Benson, with whom he had happened to be alone in the common-room during a free period but who had refused on the grounds of having a personal objection to gambling of any kind. Alan had then had the idea that the billiard-room might be the best place to try out the battery in, because those of his colleagues who went there would be less likely to disapprove of gambling. Now, however, arriving in the small lobby outside the billiard-room, he was uneasy, and instead of hanging up his gown on one of the hooks provided there he kept it wrapped round the battery as he went into the room.

Everyone inside the room seemed to be expecting him. From the far corner near the scoreboard Brook, Buckle and Railton, standing with cues in their hands, were all looking towards him across the table, and Railton, being very tall, had to crane his head sideways to get a view of him past the big green lightshade that was suspended above the table. From the long upholstered seat on a daïs against the wall other colleagues, who were there to watch the game, turned their faces towards Alan as he came in.

Then Brook said, 'Oh God, it's only Rasputin.'

'Do you know where Chiddingfold is?' Railton asked, and Buckle reinforced him with, 'Yes, where's Gus? Where's the red-headed horror? What have you done with him? He's due to partner me at snooker and we've wasted five whole minutes waiting for the old basket.'

'I haven't seen him,' Alan said.

'Serve him right if we found a substitute,' Railton suggested.

'Oh no, the old Haggis must be in this game,' Brook said. 'I've got money on it with him.'

'Wasn't he still at lunch when you came away?' Buckle asked, coming towards Alan.

'No.'

Buckle came closer. He was brown-eyed, pale-faced and physically strong in a way that made Alan think of a jockey, and his movements had a slight eager jerkiness which, if he had been less athletic, might have caused him to be regarded as highly strung. When he was within a yard of Alan he abruptly asked, pointing at Alan's gown, 'What's that you're hiding under there?'

'I'm not hiding anything,' Alan absurdly asserted, and as if to prove the point he quickly pulled the battery out from under the gown and held it towards Buckle.

186

'What's it for?' Brook asked, having also come towards him.

'It's a battery—'

Lexton, sitting at the near end of the long upholstered seat, interrupted ironically: 'I could have guessed as much.'

'It's a kind of gambling machine,' Alan added, and he at once had the silent attention of everyone in the room who was able to hear him. 'You choose one of these numbers here, any number you like – there are over two hundred of them, and you stick this plug through the paper into the socket below, and if you've chosen right this bulb will light up. You pay me fourpence for each go you have and I pay you one-and-sixpence each time you win.'

'Fourpence?' Railton almost seriously complained. 'That's far more than I could afford.'

'Make it a halfpenny,' Lexton said, 'and I'll bite.'

Alan had the impression that soon, with or even without some further persuasion, one or other among them wouldn't be able to resist paying to try his luck. Buckle seemed already to be handling coins in his trouser-pocket, but was checked by a suspicion which made him ask, 'What's this in aid of?'

'The Teachers' Anti-War Movement,' Alan unemphatically said.

'Oh-ho, so that's it, is it?' Buckle's voice was sharply exulting. 'I suppose it's one of your pet Moscow organizations. So that's what he's trying to get money out of us for, the creeping crawler.'

'It has nothing to do with Moscow.'

Buckle triumphantly went on, 'He's going round with the battery just to give himself a rest after distending his navel by carrying the banner-pole in the demonstration.'

They all laughed, except Brook, who when they had stopped laughing said as if not unsympathetically, 'By the way, I got hold of a copy of that newspaper of yours for the first time the other day – the *Daily Worker* I think it's called. And I've only one criticism to make against it.'

He had the air of being amazed at how much he'd found unexceptionable in the paper.

'What's your criticism?' Alan asked, rising to the bait.

'The paper's too thin.'

They laughed again. Alan grinned. He felt that an answer was due from him to these attacks on the *Worker* and on the T.A.W.M., but he was in difficulty about what tone to adopt in answering. If he tried to retort in a coarsely humorous way – which he might find himself without the inspiration to do successfully – he would not only be debasing the cause he stood for but he wouldn't further his purpose of raising money either. On the other hand a serious answer would sound as out of place here as a giggle during a funeral service. And yet he couldn't just go on grinning. He said, 'The Teachers' Anti-War Movement is British. Its only foreign connection is with the International Anti-War Movement which was started at the Amsterdam Congress by people like Barbusse. It is affiliated to the National Peace Council here, which you may know is a respectable organization.' He added with a touch of aggressiveness, 'The T.A.W.M. hopes to bring together all teachers, whatever their politics or religion, who want to do something to prevent the world war that's bound to come if we do nothing.'

'What rot!' Railton said, with a seriousness which neither he nor any of the others had shown up to now. He was an older man than Buckle or Brook. He had tight skin over his temples and it emphasized his skull, but his eyelids were heavy. Alan, who had for a moment been dubious about the wisdom of having spoken a little provocatively, was now glad that he had, since Railton's serious antagonism was more promising than the others' frivolous scoffing. Railton continued, 'In the first place, there's not going to be a war; and, in the second place, if there is going to be one nothing you

188

or I can do will make the slightest difference. We ought to mind our own business and leave these things to the experts.'

Alan was aware of so many exasperating philistine fallacies in what Railton had said that he couldn't easily decide which he ought to refute first.

'If a majority of people in this country, especially the workers in key industries, were determined we shouldn't go to war – then we wouldn't.'

'There speaks the Menace,' Brook said. 'What he wants is a good bloody revolution.'

Alan, ignoring him, said to Railton, 'I don't see how you can be so sure there's not going to be a war when only recently the Italian Fascists invaded Abyssinia, and now Hitler has re-occupied the Rhineland.'

'It's a good thing he has, in my opinion,' Railton said equably, disregarding Abyssinia. 'The Rhineland's German, and it was bound to be a source of ill-feeling so long as Germany was deprived of it. Hitler's re-occupying it will make war less likely, not more likely.'

No one in the room other than Alan seemed to disagree with this. Their stupidity would have made him angrier if he hadn't remembered that every newspaper including the Labour *Daily Herald* and the Liberal *News Chronicle* – though excepting the *Daily Worker* of course – had expressed approval when the Nazis seized the Rhineland. Press lords and the capitalists generally were the ones to blame for encouraging Nazism, not his colleagues whom they misled and whom it was his task to try to enlighten. He said, 'Re-occupying the Rhineland is only a first step. Next will be Austria, and then Czechoslovakia, and then Poland.'

'You've no grounds whatsoever for suggesting that,' Railton said.

'Of course I have.'

'What grounds?'

'The Nazis happen to have published a map showing

which countries they are going to invade and when.'

'It sounds like a piece of Communist propaganda.'

'It isn't. And in any case anyone who takes a serious interest in politics at all,' Alan unwisely said, 'knows perfectly well that Nazism is an aggressive movement aiming at military conquest of other countries.'

'That's simply an assertion,' Buckle said, 'with no facts behind it.'

Alan, in little doubt that Buckle was serious and was not merely baiting him, could not help being taken aback by the outrageous ignorance revealed, and he said without sufficient thought, 'If you want facts, what about the recent Nazi statement that they intend to spread Nazism all over the world?'

'Where did you read that?' Buckle sharply asked.

'Not in the popular press here' – Alan tried to avoid sounding as though he was making a damaging admission – 'because that's just the kind of thing they prefer not to tell their readers.'

'But it's the kind of thing that the *Daily Worker* does tell its readers,' Brook said ironically, though truly.

'In fact the statement was never made,' Buckle decided.

'Of course it was,' Alan said. 'It was in all the German papers.'

'Prove that,' Buckle challenged him.

'I could. But getting the papers would take time, and when I got them and showed them to you you'd ask, "What's all this about?" and pretend you'd never denied that the statement had been made.'

'He's wriggling,' Brook said, 'the Menace is wriggling.'

'I wish this conversation could be taken down in writing,' Alan said, not altogether hiding anger. 'It would make good reading in ten years' time. I think I will put it down. How you can be so blind I don't know. If people like you could be made to see what's in front of their noses, then there might be some hope of stopping the war that's being planned.'

'At any rate we can smell what's in front of our noses,' Brook said.

They all laughed at Alan, not ill-naturedly. Brook then, in the lowered voice of one having inside information to impart, told them, 'Talking of war and Reds, a letter came from the War Office some time back inquiring about the number and condition of the rifles in the school armoury. If there are civil disturbances the armoury will be put under military guard. Twenty of the rifles are in really good condition. And the ones with Morris tubes could be quite useful.'

The door was vigorously opened and Gus Chiddingfold came into the room. At once there was a confusion of voices cheerfully calling out insults against him. When it had subsided he said smoothly to Buckle, Brook and Railton, 'I'm not late, am I, boys? I've just come from a session in the lats.'

'All right, you don't have to tell us where you live, you great cloacal mess,' Brook said.

'Don't stand wobbling there,' Buckle bawled at him. 'Get your cue. Fetch your instrument out.'

'What? In here with all these people about?' Chiddingfold asked coyly; but a movement by Buckle that seemed to threaten physical violence caused him to hurry towards the cue-rack.

Brook spun a coin and Buckle called 'Heads.' Alan, carrying the battery, went and sat down in a vacant place on the long seat. Railton played the first shot of the game; being so tall, he had to bend low and to straddle his legs widely in order to get down to the table. As he was fidgeting his cue backwards and forwards before striking the ball, Chiddingfold called out, 'Legs a little farther apart, please.'

'You've put him off,' Brook exclaimed. 'You've put my partner off, you foul hound. Just wait till your turn comes.'

'He's rammed it,' someone from among the spectators

said, meaning that Railton had left the balls in a position advantageous for Buckle, who was the next player.

'Rameses,' someone else said, addressing Railton.

'You're in,' Chiddingfold told Buckle, meaning that Buckle ought to make a big score now.

'Urine,' someone emended.

Brook, when his turn came to make his first shot, failed to get the object-ball into the pocket that he aimed for. He shouted 'Christ!' but the ball travelled far and when it eventually went into a pocket at the other end of the table he shouted 'unChrist!'

There were comments from the watchers:

'Rasping fluke.'

'You can't handicap Providence.'

Chiddingfold, whose turn it now was to play, innocently asked the other players for advice. 'What had I better try, boys?'

'Use your loaf.'

'No, use somebody else's loaf.'

Chiddingfold's shot was unsuccessful, and at the end of it he stood exhibitionistically poised on one foot, with his rotund body leaning forward and his other foot up in the air behind him. This was a favourite posture of his after he had played a bad shot, and the usual remarks followed:

'Eros.' (An allusion to the slender-limbed statue in Piccadilly Circus.)

'If the pockets had hair round them he'd be able to go down them all right.'

Throughout the game most, but not all, of the insults and comments were aimed at Chiddingfold; a few were for Brook, fewer for Buckle, fewer still for Railton, in whom seniority was combined, if not with dignity, yet with some staidness – and Chiddingfold often gave back as good as he got from the spectators. He was called, at different times during the game, 'you soft crab' (by Brook), 'you titty-nosed bog-rat' (by Brook), 'you Caledonian coot' (by Buckle), 'you gaga Gael' (by Brook), 'you closet' (by Buckle), 'you overblown bagpipe' (by Buckle). He decisively defeated an attack by Lexton, a bumptious extroverted younger member of the staff who taught Classics and who had a habit of talking to almost everyone about the girl he was going to marry – his 'lodestar' he semi-facetiously called her. During a lull in the insults Lexton said to Chiddingfold, 'I shall call you Si – short for Silenus. You fit the part perfectly.'

'Did you tell your lodestar I was like that?'

'Yes.'

'I know what part she wouldn't fit.' Chiddingfold paused, and then, as though Lexton had shown signs of taking serious umbrage, he added soothingly, 'It's quite all right – I said "wouldn't".'

At various stages of the game he called Railton 'Rail-whiskers', and Ampleforth – a very reserved man who had contributed only one remark to the many made by the spectators – he referred to several times afterwards as 'Ample-rump'. He told Brook, who was trying to put him off a shot by hissing through the teeth like a horse-groom, 'Hold your udder.'

When someone said to Buckle, who was taking his time over a shot, 'Don't rush it,' Chiddingfold commented, 'He's the Tsar of all the Rushers.'

When Buckle was briefly in doubt once about which of several not very inviting shots to try, Chiddingfold advised, 'Do him a bit of dirt,' meaning 'Lay him a snooker'. Buckle followed the advice and succeeded in laying a snooker for Brook, who was the next player. 'Laugh that one off if you can,' Buckle said. Chiddingfold dangled a hand over the table, pretending to show Brook the right spot on the cushion to aim the cue-ball at and whispering, 'Hit my finger'. Brook quickly hit out with his cue at Chiddingfold's hand, saying, 'Remove those fillets of Scotch haddock,' but missed. As

Brook was about to make the shot Chiddingfold urgently warned, 'Look, he's going to foul the brown with his elbow.'

Others joined in:

'Brown's his favourite colour.'

'Watch it like a hawk.'

'Watch it like two hawks.'

Brook succeeded in extricating himself from the snooker without obviously fouling anything, and in hitting the object ball that he meant to hit. There was a cry of, 'He's got it.'

'He's had it for years,' Chiddingfold said.

When Railton, after fetching the 'rest' from the cue-rack for one of his shots, was leaning over the table on his elbows so that his long thin forearms rose vertically and one of his hands was as though jointed to the butt of his cue and the other to the butt of the 'rest', Chiddingfold said, 'Look at the praying mantis.' Later when Buckle, in order to avoid wasting time fetching the 'long rest' – or 'fishing rod' as it was more often named – played a shot left-handed, Chiddingfold called him 'ambisextrous'. When Chiddingfold himself had a run of successful shots there was an outcry of:

'He's gone mad.'

'He's diseased.'

'Send for a vet.'

'Send for an alienist.'

'Send for an ambulance.'

'Send for a padded ambulance.'

And then, as Chiddingfold at last made a shot that did not score:

'Cancel the ambulance.'

'He's sane again.'

'Send for an incinerator.'

The game was a close one, and it was still undecided after all the coloured balls except the black had been potted. Chiddingfold's final shot made Brook and Railton the winners. Though the black had been left comfortably over a middle pocket, he not merely failed to pot it but sent his own white ball into the pocket instead. He might have done this deliberately, deciding that he would get more pleasure out of annoying Buckle than out of winning the bet with Brook, Alan thought. Anticipating Buckle's fury, Chiddingfold in mock terror began to run. Buckle chased him half-way round the table and, unable to catch up with him, pointed ahead of him and shouted, 'Stop him that way,' then abruptly turned right-about and chased him in the reverse direction shouting, 'Stop him the other way,' while spectators advised, 'Stop him both ways.' The chase ended in a tableau: Chiddingfold cowering, with his hands raised to protect his head, and Buckle and Brook standing on either side of him with their cues menacingly lifted. Railton stood a little apart from them, faintly grinning, his heavy eyelids lowered so that the upper halves of his pupils were eclipsed. Buckle broke up the tableau by giving Chiddingfold an actual prod in the kidney – not so gently that it could be regarded as only a token – with the cue-butt.

As the spectators began to go out of the room Alan remained sitting, holding the battery quite conspicuously on his knees but thinking that nothing would be gained by saying any more about it. Brook lingered behind the others and, when only he and Alan were left in the room, said, 'Let's have a look at that thing once again.'

Alan handed it over to him.

'Seeing who's brought it here,' Brook mildly sneered, 'it's bound to be some sort of a swindle.'

'Not at all. The odds are quite generous.'

Alan was doubting whether he'd got his betting terminology correct when Brook said, 'All right. Call me a sucker. Here's fourpence.'

He actually gave Alan the money. Then, after a long pause for thinking, he decided on a number and pushed the plug through the paper into the socket. The bulb did not light up. He brought out a sixpence for another shot, and Alan – who had plenty of small silver but had neglected to provide himself with coppers – was able to give him change out of the fourpence already acquired from him. Brook's second attempt was unlucky also. So was his third – after which he looked at Alan with real suspicion and said, 'I don't suppose the ruddy bulb ever lights up.'

'It certainly does if you go on trying,' Alan said, wondering whether it might be defective.

Brook, who had now received back his original four coppers, produced a shilling to pay for 'another two shots and no more', and when Alan admitted to having no change he kept the shilling and took the next shot on credit. This time the bulb lit up. Brook looked as pleased as though he had won ten pounds. However, he said sharply, as Alan gave him a shilling and a sixpence, '*And* fourpence, please.'

'Why?' Alan ignorantly asked.

'The bettor always gets his stake back when he wins. Haven't you ever laid a bet with a bookie?'

'Oh yes.' Alan felt foolish.

'But since you've no change I'm prepared to take another shot instead.'

Brook made three successive attempts without having any luck, but he showed no disappointment. He seemed to be working on a system, choosing his numbers so that they formed a triangular pattern. His pauses for thinking became shorter as he continued to jab the small plug through the paper into various sockets. Alan forgot to count how many shots he was having. At length Brook, unlucky still, became angry and stopped.

'Take the damned thing.'

He gave Alan the battery and began to go towards the door. Alan might not have been able to bring himself to ask Brook to pay up, but he didn't have to ask, because Brook – with one hand on the door-handle and after an obvious inward struggle between his anger and his gambler's honour – grudgingly brought out from his pocket a half-a-crown, which Alan thanked him for, though suspecting that it was an under-payment. Clearly Brook had quite forgotten that the money would go to the T.A.W.M., but even if he had remembered – Alan thought – he would probably have felt in honour bound to pay up just the same. They went out through the lobby and on to the quad together, Alan privately becoming triumphant at having got something for the T.A.W.M. and of having got it from Brook.

And Brook seemed soon to recover from his defeat. He asked almost amiably, 'Will you be watching the Second Eleven match?'

'Yes.'

'I'm refereeing it. I ought to go and get changed now.'

As soon as Brook had begun to walk away, Alan's feeling of achievement was deflated. He recognized that, though he had now genuinely collected a little money which he would be able to hand over to the committee together with what he would collect later, he had not succeeded in making Brook better disposed towards the T.A.W.M. but had if anything made him even more hostile to it than he would otherwise have been. And in getting Brook's money Alan had done nothing to further the purpose for which the T.A.W.M. existed, had not made Brook more keenly aware of the danger of war or persuaded him to join with others in opposing the Government's pre-war policy, had temporarily been as forgetful of that purpose as Brook had been of the T.A.W.M.

Alan, depressed, was approaching the door to the main building when Barnet came out, probably about to cross the quad towards the school library, of which he was the librarian and in which he had recently been spending most of his half-holiday afternoons at work on the catalogue. Alan was carrying the battery unconcealed now, and Barnet noticing it asked, 'Had any success with that toy yet?'

Though Barnet was sympathetic to the aims of the T.A.W.M. and had allowed himself to be persuaded by Alan to attend several T.A.W.M. meetings, he had been laughingly contemptuous of the battery when Alan had shown it to him on the previous day.

'Yes. I got some money out of Brook. In the billiard-room.'

'That was an achievement, I admit. Though what real good you're going to do the T.A.W.M. by mulcting our sillier colleagues of some of the small cash which would otherwise have gone into the till at the Green Lion, I don't know.'

'You may be right. All the same the T.A.W.M. does need money.'

'Let the converts supply that for the time being, and let them concentrate on converting others who'll supply more later.'

'Getting people to give money can lead them sometimes to be interested in what they've given it to.'

'I doubt that, as far as our dear colleagues are concerned. I even doubt whether anything short of bombs falling about their ears will ever convince most of them that war's coming. The poor mutts are so trustful of the governing classes. And they'll go on being trustful, whatever the governing classes do to them.'

'Oh, I don't think they're all quite as hopeless as that.'

'Aren't they? Most of them think Hitler's rather wonderful putting down the Reds and the Yids and they hope he'll go on and put down the Soviet Union too. Their outlook is just like the Government's, and even when Hitler smashes up their houses and their families they'll no more blame the Government than they'll blame themselves.'

'If you're right – which I don't believe you are – we still ought to do what we can to influence them. They may not be capable of learning from experience alone, but when it's reinforced by what we've persistently told them it may take effect at last.'

Alan, having said this, doubted its logic; but it caused Barnet to change his pessimistic tone.

'Yes, I know we must go on trying. Though there are times when the cloddish stupidity of the blighters makes me wish they could go to hell, if only they could go there without dragging us down after them.'

The normally rich redness of Barnet's cheeks seemed to grow richer as he spoke, and his head jerked like a bird's. The skin at the sides of his face and over his chin was bluish with hair beneath the surface. His nose was Jewishly hooked. A tuft of wiry black hair stuck out backwards from just below the crown of his head. Vitality seemed to well up out of him like heat from a sun-warmed surface on a July day. He was a bird from the forests of the Amazon. He was an oriental from the near-East, a Phoenician. He was a stranger from a foreign country. But all at once he was not a stranger. The others in the billiard-room were the strangers, and this school was the foreign country. Barnet was suddenly someone belonging to the same country as Alan, who now felt as close to him as though they were near-relatives meeting each other abroad.

Alan said, 'I don't know why I haven't asked you before, but have you ever thought you would like to join the Communist Party?'

Pleasure, mixed with a surprising diffidence, showed in Barnet's face. 'I'd like to, but I doubt whether I'd be up to it. They set such a high standard.'

'Not all that high, or I should never have been accepted as a member myself.'

This obviously carried weight with Barnet, who said, 'I suppose I'd be on probation for a time.'

'Yes. Probably not for long, and you'd be able to attend

meetings just as though you were a member. There's a meeting of Party teachers tonight. I know they'd be glad to see you.'

Doubt came and quickly went in Barnet's face. 'At what time and where?'

'Seven-thirty at number sixteen Fortescue Road. You know the road?'

'Yes. I may manage to be there.'

A lingering guilt made Alan unwisely say, 'I ought to have asked you long ago whether you'd like to join the Party.'

'Well, why didn't you ask me?' Barnet was keen to know.

'I suppose I must have thought of you, quite unwarrantably, as a – don't let this offend you – as a kind of Diogenes, or a Timon of Athens.'

Barnet was offended. He said, 'I'm not a cynic. I may let my colleagues have the rough edge of my tongue at times, but it's not just in order to relieve my own exasperation. I do have some hope, however faint, of making them see a little light at last.'

'Of course you do.'

'I'm due in the library now. I've told a couple of boys to meet me there, and it's locked. I'll see you this evening, perhaps.'

'I hope so.'

As Barnet walked off across the quad Alan had, just as after separating from Brook a little earlier, a feeling of failure. But, going through the door into the main building, he told himself that Barnet would certainly come, if not to the meeting this evening, at any rate to some Party meeting quite soon. Then, ascending the stairs towards the common-room, Alan recognized with sudden joy that after many petty defeats he had at last achieved at this school something of value for the cause of the working class. He had won the Party a new member.

10

E ARLIER IN THE HOLIDAYS Alan and Elsie had
agreed to get married some time soon, and now five days
before the beginning of his school term he was travelling up
from his home to meet her in London so that she could show
him a flat to let which she had discovered and which she had
thought might be suitable for them. Through the glass of
the carriage window he watched the recession of a treescape
lumpy with separated knolls of foliage whose green was
darkened by a September staleness but was freshened for
him by his associating it with his home in the country and
with the poetic leisure which the train was carrying him
away from. Houses, scattered at first but soon more closely
grouped, succeeded the trees as he watched; and then green
weakly reappeared along a stretch of suburban common
that showed patches of dusty baldness and one larger patch
where children were using iron seesaws and swings; but then
the houses joined together and closed in on the railway,
echoing its racket, exposing to him their backyards, their
penthouse sculleries with galvanized iron tubs hanging from
nails, their sodden yellow-brown brickwork, their occasional
grimy flagpoles, their child's scooters fallen beside dustbins
or leaning against broken palings, their wretchedness which
he associated with his own life in London, with school, with
the lack of time for writing poetry. The sunlight on the roofs
of these houses seemed to him like the feeling of someone
regaining consciousness after a terrible accident. And he had
come back here five days before he need have done, and after

his marriage he would be here for most of the time during the holidays as well as for all the time during the term. But there could be no escape now: to tell her once again that he'd changed his mind – as he had told her on two previous occasions when they had intended to get married – would be too shamefully contemptible. And what right had he to wish to spend his holidays in pleasant surroundings while working-class people, whose cause he ought to be ceaselessly fighting for, were compelled to continue living in these houses here? He must go through with this marriage. More, he must annihilate in himself all bourgeois misgivings about it. There must be no sign on his face, when she met him at the terminus, of the disloyal feelings towards her that he had had in the train.

He must not visibly wince if she appeared beyond the ticket-barrier wearing the cheap and cheaply decorative wavy-brimmed white linen hat which she had worn when she had come to visit his parents at the beginning of the holidays. He must not wince inwardly either; he must allow no recrudescence of that disgraceful revulsion, painfully disgraceful to him as he remembered it, which he had had when seeing her off at the station after her visit. They had been standing on the up platform waiting for the train which was to take her back to London, and he had recognized on the down platform a public-school acquaintance named Tom Cumbers, who had had a girl with him. If she had been a platinum-blonde female clown on stilt heels Alan might have been unaffected by seeing Cumbers with her, but she had had the look of a 'lady', had been pleasant-faced and pleasantly dressed, and in an instant Alan had become ungovernably ashamed of Elsie and had turned his back on Cumbers in the hope of not being recognized by him. During the next few minutes before the arrival of Elsie's train he had done what his parents' undisguised and snobbish disapproval of her had failed to make him do: he had told her he could not marry her. But that evening he had felt shame at having been ashamed of her, and this had become more intense than his earlier shame on the station had been. By the following morning he had known without doubt that he needed her, and that his objections to her were prejudices derived from his anti-working-class upbringing and education, enemy prejudices which he must utterly destroy. He needed her still, would always need her. Let this thought be his main weapon against any enemy feelings which might attack him when he caught sight of her at the terminus in a few minutes' time.

The trackway broadened, was joined by tributaries, pushed back the buildings that banked it in on either side. The train slowed, and the Gothic-looking multiple-shafted iron pillars that supported the terminus roof came into view outside the carriage window. An optimism sparked up inside him, but it was extinguished as he stepped out on to the platform. He tried to think what had caused it, hoping that if he could discover its cause he might be able to revive it. He stood still for a moment on the platform, looking back towards the rear of the train and towards the open daylight beyond the glass vaulting of the terminus roof. He recognized that his optimism had been connected with his first sight of the pillars. They had momentarily made the same impression on him today as they had very often made on him during the time when Richard had still been living in England. This terminus then had seemed in every detail of its architecture to reflect the excitement of imminent journeys leading at last to the poetic life; it had been an iron cathedral where the mechanical triumph of man over nature was ceremonially celebrated and where the hope of happiness on earth was offered to the believer; and in the sky beyond the high glass vault birds gliding had signalled freedom. Even after Richard had gone to live abroad, and even recently – most often at the beginnings of school holidays –

this terminus had seemed to incorporate in its very structure, as though by intention of the engineer who had designed it, the promise of a time soon to come and a place not far off when and where everything that Alan most wanted would be realizable – leisure on downs or in woods, hours of imagination spent in history or science or art, liberation from the no-life of the classroom where only that superficial part of consciousness which is concerned with immediate external action had been awake. But Alan's discovery now of why the iron pillars had temporarily made him optimistic did not help him to revive the optimism. They, and the high glass roof above them, were cold and utterly denuded of promise. Like the world in the short story written by, he believed, Conan Doyle, they had had the atmosphere ripped off them.

He began walking along the platform, quickly, relying on vigorous physical movement to limit consciousness and to prevent negative feeling from invading the blankness left by the extinction of his optimism. He saw Elsie as soon as he arrived at the ticket-barrier. She was less than twenty yards away from him on the other side of the barrier, but she did not see him yet. She was not wearing the white linen hat. Her stance gave him, as it had given him often before, an impression of momentarily arrested activity rather than of stillness. Her round face, triangularly framed with uncontrolled curls that rose to a peak above her broad forehead, looked solemn. She was dressed in a cotton-print dress which at first sight had nothing about it that disheartened him. He went towards her, walking even faster than he had walked just previously along the platform, wishing to allow his eyes no time to focus her face again and meaning to reach her before there could be any wavering in his contrived and already aching smile. He came up to her, and he was still holding on to the handle of his suitcase with his left hand as he and she closed with one another and kissed. The physical contact renewed his courage, was like a warm stimulant given to someone suffering from shock. Nevertheless, he could find nothing to say to her immediately after the kiss. And she, though he was sure that she had no such weakenings as his to inhibit her, wouldn't speak to him either, possibly because of a strangely unCommunist characteristic in her which he had noticed before now – she had always seemed femininely unwilling to take the lead in the relationship between them. But as he stood there with her and not facing her, he saw passing in front of the left-luggage office near the station entrance a man whom he thought he recognized, and he spontaneously said, 'Look. Isn't that Jimmy Anders?'

She quickly looked, couldn't see Anders, said, 'Let's try to catch him before you lose sight of him.'

'I think I have lost sight of him, and I'm not sure it was him anyway.'

She wouldn't accept this, began to move off in the direction in which Alan had been looking. He followed her, asking, 'But isn't he in Spain?'

'Not yet. He's going next week. His cousin came back from Barcelona two days ago, by the way.'

'The one who was wounded driving an ambulance?'

'He has had his right arm amputated.'

'How dreadful.'

They came to a stop near the station entrance, having sighted no one resembling Jimmy Anders. Elsie wanted to go out through the entrance on the chance of seeing him at one of the bus stops outside, but Alan said, 'We'd never find him now, even if it was him I saw.'

'All right. Then we had better make our way to the Tube and go to see the flat I told you about in my letter.'

He felt relieved at this, and did not immediately know why.

On their way down the slope that led to the booking-office

he said, 'It isn't easy to imagine what it must be like to have lost a right arm.'

'He used to have a job in an architect's office and he played the clarinet for an amateur dance band.'

They were descending on the escalator when she said, 'This flat I'm going to show you is really a maisonette.'

The word would normally have been repulsive to him, and he was surprised that it wasn't now. 'How does that differ from a flat?' he asked.

She explained that it was called a maisonette because it was not part of a big block of flats but was in what looked like a two-storeyed semi-detached house. It was completely self-contained and even had its own strip of back garden. It was newly-built; in fact the builders hadn't quite finished work on it yet, but it would be ready for occupation within a month. Its rent would be one hundred and four pounds a year. He asked whether other tenants' wirelesses would be audible from above or below. She said she had taken care to inquire about that and the agents had assured her that the floors and walls were sound-proofed. He asked whether it had sham Tudor beams outside. She admitted she couldn't remember. He asked whether it was upstairs or down, how many rooms and what sort of heating it had and whether the windows had metal or wooden frames. She told him, and added other particulars, but while she was speaking and even while he himself was questioning her his thoughts were more than half elsewhere. He was uncomfortably wondering why he had felt relieved at not being able to catch up with Jimmy Anders.

'It certainly was Anders,' Alan thought as he and Elsie got into the crowded carriage of the Tube train. And simultaneously with his certainty came the recognition that he had wanted to avoid Anders because Anders made him feel guilty. Why wasn't Alan himself going to Spain? If he tried to justify his not going on the grounds that he was in a regular professional job which couldn't be abandoned, he would be dishonest: Anders too had a regular job, and was unlikely to be able to return to it. Nor could Alan make the excuse that he would be incompetent as a soldier: Jimmy's cousin had gone as an ambulance-driver. Nor could he plead that by staying in England he would be saving himself as a poet: poetry was being written in Spain, whereas during this summer holiday the news of the civil war and of the British Government's pro-Fascist attitude had so lashed round in his head every morning that he had been able to write very little. If the Fascists won they would be free to start a world war, and what would become of his poetry – and of culture and civilization in general – then? He had no doubt that he ought to go to Spain; and yet, standing in the Tube carriage next to Elsie, he knew that he would not go. But this inconsistency, he told himself, must not be the beginning of a political demoralization in him. If he wasn't going to Spain he must exert himself far more than ever before in the anti-Fascist and anti-war struggle here at home.

Partly because the carriage was crowded Alan was pressed close up to Elsie. They did not try to talk against the noise of the train. He asked himself why his awareness that he ought to be in Spain did not make him more dubious than before about his intended marriage but on the contrary tended to reconcile him to it; and he arrived at the answer that what was happening in Spain was so momentous that thinking about it made him regard his own possibly unsuitable marriage as insignificant. However, a quite different answer also occurred to him – that the horrors in Spain and the coming horrors they seemed to foreshadow in the world were so monstrous that even an unsuitable marriage would by contrast be a comfort. He began to be aware of comfort already now. The gentle resistance of Elsie's clothed body against the pressure of his own reminded his senses of nights spent in bed with her at week-ends when he and she had gone into the country together. Marriage with her would be suitable both politically and physically, he told himself; and there came over him a half-ashamed feeling of sensual release, as though he had at last allowed himself to succumb to a seducer against whom he had for a long time held out. But there had never been anything of the seducer about Elsie. All the advances had come from him. It was his pressure against her in the carriage here that had evoked her counter-pressure. And now with a long stare into her eyes he tried to suggest how much he desired her. She understood his stare, and liked it. He was glad to find as he watched her face that today her rather broad nostrils did not give her the pug-nosed look which he had sometimes distastefully noticed.

After the Tube train they took a bus. They passed quite near his lodgings but decided, in order to save time, not to break their journey there, even though this meant he would have to carry his suitcase with him to the flat. Soon they arrived in the High Street, from which a side-road led off towards the site where the maisonettes were being built. Getting off the bus, Elsie commented that if they decided to live here they would still be sufficiently near to their old haunts – she used that word – to be in with the same Party comrades as before. The High Street and some of the people walking along it looked flashily well-to-do. The shops seemed good, Elsie said, but were probably twice as expensive as in the district where Wally lived, for instance. One shop was full of flowers, another specialized in umbrellas and cutlery, another showed evening gowns. But there was also a cut-price shop and a milk bar. Above the shops were blocks of new-looking flats, set back here and there from the street so that the roofs of the shops formed terraces on which stood shrubs in green tubs. Among the passers-by along the pavement Alan noted three girls together of school age but of varying heights, who wore jodhpurs and black velvet caps and gold-pinned stocks, and with them – though somewhat apart from them – was a young man in cord breeches who had a thin black moustache and carried an ivory-handled riding crop. 'I wonder whether their parents are *nouveaux riches* or are living on credit,' Alan remarked to Elsie. The High Street as a whole, he thought, gave a similarly enigmatic impression: did the show it made represent real capitalist wealth or only fraudulent pretension? The impression remained with him when Elsie and he turned out of the High Street into the side-road, and it wasn't removed when they came to the other and recently constructed side road along which the maisonettes had been built.

Most of the maisonettes were already tenanted and had curtains in their windows. A few at the end of the road had not yet been completed by the builders – though all had reached the stage of having been roofed – and among these was number twenty-nine, which Elsie was looking for. 'Ours is the upper flat,' she said. The front door was in place, though as yet its undercoating of pink paint differentiated it from the dark green doors of maisonettes that had been finished. 'At least it isn't made of studded oak,' Alan thought, trying to keep up his morale. Side by side with the door of number twenty-nine and very close to it was another pink door, belonging to the self-contained flat that would be below theirs. There was no front garden, but the space between the doors and the main pavement was covered with imitation crazy paving made of concrete, in which there were two small islands of soil – one of them oblong and the other circular – and in the soil there were plants that had come recently from the nurseryman, looked dubiously viable, were still labelled though illegibly, and might be cotoneaster. Elsie went up to the door, which wasn't shut. Inside, there was a very small hallway that allowed him just enough space to deposit his suitcase lengthwise between the door and the bottom of the staircase. No sound was audible of anyone at work above in the flat.

'I expect the builders have finished and now there's a pause before the plasterers get going,' Elsie said as Alan followed her up to the flat.

He tried to hold on to what remained of his resolution, but as he ascended the stairs it dropped back from him, like builders' cement pouring from a damaged package. The thought that not only was he committed to marriage but that also he would be living in this petit-bourgeois maisonette brought upon him a depression too strong to be prevented from showing in his face. Luckily Elsie at the top of the stairs did not look at him but went eagerly into the kitchen.

'This is the Ascot heater,' she said. 'It lights up automatically as soon as you turn on the hot tap. The hot water for the bathroom as well as for the sink comes from it. It's quite different from the old type of geyser.'

Alan looked at the flat white-enamelled surface of the heater and remembered with brief nostalgia the cylindrical copper-coloured geyser over the bath at his home. He did not really try to restrain himself from saying pessimistically, 'The bathroom's rather far off from the heater. Won't the water become tepid on its way there?'

'I asked the house agent about that, and he said it might run rather cool for a short while after the bath-tap was turned on, but then it would become really hot, better than you'd get from any old-fashioned boiler because it would be unlimited unless the gas-works went phut.'

The pleasure she took in this kitchen made her not notice his depression.

'We'll have an electric cooker, don't you think?' she said. 'It'll be cleaner than a gas one and less smelly.'

'I expect so.'

'Well, you had better make up your mind which you'd prefer, because you're going to have quite a lot to do with it when we get it. Quite as much as I am, my boy. Our shares in the household drudgery are going to be fifty-fifty.'

'Haven't I often said that I think the husband ought to do just as much as the wife in the house if she goes out to work?'

'Of course you have.'

She noticed his gloom now, but she attributed it to her having appeared to cast doubt upon the genuineness of his belief in sex-equality.

'I was only being humorous,' she said. 'I know you are more progressive in your attitude to women than many other men comrades are.' She added lightly, 'That's why I'm willing to marry you.'

They went into the bathroom. Boards glossily and streakily painted to resemble marble enclosed one side of the bath, and the other side contacted the white-tiled wall. Elsie commented how much better this type of bath was than the old type under which dust and worse things than dust could accumulate for years out of reach of any broom.

'You seem to be well up in domestic science,' Alan said, attempting to sound jocular.

'I wouldn't say that, but I will say that what knowledge of housecraft I have is soundly based on practical experience: girls living with mother seldom go scot-free from housework as boys do.'

There were four other rooms besides the bathroom and kitchen. Two of them were quite large, one was medium-sized, one rather small; and Elsie suggested that the small room – which she showed him first – should be for visitors, and that the large room with the built-in cupboard (another very useful modern invention, she said) had better be their bedroom, since she would need the cupboard for her clothes. Just before they stepped into the second large room she asked him to consider whether he would prefer to have this or the medium-sized room, which she would show him next, as their main sitting-room. While she was speaking an idea came to him which, though it could not make him cheerful, had the effect of partly neutralizing the unhappiness he had been feeling. Suggested to him perhaps by the word 'visitors', or perhaps even by the proletarian austerity of the bare floorboards and the as yet unplastered walls, his idea was that if he had to live here he would make this petit-bourgeois maisonette a place of constant Communist activity where local comrades would come for meetings and where provincial and foreign comrades who were in London for congresses could stay for as many nights as they liked. Working-class Party members would come walking or even cycling down this snobby little road, and the neighbours would see them stop and see them stride across the crazy pavement to his front door. But as soon as he had thought this about the neighbours, he rebuked himself for inverted snobbery. What mattered was not that the arrival of comrades here should shock the local petit-bourgeoisie but that it should help to prevent him and Elsie from ever beginning to live the restricted and philistine kind of life that these maisonettes seemed designed to encourage. Not this flat but the whole world of working-class struggle must be his place of residence.

'What do you think of it?' Elsie asked, referring to the room in which they stood.

'I think it would make a good sitting-room. We could get plenty of chairs into it.'

'Now you must see the other.' As they went across the landing towards the medium-sized room she added, 'This one might be suitable for you when you want to work on your own.' She did not say, 'When you want to write poetry,' which was what she meant.

She took his hand and brought him over to the window. 'Here's a little surprise for you.'

He looked out of the window. Instead of the blocks of flats or rows of houses that he had expected he saw a strip of field, and beyond this an old red-brick wall overgrown with creepers, and beyond the wall a garden with a large-windowed house in it, shadowed by trees, one of which was a very tall cedar. Something brown moved in the field close to the wall.

'Good God,' he said, 'this flat's even provided with a cow.' He put his arm round her waist, adding with facetious anti-gallantry, 'Or should I say it's provided with another cow out there?' She giggled briefly. 'But how did it get there?' he asked.

'It belongs to a small farm which has somehow survived in these parts.'

'I don't suppose it'll survive much longer. Enormous build-ings will be going up all over it, and all over that walled garden, before we've been here a year.'

'I asked at the house agent's about that and I got an admis-sion that attempts have been made for some time to buy out the man who lives in the house over there, but he only pays a peppercorn rent – whatever that may be exactly – and he refuses to budge.'

'Long may he refuse.'

As Alan said this an emotion whose beginnings he had obscurely felt when he had first looked out of the window and seen the walled garden now became steadily stronger in him. It was connected with the cedar tree, his initial impres-sion of which had had on him the effect of a shock too abrupt to be fully felt at once. And his initial impression was still the one that dominated him as he looked at the tree again, though his second view did help to thaw out the temporary emotional numbness caused by his first. There came upon him now the memory, like an emanation from this cedar, of the home and the poetic leisure he had left behind him that morning. The flat black-green foliage, resembling terraces in the sky or shapes seen distorted through clear water, and evoking Tennyson's 'O art thou sighing for Lebanon', seemed to revive here at this moment for Alan the possibility – that had existed but never been realized in the past – of living the poetic life with which no other life could compare. He was filled with an agitation of joy; and, removing his arm from Elsie's wrist, he went over and leant on the window-sill. Then the joy was suddenly stopped, like an engine that having been revved up is choked into silence when the ignition is switched off. He remembered that from now on he would not be able to spend his holidays at home in his parents' house, and that the poetic leisure he had enjoyed there would be lost to him. A bitterness he could not control made him say to Elsie, 'I shall never be able to live in this flat.'

She was at first no more than surprised. 'Why? What's the matter with it?'

'Everything. It's so mean.'

'We could find another.'

A hurt suspicion of what might be the implication behind his words appeared in her face. Pity for her began to encroach on his bitterness, but he continued, 'Another would be just the same. Oh, I wish I didn't feel like this but I can't go on pretending I don't. I know that our marriage will be a mistake.'

Her face became expressionless. A misery rose in him at the thought of how he had betrayed her, of how he was injuring her. But at the same time a fear was in him that he might weaken, might retract what he'd said, might betray the poetic life. He was impelled to add something outrageous, something that he would not be able to go back on and that she could never forgive.

He said, 'Oh Elsie, you are so ugly.'

But his voice, which was meant to sound offensive, had the tone of a pathetic and wailing query. Her look showed resentment, though to his extreme relief she did not – as he knew he deserved that she should – turn her back on him and walk out of the flat. She did not even sound angry when she answered him. 'It's not true that I'm ugly. I may be no beauty queen and I wouldn't do for a film star but I'm not ugly. Anyone who knows me would tell you that. Some would say that I'm quite good-looking.'

'Of course you are.' He was eagerly repentant. 'I wish I didn't come out with such swinish things. I don't mean them. I didn't mean that I couldn't live in this flat. I don't know what made me say what I've been saying.'

He moved towards her, but her look did not encourage him to touch her.

'Yes, I do know,' he corrected himself. 'It was the thought that after our marriage I shall have much less time for poetry. It occurred to me suddenly as I looked out of the window and that's what caused my unforgivable outburst.'

She was not mollified, but she seemed to be trying to resist the feelings of injury which he had caused in her. She said, 'I don't see why you will have less time for poetry.'

He was surprised to find that he couldn't immediately see why, either. Then he said, 'I shall be doing Party work during the holidays as well as during the term.'

'Not necessarily. You could ask to be given time off for writing.'

'I wouldn't have the nerve to ask.'

'As a matter of fact I've already sounded comrades on the district committee about it, and they understand your position. You've only to ask and you'll find they'll be quite willing for you to cut down on your political work. They see the point too that your poetry is indirectly a kind of political work.'

'All right, I will ask.'

He moved close to her and put his arms round her. She did not repel him.

'I wish you could forget the poisonous things I've just said.' She did not answer. He went on, 'Will you still marry me?' She ignored the wheedling question. 'Though I don't know what should make you want to,' he added. 'I'm so unstable. I shall never shake off the effects of my bourgeois upbringing.'

'I've got no illusions about our marriage,' she said. 'It may work and it may not. If it doesn't we shall have to separate, that's all.'

'I don't deserve you.'

His arms brought her closer to him, and the love he felt for her now seemed to have only one objection to overcome – which was that being allowed time off for writing poetry during the holidays would not be the same as going home and getting right away from political work as he had hitherto done. But what sort of poetry was it, he suddenly asked himself, that required him to spend fifteen weeks of each year in bourgeois surroundings away from his comrades? If he wanted to be a militant pro-working-class poet – which he did above all want – then the sooner he pulled up the remaining roots that attached him to middle-class life the better. Elsie's response to his embrace seemed to be willed rather than spontaneous. But he knew, from experience of what had happened on the one or two previous occasions when he had misbehaved in a similar way towards her, that within the next hour the feelings he had upset would right themselves again in her.

'Let's go to my lodgings,' he said.

'Yes.'

On their way down the stairs from the flat he thought, 'Up to the present I've really been no more than a part-time Party member. Now I'm going to marry into the Party.'

11

AN HOUR AND A QUARTER before the Blackshirt meeting at the Mawney's Road Baths Alan and Elsie were sitting opposite each other in armchairs in their maisonette, and he had just finished reading a *New Statesman* book-review which antagonized him sufficiently to make him temporarily forget that they would soon be going to the meeting and might get beaten up there.

He asked her, 'Have you seen this by Philip Jordan?'

'I'm not sure. What's it about?'

'He's attacking left-wing modern poets for being too obscure.'

'Yes, I believe I did read parts of it.'

'What did you think of what you read?'

'Well, you know my sentiments about the kind of thing that most modern poets turn out. I don't begin to guess what they're aiming at. Give me Shelley and Burns every time.'

Alan started reading the *New Statesman* to himself again, but soon said argumentatively, 'Of course he's perfectly right when he says that the anti-Fascist cause is more important than literature. But he implies that the best anti-Fascist writing is the kind which is most easily intelligible to the greatest number of readers.'

Elsie's look showed she didn't think the implication at all outrageous; however she did not say so.

'This may seem logical,' Alan went on, 'but is it? Would you call Marx easily intelligible? Yet he has had an immensely greater influence even than a popular socialist writer like Blatchford for instance.'

'That's true.'

As soon as Alan became aware that he might be beginning to convince Elsie he was impelled to oppose his own argument and to side with Jordan, the disturbing effect of whose review upon him had been due to its having expressed all too well the misgivings he himself had often had about poetry. 'But Marx's intention in *Das Kapital* was scientific, not poetic. To criticize him because not everyone can understand him would be almost as absurd as to criticize Einstein for expressing the Theory of Relativity in mathematical instead of in popular terms. Whereas if a poet writes in such a way that only the cultured few can make anything of him he's failed as a poet.'

'I think so.'

'Of course it could be argued that, just as the work of the pure mathematician does eventually affect everyone, so the work of even the most precious of modern poets does influence the masses indirectly through the intellectual élite. But the trouble is that the poet, unlike the scientist, can't write for a limited public without limiting the value of his work in itself.'

'Yes.'

'On the other hand if a poet were to appear today who could write as marvellously and appeal to as wide an audience as Shakespeare did, wouldn't he be wasting his time?'

'I don't see what you mean by that.'

'I mean, wouldn't he be better occupied not writing verse at all but writing the simplest possible prose and making himself understood by a maximum number of people?'

'I don't think so,' Elsie said decisively. 'Good poetry can have an effect on people's emotions which is quite different from the effect got by prose, and which is just as useful.'

'Suppose the poet isn't a Shakespeare but only someone like myself, oughtn't he in the present state of the world to use what literary gifts he has in writing political pamphlets rather than poetry?'

'Certainly not. Pamphlets may be more important than poetry, but other comrades can write those better than you can, and you can write poetry better than they can.'

He was warmed and pleased by what she said, all the more because he knew that she said it not just out of love for him but out of genuine conviction. And yet he was not convinced by it, partly because he had paid less attention to the sense of her words than to their encouraging tone. He again looked at, but did not begin to reread, the *New Statesman* review. The question 'Why write?', which he had been asking himself more and more often since he had joined the Party, came into his mind as sharply as though it had been spoken aloud to him. While Elsie resumed her reading of *World News and Views* he considered his old answers to that question, and his counter-answers to those answers. He must write because he wanted to: but merely wanting to do something was no justification for doing it. He must write because if he didn't his life would become a desert: but to make such an answer was to imply that Party work was arid and worthless. He must write because, although the political fight must always come first, writing was his best weapon in the fight: but in this epoch of wars and revolutions how feeble a weapon poetry was, 'whose action is no stronger than a flower'. Poetry had lost its influence. Life moved men so much that they no longer had any emotion to spare for imaginative literature. The tears no longer fell on 'holy poets' pages'. He would do better to write political tracts. At this point in his thinking Alan remembered, and for the first time grasped as a rational and relevant statement, Elsie's saying that other comrades could write better pamphlets than he could. For a moment it seemed to him that she had given a final answer to his doubts. But then he thought, 'My pamphlets, however inferior to those written by other comrades, might be of more use to the movement than my poems, however good.' He was trying to find a flaw in this new doubt when he was interrupted by the sound of a playfully rhythmical septuple knock on the front door downstairs.

'I'll go,' Elsie said.

Before she had reached the bottom of the stairs he was sure that the knock – which was not aggressively loud – must be Wally's, and as soon as she opened the door Wally's 'Hullo, comrade' sounded up into the room. The friendly and happy voice had the effect of bringing Alan instantly back to an actuality that was dominated by the unpleasant prospect of the Fascist meeting. Wally came smiling into the room with the look of someone on a holiday outing. He was wearing a new brown suit and carrying a brown trilby hat. Alan had not seen him dressed up like this before, but, though on sufficiently familiar terms with him to be unafraid of making a facetious remark about his smartness, Alan refrained from making one – partly because this new flat, with its pale green damask curtains and its new armchair and sofa, carefully chosen for the ascetic simplicity of their design, invited a retort in kind.

'Feeling strong?' Wally asked, and before sitting down on the sofa he hitched up his trousers to avoid spoiling their creases.

Alan gave him a grin which he hoped had nothing sickly about it. He wondered why, in view of the possibility of a fight at the meeting, Wally had not come dressed in working clothes. The unasked question was half answered by what Wally said next: 'We shan't try to break up the meeting.

There'll be too few of us for that. It would be different if Mawney's Road was a real working-class district instead of mostly petit-bourgeois. And the Fascists are bringing in supporters by motorcoach from outside London. We think our best plan will be to leave the meeting in a body when Bill Fenton gives us the signal.'

'Why Bill Fenton?' Alan asked, trying not to show the relief he was ashamed of feeling.

'You ought to know that he's our branch secretary now,' Elsie reproved him.

'But he hasn't been secretary for long,' Wally excused Alan. 'In fact he's only been in the Party for just over a year. He's a first-rate comrade.' With pride Wally added, 'I brought him into the Party. I met him at work.'

'By the way, how's your latest job going?' Elsie asked, humorously stressing the word 'latest'. This allusion to the fact that Wally was so often changing jobs struck Alan as an indelicacy, but the pleased way in which Wally received it suggested that Elsie's customary robustness of comment might sometimes make for better comradeliness than his own delicacy.

'Not so bad. I'm with the Lea Plywood Company now. You'd have laughed at an incident there yesterday. We've got an architect who's a German refugee and doesn't speak English well.' Wally got up from the sofa, stood rather stiffly and put on a serious expression of face; evidently he was impersonating the architect. 'One of the labourers – a young lad who's a boxer – was walking around looking for somewhere to relieve himself.' Wally became the young boxer, moved with a sturdy gait towards a corner of the room near the door. 'At last he found a convenient wall.' Wally came to a stop facing the cream-distempered wall of the room. His hands went down to his flies, and for a moment he seemed to be about to perform the urinating part of his story in earnest, but instead he transformed himself into the German refugee architect once again and then continued the commentary: 'Just as he was finishing, the architect came up behind him and called out, "Offeece, offeece!" So this lad followed the architect to the office, expecting to get instructions there about steel rods, but what happened was that the architect reported him for using the wall.' Wally became the boxer, looking resentfully surprised and powerlessly aggressive; then he became himself, laughing at the remembered situation, and he returned to the sofa and sat down again. As he did so Alan knew that the story had been told with a purpose: Wally had meant it to counteract the tension which, though not felt by himself, he had guessed Alan and Elsie might be feeling about the meeting at the Mawney's Road Baths. Alan now knew too that Wally was wearing his new brown suit not because he believed a scuffle with the Fascists to be wholly improbable this evening but because he liked changing into it after work and he wasn't going to let the Fascists stop him.

Neither Wally nor Elsie nor Alan said anything further about the meeting before the time came for them to go to it. Until then their conversation consisted mainly of gossip about various Party comrades. Elsie wondered how Eddie Freans was getting on now that he had left London. This reminded Wally of an incident during the Jubilee when Eddie and he had fixed up from the roof of a building on the Manor Estate a Red Front banner which was to be opened out by the pulling of a string at the very moment when George Rex would be passing by on his visit to the borough. Eddie had neglected to make a preliminary investigation through the window of the drying-room, so they unscrewed the wrong bars and had to unscrew another lot before they could get out on to the parapet, which was very narrow and very high up, and they tied one end of the banner to a curving bit of metal at the corner of the tiled roof and the other end to a nail which Wally had to drive in under the tiles.

More than once the bunting and festoons and suchlike which were already there below them made a rustling sound that startled them into thinking the caretaker was creeping up after them. And the nail which Wally had driven in under the tiles came out during the night. This Jubilee story reminded Alan of a trick question which Brook had put to various members of the common-room at the time of the Coronation: 'Are you going to the Town Hall tomorrow?' The victims had asked, 'What for?' and Brook had explained, 'To get your arse painted red, white and blue for the coronation.' Alan now told Wally about this trick question, but after he had spoken the word 'arse' – and in spite of Wally's having so frankly mimed the urinating of the boxer – he felt an embarrassment that was strong enough to overcome for a moment the underlying uneasiness caused in him by the prospect of the Fascist meeting. Perhaps he was embarrassed because he sensed that in using the word 'arse' he was not living up to Wally's conception of him as a Marxist intellectual. The uneasiness soon reasserted itself; but it disappeared, as though wholly transformed into physical movement, when, Elsie having called attention to the time, the three of them got up to leave the maisonette.

Outside the front door they met Barnet, who said he had been coming to call for Elsie and Alan on his way to the Baths. He carried a brown paper packet, with no string round it, under his arm.

'What have you got there?' Wally asked him. 'Cordite?'

'No, leaflets.'

Barnet produced one of them out of the packet. In thick black type on yellow paper it was headed with the words 'Smash Fascism Before Fascism Smashes You.' He said, 'I might be able to get rid of some of these at the meeting.'

'Yes, when we walk out,' Wally suggested, and went on to explain Bill Fenton's plan, which he had already told Elsie and Alan about. He added, 'We're to meet Bill and the other comrades at the corner of Church Street, and then we can all go on to the Baths together.'

The four of them were moving unhurriedly along the pavement past other maisonettes outwardly identical with the one in which Elsie and Alan lived. On the low wall which separated the pavement from the concrete crazy paving and small shrubs in front of one of these other maisonettes Alan noticed that the symbol of the British Union of Fascists had been painted with white paint. He was sure it had not been there on the previous day. A circle enclosing a squat squiggle which was meant to represent lightning, it called to his mind a name given to it by some politically Liberal humorist: 'the flash-in-the-pan'. But Alan was contemptuous of the mentality that could be so optimistically funny about what was really the symptom of a plague which had already infected millions on the continent of Europe and would inevitably spread over Britain also unless the most energetic steps were taken to check it. Overnight this symptom had appeared in the road where he and Elsie lived, and on the wall in front of a maisonette similar to theirs. Invisibly the danger which the symbol visibly stood for was closing in on them every day. And now, as they came out of their road with Wally and Barnet into another side-road, he saw chalked on the pavement the letters P. J. – meaning Perish Judah – and only a few yards farther ahead on the surface of the road itself the words, 'Save our King from the Yids'. The sinister lynch-mob-rousing flavour of these words was still sharply upon his mind when, arriving with the others at a T-junction where the side-road joined the High Street, he noticed that the road nameplate fixed to a house wall had something written in pencil on the white part of it below the black lettering of the road name. He detached himself from the others for a moment to go and read the writing: 'You are a product of your father and mother? Take a good look at yourself.' Though the tone of this was unpleasant, seemed even in some way anti-human, he had to admit to himself that it wasn't specifically Fascist. It served to make him recognize that he had been running into a danger opposite to that of regarding British Fascism as comically ephemeral: he had been seeing the hand of the B.U.F everywhere.

Nevertheless, when they got into the High Street he didn't think he was deluding himself in observing that fewer of the people moving along the pavements seemed to be going in the direction that led away from the meeting than were going in the direction that led towards it. And on the far side of the street he saw within less than a minute three unconnected individuals stop and buy from a boy copies of a paper which – as Alan, Elsie, Wally and Barnet came nearer to him – appeared to be the Fascist paper *Action*. When the four of them had arrived opposite the boy, Barnet unexpectedly turned and crossed over towards him. Alan, alarmed by a look he had caught sight of in Barnet's face and by the jerkiness of his striding across the roadway, followed; while Elsie and Wally disapprovingly came to a stop on the pavement where they were. Barnet, however, did not do or say anything wild. He spoke to the boy in the tone of a schoolmaster being reasonable: 'I'm not asking to buy one of those. I only wondered whether you'd mind telling me something. Why are you selling them?'

'Because I'm proud of the paper,' the boy said. 'I don't mind telling you that.'

His face reminded Alan of young George who had worked in the still-room at the big hotel on the cliff and who had admired Basher so much. This boy had the same monkey look, rather sad, though his skin was sallower than George's. He wore a tweed sports-coat that was clean but shoddily ill-shaped.

'Are you paid for selling it?' Barnet asked.

'No, and I don't want to be. I'm selling it because I believe in it. I believe in Fascism. There's nothing I wouldn't do for our Leader.'

'Why?'

'I'd willingly die for him.'

'But why?'

'Because when he comes to power he's going to clean out the Jews from England.'

'What's wrong with the Jews?'

'They're poisoning our national life. There's no dirty crime they wouldn't do if they thought it would help to bring England down.'

Barnet said with careful mildness, 'I am a Jew. Do you think I'm the kind of person who would go about committing dirty crimes? If you do you're quite mistaken.'

The boy looked embarrassed, giving the impression not that he believed Barnet to be incapable of crime, nor that he lacked the courage to accuse him directly, but that he was deterred by a civilized scruple from being personally rude.

'There may be some Jews who are different,' the boy said.

'There may be one or two who are almost as evil as Hitler says all Jews are, though I doubt it. There are bad Jews just as there are bad Germans and even bad Englishmen, and there are good Jews too.'

The boy's face seemed to wince as though he was shocked at a Jew's suggesting there might be bad Englishmen. Barnet went on, with a barely controlled vehemence, 'Some of the men who have done most for humanity in the sciences and the arts, some of the world's greatest men, have been Jews. Don't you realize that even Hitler himself doesn't believe a word of the anti-Semitic propaganda he's been putting out? He admits as much in his book *Mein Kampf*. You should read it, you know. Don't you realize that all these lies about the Jews are deliberately intended to fool young chaps like you, so that your rightful anger against social conditions will be worked off on the Jews instead of on the whole ruling class who are really to blame?'

The boy's look changed from wary to fanatical. 'The Jews are to blame. I don't need Hitler to convince me of that. I know it from personal experience. My first employer was a Jew. He messed me about. That's why I'm still impotent with girls even now.'

Barnet's lips opened as though he was going to argue further, but he thought better of it, turned and began moving away, and Alan followed him. They boy said, not loudly, after them, 'Heil Hitler.'

As soon as they had crossed the street again and were walking to catch up with Elsie and Wally, who had gone slowly on ahead, Alan said, 'He's psychopathic.'

'Don't be so sure of that,' Barnet advised. 'We're a bit too fond of using this fashionable psycho jargon to explain every sort of criminality. I know I may sound reactionary, but there's a danger of our not distinguishing between the manic depressive who tries to bash someone in the asylum and the Nazi storm-trooper who knocks down an elderly Jew in the street at night. That boy may be a mental case, but he may not: he may be deliberately lying.'

'I doubt it.'

'Perhaps you're right, but perhaps in his small way he's doing what Hitler did: he's consciously trying to rouse loathing against the Jews in the hope of weakening the socialist movement. You noticed his clothes? Poor but clean – I expect he has pretensions to gentility. I should guess that he hates the guts of the working class.'

'It has often puzzled me how we as determinists can make any distinction between what's done deliberately and what isn't,' Alan said speculatively.

Barnet, who normally did not dislike discussing philosophic questions, was uninterested. He said nothing further until they caught up with Wally and Elsie. In answer to

Elsie's 'What were you up to – trying to convert him or just buying a copy of *Action*?' he said, 'It would take more than me to convert him. Mere talk could never reach down to the disease in him. He's got Fascism very badly.'

Barnet's tone made them realize how much of a shock the incident had been to him. He had presumably expected, Alan thought, that by making personal contact he would somehow moderate the hostility which the *Action*-seller must feel against Jews but had come away with the impression of having intensified it. Not till they reached the corner of Church Street and saw Bill Fenton standing there with about fifteen other comrades did Barnet break his depressed silence. 'They're here very punctually,' he said, with emphasized surprise.

Alan wondered whether those whom the prospect of trouble had not attracted here early would now come at all. Bill Fenton smiled towards the four of them, and said, 'We'll be waiting here another minute or two.'

Jean Pritchet, Lily Pentelow, Jock Finlayson, Sam Cowan, were among the others, most of whom Alan knew by sight. Bill Fenton was the tallest comrade there. The skin of his face had a pale gold-brown tinge, as though olive oil had been rubbed into it, and he wore glasses and might have been taken for an intellectual. He was staring over the heads of the others at something across the street. A group of tough-looking young men were moving along the opposite pavement. Perhaps recognizing the Communists, they suddenly shouted, 'Yid, Yid, we must get rid of the Yid.'

Sam Cowan bawled back, 'Rats, rats, we must get rid of the Blackshirt rats.'

The Fascist group paused, seemed about to cross over for a fight, then possibly because they saw that the Communists outnumbered them they walked on. Several of them, looking back as they began to move again, raised their arms in the

Fascist salute. The Communists answered them with the clenched fist salute.

As soon as the Fascists were out of sight Bill Fenton said, 'We may as well get going.'

They moved off rather slowly, to avoid bunching on the pavement. The nearer they came to the Baths the more it seemed that everyone else in the street was going there too. The discouraging effect this had on Alan was partly counteracted by the thought that among so many they would be more likely to get in past the stewards unnoticed as Communists. Arriving in front of the Baths, they had to pause while others, every one of whom was perhaps a Fascist, went crowding in through the two separate double doors. Pillars on either side of the entrance supported a stone-seeming balcony, from the middle of which a green flag-pole – without a flag, Alan was irrationally relieved to note – stuck crudely out at an angle of forty-five degrees above the people entering. He imagined that the Leader might appear now on this balcony and start making an anti-Semitic speech beneath the two tall and narrow windows that were as close together as the eyes of a mandrill. White glass globes with lights inside them were supported on fluted bronze columns near the windows. The group of Communists began to move in through the doors. As Alan had hoped, the stewards were not suspicious. One of them, wearing a black shirt beneath a slick sports-coat, even gave him what seemed a look of welcome.

Another steward, when Alan and Elsie had come through the vestibule and were entering the main part of the building where the meeting was to be held, moved as if to guide them to seats, but they ignored him and followed Bill Fenton, who was leading their group towards a still vacant row of chairs nearer the front of the hall, Fenton's idea no doubt being to choose a position which, while making the group's exit fairly conspicuous, would not be so far from the doors as to allow the Fascists time for interception. Under the jacket of an ordinary lounge-suit this steward too wore a black shirt, obeying the letter of the Public Order Act which prohibited the wearing of political uniforms. After Alan had sat down on a chair between Elsie's and Barnet's, he remembered with resentment the phrase that a Conservative MP had aimed against both Fascists and Communists during the debate in Parliament on the Public Order Bill – 'A plague on both your blouses!' This seemed to him a vivid example of the kind of silly thinking which fashionably refused to distinguish between Communism and Fascism, and which in effect tried to hold an impartial middle position between right and wrong, between truth and lies. But the MP's facetious phrase refuted the very point he was trying to make, since in order to show the similarity of the two opposites he had had to imply the falsehood that British Communists wore uniforms. Alan, looking at the faces of some of the stewards who stood in a line at short intervals from one another along the nearer side wall, could imagine nothing in common between the natures he guessed at behind those faces and the natures of his own Party comrades. Among the audience also there were people whose appearance suggested that if he had met them personally he could have found no topic of conversation, however trivial, on which he would not instantly have been at odds with them. A slim young man came with his young woman up the main aisle between the rows of seats, and when he had found a row in which two seats were vacant he stepped smartly back from her, then bowed to her very graciously and ostentatiously before extending his hand to indicate that she should precede him along the row. Sitting almost directly in front of Alan were a big-boned middle-aged couple exchanging occasional remarks in voices which were penetratingly refined and but for which the man's posture and face might have led Alan to mistake him for a retired naval commander. Very likely they kept a small sweet-shop, and when speaking to their better customers claimed in sympathy-seeking tones that house property had deteriorated since they had first come to the district because of the influx of a more 'common' type of tenants, among whom there were even some aliens. These two, Alan guessed, would condone any measures, however bestial, which a future government might take against active members of the working-class movement. Farther in front of him a pallid mole-dotted face topped with crimped wiry hair was side-turned for a moment and he thought he recognized it as belonging to a youngish Fascist who at an earlier Mosleyite meeting, which Alan had attended when the Public Order Act had not yet been passed, had come on to the platform wearing a black shirt and had tried to play classical music on a baby-grand piano before the arrival of the main speaker; but the audience – unlike the present one which, symptomatically of a sinister worsening since then of the political situation, appeared eager to give the Fascists a hearing – had been largely hostile and had blown raspberries and catcalled, till at last the pianist had got up from his stool and had stamped his foot on the boards like a spoilt child in a furious pet. No doubt his parents had given him at least four fancy names at his christening, and he had been brought up to think of the workers as dirt. More startling to look at, however, than any member of the audience was one of the stewards, whom Alan now for the first time caught sight of. This man, who had a drooping bull-frog's jowl and whose eyes were glazed under almost hairless eyebrows that slanted downwards, as did the corners of his long mouth, might have been a depraved aristocrat or a punch-drunk ex-boxer or neither, but in any crowd he would have seemed conspicuously abnormal. Probably he had exquisite daydreams of torturing Reds in cellars, and had already tried out his hand at sjamboking South African natives. Standing next to him, another of the stewards had a baby face evenly coloured like a nectarine painted in smooth watercolour on cream paper. This steward seemed to be watching Alan, who, assuming that his outward innocence must be deceptive, found him still more repulsive than the bull-frog.

'Do you see that one staring at us?' Alan asked Elsie. 'He looks the nastiest bit of work among the lot.'

'He seems quite an ordinary young fellow,' Elsie decided. 'The fact is that just because he's a Fascist you think he's got an unpleasant face. But he hasn't. I'd go so far as to say he's good-looking.'

She was right. Alan knew that he had been viewing not only this steward but members of the audience also – and even the bull-frog – through the eyes of prejudice. He had seen them as incarnate political and social attitudes instead of as actual human individuals. Ignorant of everything about them except that they were stewarding or merely attending this meeting, he had labelled them in his mind as out-and-out reactionaries, had made demons of them. He had himself behaved like a Fascist, had imposed his unbalanced preconceptions upon them much as the boy *Action*-seller had done upon Jews. The truth about this audience might well be that at least half of them were apolitical and had come here out of curiosity; and not impossibly quite a few even of the stewards didn't yet fully understand the nature of the movement they were in and would come out of it when they did. Many supporters of Fascism here and outside in the country as a whole might be curable if understandingly approached. Others – and Alan feared that their numbers were increasing every week – had been too deeply infected and would have to be fought, and this meant that they and the bitter social conditions which had laid them open to infection must first be known not as hypostatized abstractions but as actualities. He must keep his head and see things for what they were if he was to be of any use in helping to deal with this fever.

The idea of fever may have been suggested by a movement

among members of the audience sitting at the front near the platform. They seemed to shiver, then they abruptly stood up, and nearly everyone behind them except the Communists did the same. The Leader was coming out of a side-door that opened on to the platform. Arms among the audience went stiffly up in a salute that unpleasantly was almost unanimous. There were cries of 'Hail' and there were even a few of '*Heil*' – these sounding not at all ironical but as though they came from the Leader's most fanatical supporters. So much for the Union Jack that was draped over the speaker's table on the platform, Alan thought. These British Fascists, as soon as the working class here showed the first signs of making a serious bid for power, would feel no more scruples about having their countrymen shot down by invading Germans than Caudillo Franco had felt about getting the Moors and Italians and Nazis to help him against the workers in Spain. The Leader came to the front of the platform and stood with the Union Jack for a backcloth behind him. He wore a double-breasted grey flannel suit, had a prominent bird-of-prey nose with a thin black moustache beneath it, and his lower jaw was prognathous and Hapsburg-like, as though he was thrusting his tongue down over his lower gums and causing the flesh between his lip and chin to protrude. Throughout his speech he seldom changed his posture, standing most of the time with the backs of his hands resting curled on his hips and his elbows sticking out sideways so that he resembled a double-handled challenge cup. He had no doubt got the pose from Mussolini.

He began by speaking of the economic situation, in a tone that unexpectedly had nothing rabble-rousing about it but seemed studiedly gentlemanly, almost donnish, as though he was addressing a gathering of the most respectable Tories of the district. The audience were stolidly silent, showing no tenseness at all, giving the impression that the words of the speech meant nothing to them but that they had been disci-

plined to sit through it. After about twenty minutes the
Leader abruptly changed his tone. Like an engine that had
hitherto been idling, he revved himself up and began to
show what he could do at full power. His voice became hard
and loud. Words of incitement flashed out from him. The
phrase 'international Jewish finance' affected the audience
like a military command and a seemingly unanimous growl
went up from them, which became a howl, vicious and deep-
felt but nevertheless controlled, loathsome as the disciplined
fury of a bully's dog whose master at last gives him leave to
bite. Bill Fenton stood up and signalled to the other comrades
that the time had come for them to leave the meeting. They
moved in file unhurriedly out from their rows of seats and
along the middle aisle. The stewards, taken by surprise and
uncertain whether or not anything could be done against
this demonstrative exodus, merely watched them go. Only
when the Party members had begun to push through the
swing-doors into the vestibule did Alan become aware that
Barnet, who had been sitting next to him, was no longer near
him and must for some reason be lingering behind.

Alan stopped to look back, while the other comrades went
on through the vestibule, and Elsie stopped beside him.
Barnet was moving along the row which the Party group
had just left and was distributing some of his yellow leaflets
on the empty seats. He turned before reaching the side aisle,
where he would have had to run the gauntlet of the stewards
ranged along the wall, and, coming back along the row as
fast as the chairs would allow, emerged into the middle aisle
and hurried towards the swing-doors, but found time to drop
leaflets into the laps of several members of the audience on
his way. He joined Alan and Elsie, who preceded him quickly
into the vestibule, Alan thinking they might just have time
to get out of the building before any of the stewards caught
up with them. But they did not have time. From a side-door
a steward came springily striding into the vestibule just as

they were crossing its floor. To have made a dash for the main entrance would, Alan felt, have had the same effect as running away from a dangerous animal, would have invited an instant assault. The steward wore plimsolls, like a male nurse in a private mental home or a flogger in a naval cadets' gymnasium, and his face looked sick with hate. He advanced crouchingly upon Barnet, his arms extended towards him at groin-level and his hands clawingly upturned, his posture as a whole resembling that adopted for 'ball-fighting' by boys at a public school. The steward was recognizable as the innocent-seeming one who had watched them before the meeting had begun. Alan stood still between him and Barnet, and tried to fix him with a frigidly pacific look, while not at all sure whether Barnet mightn't be making counter aggressive gestures in the background. The steward gradually relaxed, letting his arms drop to his sides but maintaining an expression of venomous contempt, and they judged that now he would not move to the attack when they turned their backs on him. They pushed through the swing-doors of the main entrance, Alan choosing to bring up the rear, and came out on to the broad steps in front of the Baths.

Elsie gave a short laugh, as of relief, but Barnet said to Alan, 'That was a close thing. He would have liked to tear my testicles out. If this had been in Germany he would have been able to. You saw his face. For two pins he'd have done it. If ever his lot comes to power here we know what to expect.'

On the pavement across the street, at the corner of a side-road opposite the Baths, a speaker was talking from a portable rostrum to a small crowd surrounding him. He might be a Fascist addressing Fascist sympathizers who had been unable to get into the main meeting. He didn't look like a religious preacher. The three of them walked over to investigate. One or two other Party members, including Wally and Sam Cowan, were there. He was speaking in a cockney accent, not very loudly. Alan heard the phrases, 'wash their shirts for them' and 'their carpet-biting German Führer, Herr Schickelgruber', and knew with surprise that the speech must be anti-Fascist, and saw that the crowd were listening without disapproval. 'I'm told that this is the district of the three P's,' the man said, 'pride, poverty and a piano. That's why the Black rats have selected it for their meeting this evening. They've not forgotten what sort of welcome they got when they tried to march into the East End.' He had a round and amused face and was like a cruder Dean Ayres. Alan was ashamed of his own lapse in morale, which had been causing him temporarily to regard Fascism as though it were invincible. The man's language, however, had a fruitiness and an individuality bordering on eccentricity which suggested that he could not be a member of the Party. He seemed to be here on his own initiative like a speaker at Hyde Park Corner. He went on to speculate in detail about the Leader's private life. The thought abruptly came to Alan that the man might be a provocateur, might even be in the employ of the Fascists. Elsie and Barnet, to whom the same thought may have come, began to move away from the crowd. They looked round for Alan, and he followed them.

As the three walked on together the pessimism which the man's speech had temporarily expelled from Alan's mind began to return. Now, however, the danger seemed not that the British Fascists might in the near future gain power but that they might already be strong enough to counteract the Party's struggle against the pro-Hitler foreign policy of the British Government. They could help Chamberlain to clear the way for the world war that Hitler was preparing. Suddenly in the High Street this danger was like a physical presence, an invisible gas heavily advancing, weighing on the traffic, thrusting against the plate glass of the shop-fronts, penetrating to the very centre of Alan's nervous system. A terrible woe was in him. And he thought of what Elsie had told him nearly a week before, that she believed she was pregnant. Once, soon after their marriage, he had said to himself that never would he breed in captivity, meaning in the captivity of his enforced job as a teacher, but now he was to be the father of a child who would be born at the beginning of a deadlier war than there had yet been in all history, a war which would murder and starve millions on millions of men, women and children; a war in which any wish he might still have to write poetry must be dismissed as the most contemptible, the most ludicrously impracticable egoism.

12

IN THE DREAM ITSELF nothing ominous happened. The afternoon was cerulean above a field full of drowsy cows with no bull lurking among them as Alan and Richard walked or floated together along the path towards the stile. A road between umbelliferously-flowered ditches led down to a hump-backed bridge built of stone, on which were blotches of gold-brown lichen, and pausing to point at one of these blotches Alan said with certainty and joy to Richard, 'This is why we were born.' Just beyond the bridge the road went between the open white gates of a single-line railway crossing, and then, passing beside a watermill whose under-shot mill-wheel was broken-boarded and out of action, met the overlapping edge of the mill-pond, on which Alan saw grey rowing-boats moored near to where the downsloping lawn of the mill tea-gardens reached the water; and wasps humming over the cakes and jam-pots on the open-air tea-tables brought to mind unexpectedly the happy security of childhood, and the smell of the pigsties that were hidden somewhere behind the gardens did not depoeticize the scene but on the contrary tended to make it less dreamlike and more convincing. The fact that, when Alan came to the level crossing and was stepping over the sunken rails, Richard was nowhere within sight seemed of small importance, because the air and the mill and the tea-gardens had as it were grown conscious of a long yearned-for and never despaired-of event which was going to happen next, and which had already begun to happen. A greenhouse door was opened at the back of the tea-gardens and a girl in a summer dress, whom even before Alan could see her face he knew to be Peg, came out on to the lawn, was walking down it, was stepping into one of the rowing-boats, was across the pond and was at his side, pressing close against him. She showed him her right hand, saying with the frankest love, 'You gave me this ring.' But his eyesight was becoming too weak for him to see the ring and at this moment for the first time he understood clearly what was ominous: the dream from its beginning – in spite of brief contrary phases of reviving vividness – had been getting less distinct and was now disappearing. He foreknew that outside it, if he allowed himself to lose it, there would be something to make him afraid.

He must not, need not, lose it. By straining his eyes he succeeded in focusing the ring, which he discovered to be an amethyst set in platinum. He was even able, soon afterwards, to see as far as the garden tables where wasps, with their tiger-striped abdomens twitching, were settling on the rims of jam-pots; though he couldn't see so far for long. Like water-colours running together in a child's painting the black and yellow of the wasps' stripes and the grey-white of the jam-pots were intermingling, were coalescing into a unity that was inexplicably luminous, and this unity quickly expanded, absorbing within itself other colours and shapes such as the crumbling buff dustiness of the road ahead and the mauve circlets that made the pattern on Peg's dress. The warmth of her body ceased to be localized at his side, began to merge with the surrounding luminousness until he found himself enclosed as by pinkish-golden cotton wool, which he vigorously clutched to prevent it from vanishing; but his very tenacity betrayed him, because the wool proved to be the bedclothes of the real bed in which he was lying and the pinkish gold became the sunlight on his closed eyelids. He was irrevocably awake. For a short while he hoped that the bed might protect him, even though the dream had been withdrawn; then a sudden acceleration of the beating of his heart disillusioned him, and there came to him like a blunt bullet entering his body a concentrated pain, which was not yet but would soon become an awareness in detail of what he was waking to – his struggle at school, Fascism's unchecked advance in Europe, his child that Elsie would before long give birth to, the powerlessness of poetry, the world war that was approaching.

He opened his eyes, trying to exorcise the misery in his mind by looking at the actual bedroom in which his body was lying. The sunlight coming through a very small gap at the top of the curtains made a faultless circle, like a reflected image of the sun itself, on the wall above Elsie's bed. He knew from former observation that this circle would gradually move towards the corner of the room, where, straddling over from one wall to the other, it would become elongated and be transformed into an ellipse. Watching it one Sunday morning when he had felt under no compulsion to get up, he had been happily reminded by it of his seaside days with Richard. Now it was as different in its effect on him as though it had become dead black, like a brilliance translated into its opposite on a photographic negative. It reminded him that this morning was Monday morning. Everything he hated was here once again and there was no way of escape for him. He must get ready to continue to sweat out his life at a job in which he was bound to injure not only himself but others also, and in which he could have no better ambition than to do as little harm as possible. He must be the active supporter of an educational system whose one merit lay in its being less unfree than the Fascism that would succeed it if the pro-Hitler policies of the British Government were allowed to run their course. He must be a trickster, and he must not, would not care to, look too long out of the class-room window or consider the problems of poetry. A wave of slime was approaching, taller than the houses or the schools or the churches, a new week of work, stinking with deceit and exhaustion, and he would be in it. 'Struggle, petty hero,' he told himself; 'here in your bedroom swear never to lose the energy of your loathing, never to be wholly submerged.' Oh, he would come through, he would win once again, and compulsory dishonesty should not poison his eye for gardens, nor hymns in the school hall his ear for Shelley. But beyond this week he foresaw another, another. Weeks, years of filth were ahead, and there was no rewarding island, no time of leisure to make for. Struggle would reach nothing but struggle, heavier as he grew older. He would develop minor diseases, catarrh, rotting teeth, the infected sinus. And, dirty as the spider fighting to climb out of a kitchen sink, at last he would fall and submit and crumpled be swirled in nar-rowing circles till he went down the drain. This was his future, or it would be if the future at all resembled his pre-sent, if there were no war coming, if the newspapers and wireless did not every day threaten death by fire and torture.

There rose into his mind a question which even before it had become clearly defined he knew to be a blasphemy against Communism, but which he could not prevent from taking shape in words: 'Oh what is the use, and why, why go on?' He tried to smother it with the answer, 'Go on because there is no way out for you except through the struggle for Communism, and because only in recognizing the necessity of that struggle can you find freedom.' Then another question came to him: 'But what if necessity is slavery?' He could find no better answer to this than 'Go on not for any positive inducement but because of what would happen if you stopped.' In imagination he got up out of bed, found him-self dressed and had had his breakfast and was walking to the station. The usual crowd, many of whose faces he knew well from having seen them at this usual time so often before, were advancing along the pavements on either side of the High Street, among bus-noises too often heard to be heard this morning, passing the unfocused glassiness of familiar shop-fronts and not looking up at the terrace above the shops, where a painted hoarding set between shrubs in green tubs advertised so-called luxury flats to let; and he went with the crowd and was as devoid of feeling as the electric motors of the trains that would carry them to work. But he did not reach the station. He saw the others bunch in through its entrance, then he broke ranks to turn down a side-road which led to the public park. The park gates were open. He went in and walked beside a long pond that broadened out to surround an island where Chinese geese were asleep in the shade of shrubs. Against the far end of the pond there was a wood, and just as he was stepping in under its trees he realized that unless he turned back towards the station he would lose his job and would receive no salary in future and would be unable to live.

Nevertheless he did not turn back. 'I could live on my parents for a time,' he thought. Then the imaginary scene changed and he was no longer in the park but was beside the sea far from London. The time was nightfall. He was walking along an unbroken part of the esplanade towards the road which led into the village. There were patches of snow on the beach up against the esplanade wall, just as there had been one Christmas when – before his marriage but long after the time of his summer arrival here at Richard's invitation – a nostalgic impulse had brought him back in actuality to stay for a week-end at this seaside place. He saw again, as he had seen then, the winter sea and the obscure horizon, the slate-coloured sky and the black land. Even the chalk cliffs that bounded the bay appeared black. The tide was far out and lumps of stranded foam on the sand shivered in the freezing wind. The lights of the village twinkled like tinsel on a Christmas tree. Frost seemed not only to make the air clearer but to sharpen perception, though it did not now give him anything of the pleasure which in actuality he had felt so keenly that he had believed no other pleasure, except poetic creation, could be as great. Like the Coleridge of the Dejection Ode, he could no longer feel the beauty that he saw. This was not because of any emotional deterioration in Alan but because the beauty was fraudulent. From the darkening sky far out above the bay a sinister noise was beginning, was getting louder, and he knew it to be the noise of enemy bombers, and soon all the air over and around him was intolerably possessed with the throbbing drone of engines. But he did not need to hear the first bombs fall: his imaginings had already achieved their purpose, had reminded him that the poetic life, even if he could miraculously get enough money to lead it and at the same time to support his child who would soon be born, would be made totally impossible for him by approaching war. He must go on with the present struggle. He must go on with it because of what would happen if he tried to step out of it.

But if he did go on what would happen? Again, as he lay unmoving in the bed, he imagined himself walking with the crowd along the High Street towards the station. Dressed in neat clothes, they passed the tobacconist's projecting electric clock and the rotary washing machine in the window of the one-day cleaner's. He saw no face among them that showed discontent. In their movement along the pavements they seemed as mechanical as the traffic on the roadway. And now they had no features, had only flat pink discs where faces should have been. But among them, as he arrived with them at the station entrance, there was a young girl whose beauty startled him. Though she was going to work, she had a free and holiday look, and, seeing her, he was reminded that the others belonged to the same species, were human. They might not be rebellious yet, but they were capable of rebellion. Their servitude was tolerable to them now because of certain amenities that were offered with it, because of the cinema or the dance-hall or the ice-skating rink or their small gardens, but it might cease to be tolerable if they came to suspect that these would soon be taken from them. At present they glanced at the words on the newspaper posters outside the station without feeling any indignation against their rulers, but they might feel it if only they could become aware of the disaster that was being prepared for them all. Was there any hope that they could be made aware before destruction came? He tried to have faith in them as he walked with them through the entrance and down steps that were walled in on both sides by planks painted the colour of dung by moonlight. His imagining, however, instead of taking him down as far as the platform brought him back again to the High Street and he was again advancing with the crowd, but this was another day and the words on the posters outside the station had changed, had become still more menacing, were eve-of-war words; yet the crowd moved as mechanically as before, incapable of revolt, everlastingly trustful of rulers whose minds were like the minds of evil small boys but who had, and would use, the power to lay waste much of the world. Again he pushed in with the crowd through the station entrance, descended the steps between the pale brown plank-walls, arrived this time on the platform, and as he did so a blackness invaded his mind, a foreboding of material and human desolation, the sense of a dreadful weight of punishment that had been accumulating over many years and was now about to fall upon these people and upon all his countrymen, who had deserved it by their invincible indifference to the sufferings of other people in other countries. He walked past the windows of the general waiting-room, which were brown like the gauze of a rusty meat-safe, and he came to the edge of the platform and looked down at the live electric rail which was supported on ceramic insulators alongside the other rails in their iron chairs. Out of sight, beneath the whitewashed edge on which he stood, a vibrating signal wire gave a metallic twitter. Before very long a train would be here. He thought of throwing himself on to the line in front of it.

But simultaneously with the thought came a remembrance of how in his pre-Communist days after failing to write poetry he had had the intention of throwing himself over a cliff. And now he was allowing himself to lapse back again into that same mood of middle-class despair, as though he had never become a member of the Party. Like a snivelling philistine he had lost all faith in the people and had come to feel that the working class would leave the criminal rulers in power for ever. What had caused him to get into such a despicable state? He had not been as bad as this three days ago when he and Elsie had been talking about arrangements for her confinement: then he had succeeded in at least sounding optimistic and perhaps even had genuinely felt so.

He began to remember the conversation with her, and in his imagination he found himself standing no longer at the edge of the platform but beside her on the landing of the flat. She was just back from a day's visit with her mother to her uncle and aunt at their bungalow outside Haslemere, where she had gone to sound them about whether they would be willing to take her in if the Government decided during the next few days to evacuate school-children and expectant mothers from London. He asked her how her uncle and aunt had reacted, and she said, 'They'll take me in. But it was obvious they're not at all keen to.'

'They'd be prepared for you to have the baby there if necessary?'

'Yes, though they seemed to think I was being unreasonable. And the bungalow is quite a large one and there are only the two of them living in it. I suppose they're getting old and don't want any upset in their routine. I felt pretty fed up when Mum and I came away.'

She looked tired and he suspected that she was restraining tears. He tried to be comforting: 'Anyway there won't be any evacuation, or if there is it won't last more than a week. It's all part of Chamberlain's plan to get the people into such a state of apprehension that they'll feel nothing but relief when he sells Czechoslovakia out to Hitler.'

'I don't see there's much consolation in that.'

'No, perhaps there isn't.'

'It will only mean that war will come later for certain.'

He was going to put his arms round her so that she could burst into tears and be freed from the bleak tension he saw in her face, but there was a knock on the door downstairs. Her look said she couldn't trust herself to remain controlled in front of a visitor. He went down the stairs. He opened the door to a young man, who immediately and gladly knew him but whom at first he did not recognize at all.

'I'm Holyman, sir.'

'Yes, so you are. You've changed a lot.'

This must be the inappropriately named Holyman, Alan guessed, who had once set fire to a form-room floor with some phosphorus from the school lab. At school he had seemed always to be frowning, and his greasy forehead beneath his wiry red hair had been ridged with wrinkles like the forehead of a middle-aged worrier. Now he was relaxed and cheerful. Under his arm and slung from his shoulders he carried what looked like a postman's bag, large, its bulgy surface showing the angular outline of the parcels or boxes inside it. He explained, 'I'm going round fitting on gas-masks. I'd no idea you lived here, sir.'

Sure of his welcome, he moved forward and stepped into the small hallway. Alan gave ground, was unable to think up a way in which he could civilly and plausibly refuse both to renew acquaintance with Holyman and to submit to a gas-mask fitting that would sooner or later be inevitable anyhow.

Indefinitely Alan said, 'As a matter of fact perhaps it might be better if—'

Then, seeing how insensitive Holyman was to the tone of this, he did not finish the sentence but began to lead the way up the stairs. Elsie was where she had been on the landing. He said to her, 'Here's an Old Boy of the school — Holyman.'

Her look was almost blank as Holyman happily shook hands with her, but Alan judged that she was going to be able to control her feelings and he risked adding at once, 'He's brought our gas-masks and wants us to try them on.'

She stonily made no objection. They went into the front room. Holyman brought out two masks from his bag. He had the sense – or was he merely following advice from headquarters about the most tactful way of persuading wives to wear these things? – to ask Alan first to try one of them on. Elsie then allowed Holyman to show her how to put hers on and she obeyed when, after he had placed a postcard up against the holes in the base of the cylindrical metal respirator, he asked her to breathe in so that he could tell whether the rubber of the mask was airtight. But when she took the mask off she said to him, 'What use are these things going to be against bombing?'

'None,' he comfortably admitted.

'The Government should be forced to provide deep shelters, instead of being allowed to get away with sending round this sort of rubbish.'

Her tone blamed Holyman, but he was not in the least put out. He said mildly, 'There's always the possibility that gas might be used too.'

'What about the babies? I suppose their mothers are to stand over them wearing masks and watch them choke to death.'

She so plainly and so bitterly held Holyman responsible that Alan was a little embarrassed. However, Holyman's face, its tough-looking skin glistening slightly, remained happy. With modesty, though soothingly, he said, 'We shall soon have a respirator for babies.'

'How soon? And how do you imagine you're going to get a baby to wear some filthy thing like this?' Elsie threw her mask on to the sofa.

'Oh, it won't be like that. It will be large enough to contain the baby entirely. Air will be supplied through a filter by means of bellows which the mother can work with her foot.' He smiled. 'It will be rather like rocking an old-fashioned cradle. Though of course the mother herself will be wearing a mask.'

A dull coldness, alarming to Alan, came over Elsie's face, as though she had seen in her imagination what Holyman had described and as though the sight of it had for the moment numbed her spirit. He did not know what she would do next. She might burst into tears, or she might shout into Holyman's face that he was to get out of her flat at once.

'Well, thank you very much, Holyman,' Alan said; then moved towards the door of the room, and Holyman understood that he was expected to go, and they went down the stairs together to the front door, where Alan said goodbye quite affably.

When Alan got back to the room he found that Elsie had not moved, was standing in the same posture and with the same look as before he had gone out. Suddenly she spoke: 'I ought never to have conceived this child.' Her face came alive with misery, and she sat down in the armchair and began to weep. He was doubly shocked, was frightened both because what she had said echoed feelings that he himself had long been trying to suppress and because such pessimism – if she had ever before felt it – had never until now been too strong for her to control. He went over to the chair and sat on an arm of it, and put his hand on her shoulder, trying to comfort her. He stroked the back of her neck and of her head, and his fear increased. Her sobbing became worse, jerkier, might soon develop into hysteria. He moved away from the chair, guessing that his touch and his sympathy were strengthening not her but the emotion in her which she needed to overcome. He sat on the sofa, helplessly wanting to help, watching her in the hope that soon he would gain some hint of how he might be of use.

At last, seeing that she was no worse though no better, he risked saying, 'Lenin was pretty scathing against Party members who had doubts about bringing children into the world under capitalism.'

She was able to answer, 'I know he was.'

'To be afraid to have children is to disbelieve in the future of the working class.'

'I wonder whether Lenin himself had children.'

The mild irony and the consciousness of daring that were in the tone of this showed him she was beginning to feel better.

'Yes, I wonder,' he agreed. 'Krupskaya doesn't seem to mention any in her memoir. . . . But aren't we being a bit blasphemous?'

She smiled, and he knew that her despair had been no more than a temporary aberration and that she was already becoming herself again. But now his own optimism, having served the purpose of cheering her, began to seem factitious to him. Misgivings which, since the start of her pregnancy, had been as normal in him as confidence had been in her, irresistibly returned. He remembered how before his marriage he had sworn to himself, 'I will never breed in captivity,' and he recognized that his child would be born not only under the captivity of capitalism but during a time when capitalism was at its vilest and most murderous. A voice in his mind asked, 'What right have you to bring a child into this suffering?' But suddenly he found an answer, and he spoke it aloud to Elsie, as though he were still trying to convince her rather than himself: 'What right have we *not* to have a child? We know that the general movement of society is a forward one, in spite of the temporary disasters that are bound to happen. What right have we to say that no child of ours shall be allowed to take his chance among other children?'

'The majority of children in the world as a whole will probably survive the war if it comes,' she said, and showed no sign of any tendency to relapse into tears.

But on Monday morning, only a few days after that conversation, he was lying here miserable in his bed thinking that the people would never learn to distrust their rulers. Why couldn't he be a little more like Elsie and have something of her courage? He turned his head to look at her. She was just waking up. She put out a hand from under the sheet to reach her wrist-watch, which was on top of the wicker laundry-basket at her bedside.

'It's a quarter past seven. I've overslept,' she said.

She got out of bed quickly, in spite of the weight she now carried, and she came over to him and kissed him. His hand clasped the back of her neck and held her head down to him; but she said, laughing, 'No time for love now. You ought to have started earlier. I must get your breakfast or you'll be late.'

'Let me get it, and you stay in bed and rest.'

'Oh no, I'm feeling perfectly all right.'

After a minute he let her go. Ordinarily he would not have felt guilty about allowing her to get breakfast for him, because he had the job of making the beds while she got it – a division of labour they had agreed to in the first days of their marriage after proving in practice that their plan to take equal shares in both the cooking and the bed-making led to a waste of time. But he wondered whether at this stage of her pregnancy it was good for her to do as much as she was doing. She had assured him several times, however, that it was all right; and he knew she was not the sort to act unreasonably or to want to be a martyr. There was nothing unbalanced or romantic about her. He was lucky to have married her and not Peg.

He must try to learn from Elsie. He must put a stop to his endless bourgeois whining, to his miserable fussing about his own happiness. He must remember what he had joined the Party for. 'Was it merely in order to feel good?' he asked himself. 'Did I do it, like some egoistical religious convert joining a church, just for the good of my own soul?' Indignation against himself for his backsliding since he had first come into the Party grew so sharp in him that he could not lie any longer in bed. He jumped out and began, almost unaware of what he was doing, to strip the bedclothes off the bed, and then to make the bed, and as he did so he inwardly answered his own questions. 'I joined the Party,' he thought, 'in order to help to bring about certain changes in the external world. These changes won't be achieved easily, and perhaps not till after I am dead, but the people will turn in the end, and even though the work I am doing with the Party seems ineffectual now it will take effect then. Whether the work makes me *happy* or not is of no importance at all. The thing is to do it.' Having finished making his bed, he went over to Elsie's, and he remembered Emily Bronte's lines:

'Then did I learn how existence could be cherished,
Strengthened and fed without the aid of joy.'

He said the lines over to himself several times; and, at the thought that from henceforward he would make himself strong to go on without joy, he felt a kind of joy.

251

13

AFTER LUNCH Alan was taking round for signature by
his colleagues a typewritten letter to the Prime Minister
demanding that the Government should not agree to the
dismemberment of Czechoslavakia under Hitler's threat of
armed intervention. As he was nearing the orderly-room on
his way back from the billiard-room to the common-room
he met Brook, whose signature he had intended to ask for
last after having approached all the other members of the
staff, but his success with everyone to whom he had so far
shown the letter made him ready now to face the abusive
refusal which he expected Brook would give him. He came
to a stand in front of Brook, who had to stop walking towards
the billiard-room, and he stared into the boyishly pink face
gravely enough to achieve his purpose of preventing it from
flowering over with the kind of leer which would precede a
verbal assault on him, and he said as he put the letter into
Brook's hand, 'Perhaps you would like to have a look at
this. Most of the others have signed it.'

Brook took the letter and began to glance through it. The
flesh beneath the sides of his eyes was a little puffy, making
him seem surly, but he showed no sign of contempt for what
he was reading. Probably he was impressed by the wording
of it, Alan thought. Barnet had been right to insist on com-
posing it himself, claiming that he could do this sort of
thing much better than Alan could, and he had been right
also in suggesting Alan would be more capable than himself
of asking colleagues to sign without antagonizing them. 'You

can smarm them better,' Barnet had said not altogether
pleasantly.

Brook, having finished reading the letter, asked as though
he didn't understand a word of what he'd read, 'What's it
all about?'

Alan, over-eager not to offend, answered stumblingly at
first and in a tone almost of apology, 'Czechoslovakia. It's a
letter to Chamberlain from the staff. If Hitler is given the
Sudetenland he won't stop there. The Czechs would lose the
only really defensible part of their country. The Nazis would
soon get the Skoda armament works, one of the most important in the world.' Alan emphasized this, thinking that anything to do with armaments would impress Brook. 'Hitler's
talk about the Sudeten Germans being persecuted by the
Czechs is just to create a pretext for intervening. And
Chamberlain seems to aim at making the Czechs give way
to Hitler without a struggle. That's why I think we should
send this letter.'

Brook said enigmatically, '*J'aime* Berlin, as the French
say.'

Alan was not clear whether this was meant to show sympathy with his point of view or to mock it or merely to air
political knowledge. Brook began to read the letter again,
with apparent concentration. Alan, watching, remembered
the reaction of a householder to whom a few days before he
had tried to sell a Party pamphlet about the Czechoslovakian
situation. At all the other doors in the street he had either
been successful or, at worst, had been met with a polite
excuse, but one door had been opened even before he had
knocked on it and a black-haired youngish man had stepped
close up to him, had peered with hostility into his face,
seemingly in order to examine the shape of his nose, and
had asked, 'Are you British?' Alan, trying to sound casual,
had answered 'Yes' and had then been inspired to continue,
'Are you in the Territorial Army?' implying that every pro-

fessing patriot should be. The evident Fascist had lamely answered 'No', and Alan had pressed home with, 'At their local headquarters they are saying they fully expect Hitler to start a war soon.' This had not been entirely a fabrication, since the man who lived in the flat below Alan and Elsie's and who was a Territorial had once expressed such an opinion to Elsie. The Fascist had been silenced and Alan had moved unhurriedly on to the next door. Brook, looking up from the letter as he finished reading it, did not address Alan as Rasputin or as the Red Menace, but said, 'If there's a war I shall get into the Air Force.' He was about to return the letter unsigned, but Alan made no move to take it from him and he changed his mind. 'All right, I'll sign it,' he said lightly. He brought out a fountain pen and to Alan's alarm placed the letter up against the orderly-room wall and was going to try to write on it there with the roughcast behind it and would certainly have punctured the paper, but Alan quickly handed him the book he was carrying for the purpose and asked him to use that.

When Brook had signed, Alan said, 'You're going to the billiard-room?'

'Yes.'

'Well, I must get back to the common-room for some more signatures.'

Alan smiled, gave a very slight wave of his hand and walked off, trying not to move quite as hastily as he was spurred to do by his apprehension that Brook might think better of having put his signature to the letter and might demand to cross it out.

When Alan had entered the main school building and was going up the stairs to the common-room he began to appreciate the significance of his success with Brook. It showed, more certainly even than his having persuaded at least fifteen other colleagues before Brook to sign, that there had been a real shift of political opinion on the staff. An optimism rose in him as he reached the top of the stairs, and with it came the idea – which before now he would not have seriously considered – of taking the letter along to the Headmaster. He stood still for a moment, then instead of turning towards the common-room he went straight on along the corridor to the Head's study.

He waited, not at all uneasy, outside the Head's door after having knocked. There was a sound of movement inside the study before the Head called to him to come in. When he went in he saw the Head sitting sideways to the desk there and with a copy of *The Times* on his lap. Had he in fact, Alan found time to wonder, been reading something else?

The Head said with marked amiability, 'Come and sit down, Mr Sebrill.'

It was as if Alan was just the person whom he had been waiting to see, and for no unpleasant reason, at that very moment. So strong was this impression that Alan, sitting down in the wooden-armed chair indicated by the Head, waited for him to speak further and while waiting noted that the Head's chair also was of unupholstered wood – not uncomfortable, but why hadn't he provided himself with at least one real sprung armchair, unless perhaps because with his Riviera complexion he particularly wished as a headmaster to avoid any other suggestion of sybaritism?

Alan became aware that the Head's look of amiability was shading into one of inquiry, and quickly said, 'I wondered whether you would be willing to add your signature to this letter, sir.' He used the word 'sir' with none of the qualms he would have had if he had been speaking of some matter connected with his work at the school instead of with his work for peace. 'I'm sending it to the Prime Minister. It asks him to stand by Czechoslovakia. I feel there's a real danger of his putting pressure on the Czezchs to submit to all Hitler's demands.'

Startlingly the Head, before even glancing at the letter,

which Alan stood up again to hand to him, said, 'Of course I'll be glad to sign.'

He had probably been informed by someone both about Alan's taking it round among the staff and about its contents, and had hoped Alan would bring it to him too. He did, however, read it through now, and, having finished, he signed it, saying, 'This business has weighed very much on my conscience. Not that I feel we're breaking our word – England never has been and never will be guilty of that – but I do feel most uncomfortable about our supporting the French, who are undoubtedly breaking theirs. I mean they are obviously preparing to dishonour their treaty of alliance with the Czechs.'

Alan, while grateful for the Head's willingness to sign the letter, couldn't help reflecting how typical of the patriotic mentality was his total blindness to the fact that Britain, though not directly allied to Czechoslovakia, was in honour bound by the Covenant of the League of Nations to support the Czechs against the threat of aggression.

The Head went on, 'And there's something else at stake, still more important than any principle of law or even of honour – our standing in the world as a Christian nation.'

'Yes,' Alan said; but to have left it at that would have been dishonest, and he risked adding, 'I am not a Christian, but Christianity has certain humane values which I would defend to the utmost against the Fascists.'

The Head gave him no time to doubt whether he had been wise in revealing himself so frankly but said at once, 'I am sure you are with us really.'

At this moment Alan became aware of the glass-fronted bookcase to the right of the door and was reminded of that earlier interview when the Head had come very near to giving him the sack. Alan said, not caring whether it would sound relevant, 'I hope you find that I'm fitting in better here than I'm afraid I may have seemed to be at first.'

The Head looked surprised. 'You're the sort of person we like to have on the staff here,' he said.

'I know my discipline wasn't much good at the start. Perhaps that was because I was rather too full of abstract progressive ideas about education.'

'Perhaps so,' the Head said cheerfully, more as if agreeing with the sentiment about abstract ideas than as if remembering anything in Alan's disfavour.

'Well, thank you very much – for signing the letter,' Alan said.

'I'm glad you gave me the opportunity,' the Head said, handing the letter back.

'Thank you, sir.'

Alan moved sideways to the study door; and, with a feeling not only of gratitude but also of admiration towards this man whose views on public schools were so much opposed to his own yet who had been broadminded enough to tolerate him here at this school, he repeated, 'Thank you' as he opened the door to go out into the corridor.

Elation hurried him towards the common-room. There was still time to get one or two more signatures before he was due to go and watch a league game in which the House he was attached to as assistant tutor would be playing. Nobody as yet unapproached seemed likely to present any difficulty after his triumph with Brook and the Head. Benson, who was just coming out of the common-room as Alan neared it, would be one of the easiest. Alan stopped him.

'I wonder if you would like to take a look at this.'

Benson, showing no curiosity – perhaps he already knew – about what Alan was asking him to look at, said, 'If you wouldn't mind coming along with me to my classroom. I want to make sure no boys are loitering in it.'

The prefect on duty could see to that, Alan thought but did not say. He went with Benson.

There were no boys in the classroom. Benson not very

257

willingly took the letter from Alan, then sat down on the chair behind the master's desk – presumably in order to have a flat surface on which to place the letter when signing it. He read it slowly, his face not revealing what he thought of it. He had very light eyelashes, almost like an albino's. When he had finished reading he said mildly, as though there was just one slight doubt he wanted Alan to resolve for him, 'But supposing Chamberlain were to take note of this letter and act upon it – that's to say supposing he encouraged the Czechs to resist – wouldn't the result be war?'

'I don't think so,' Alan answered almost as mildly. 'If Britain, France and Russia were to make plain to Hitler that they would combine forces to counter any attack against Czechoslovakia, we might well find he had been bluffing. Then, unless he chose to risk certain military defeat, he would have to eat his words, and the German people might well decide to get rid of him.'

'Assuming they did get rid of him, I think war would only be postponed. The danger of it will exist for just so long as we allow Germany to remain a have-not nation.'

'How do you mean, "have-not"?' Alan's pretence of ignorance was a compensation for being constrained to keep out of his tone of voice the irritation which the phrase caused him.

'I mean having no colonies. Germany was late in becoming a nation, and so France and ourselves got the best territories, and at the end of the Great War we took away from her even those she had managed to get.'

'I'm not inclined to sympathize with the German ruling class for having no colonial peoples to exploit.' Alan was still able to make his voice sound unindignant.

'Having an empire ourselves, we can hardly adopt a tone of high moral disapproval when the Germans want one too.'

'We can, provided at the same time we're in favour of freeing Britain's own subject peoples. But there could be no justification for inviting German Fascists, who would be even worse than public-school Englishmen, to rule over African natives. Two wrongs don't make a right.'

Alan became aware that though he had kept his voice under control he had not used words which would be likely to persuade. Benson said, 'Anything is better than war.' A fanaticism came briefly to life in his eyes beneath the blink of his pale lashes, but was dowsed as he added in an explanatory tone, 'Another war would destroy the human race.'

'I don't think it would,' Alan said, conscious now that getting Benson's signature was going to be much more difficult than he'd expected. 'There would always have to be someone alive to do the destroying – I mean, the last lot of destroyers at least would survive.' But this didn't seem very lucid or a very good argument, so Alan changed his ground, adding, 'And in any case non-resistance to Hitler would result in war for certain.'

'Not if it were carried far enough.'

'You mean that if the Nazis decided to invade this country they should be allowed to without a shot being fired at them?'

'Yes.'

'And they should not be hindered in any way from putting to death as many Reds and Jews and Jewish children as they liked?'

'They should not be physically hindered, but every kind of moral and non-violent pressure should be brought to bear on them. Violence can never lead to anything but violence. Those that take to the sword perish by the sword.'

'But you seem to want the Nazis to be able to use the sword without having it used against them in return.'

'If no one resisted them they would have no cause to use it.' A sudden not ill-natured cunning came into Benson's voice. 'And when you talk about their putting children to death aren't you taking rather the same line as those old-fashioned patriots in the Great War who used to ask conscientious objectors, "What would you do if you saw a German raping your sister?" '

Alan was about to answer that the Great War had been an imperialist one in which there had been nothing to choose between the two sides, and that the stories of German atrocities had been concocted by British propagandists, whereas now the Nazis really were torturers and murderers: he was checked, however, by mortification at having not for the first time underrated Benson's intelligence, and by the thought that while there was still hope of getting Benson's signature he should avoid sounding too much like a debater. He therefore conceded, 'Yes, you're right; I was talking pretty crudely.' He added in a tone as unargumentative as he could make it, 'What I feel about non-resistance is that to preach it in the democracies, where we're allowed to, will never make the majority of the people accept it but might affect enough of them to weaken the democracies against Hitler, who won't allow it to be preached in his country. I would of course be entirely in favour of having non-violence preached in Nazi Germany.'

'So would I,' Benson said, rather to Alan's surprise. 'Though that must be left to the Germans themselves. I think our best and perhaps our only way of recommending non-violence to them would be by giving a practical example of it ourselves.'

'And letting the Nazis get away with every new aggression they chose to make? I should have thought that that would have the effect of recommending violence rather than non-violence.'

'Not in the long run. Hitler would eventually find that he had no more worlds to conquer.'

This was spoken with a lightness which might or might not have been intentionally provocative. Alan after a pause allowed himself to be provoked; and, ignoring what Benson had actually said, countered with, 'The thing I find hardest to stomach about a certain kind of pacifism is the impartial way it reads lectures on keeping the peace both to the criminal and to the victim – no, I'm wrong, it's not so impartial, it reads them mainly to the victim.'

The lightness went from Benson's look, and he said firmly though mildly, 'Nothing good can be achieved by the use of force, no matter who uses it.'

'That seems to me to be much too sweeping a generalization.'

'Who gained by the last war? Certainly not the victors. Both sides were losers. And with more modern weapons another war would destroy both.'

'I am as much opposed to war between nations as you are.' Alan was in doubt whether he would be wise to reveal his position more fully; but awareness, now, that Benson was quite intransigent made him continue, defensively rather than with any hope of convincing him. 'All the same, I believe we shall not be able to put a stop to war until we get rid of the imperialist rulers whose rivalries are the cause of it. And to get rid of them may require the use of force.'

'So you are in favour of civil war to end all wars?' Benson said in a tone of sincere inquiry but with a trace of a smirk on his face.

'The imperialists are unlikely to surrender without putting up a fight. I believe that the peoples of the world must be prepared to fight back, and that their victory will be different from any imperialist victory because it will bring lasting peace.'

'When you say the peoples of the world do you perhaps really mean the Communists?' Benson unironically asked.

'I mean the peoples,' Alan too emphatically answered, being put out at having once again underestimated Benson's astuteness, 'though they would be led by the Communists because no other political party would be willing or ready to lead them.'

'So you think that in a Communist world there would be no more war?'

'Yes, I do. The final defeat of imperialism would remove the economic motive for war. Competition would give place to co-operation. All nationalities would have a common interest and a common ideology.'

Benson got out of his chair and stepped down from the wooden platform on which it and the master's desk were placed. He leant an elbow on the desk and said with quiet combativeness, 'Habits of violent suppression are not easily unlearned. After liquidating the imperialists the next step would be for the Communists to start liquidating one another. The era of heresies and persecutions would begin.'

'I believe on the contrary that when the imperialists have been got rid of there will be no further need for dictatorial methods. An age of complete toleration will begin. If a few hankerers after the old imperialist days still survive they will merely be laughed at – perhaps rather unkindly sometimes, but that will be better than war.'

'I wasn't thinking of hankerers after the old days but of sincere Communists who might find themselves unable to go on toeing the Party line.'

'Such people might be sincere, but objectively they would be anti-Communist.' Having said this, Alan knew that it would not do at all, and he added, 'I agree that for a time there might continue to be disputes inside the Party, though they would become less intense and eventually the Party itself would pass out of existence because it would no longer be required.'

'I suggest that they might become more not less intense,' Benson said, waving the letter like a barrister's brief at Alan. 'Whole nations might become heretical, and there would be a world struggle carried on with all the bitterness of the Thirty Years' War and with the appalling weapons of modern science.'

Alan, wanting to be contemptuous about this suggestion, at first found himself unable to think of words that would sound logical and then had to recognize that the suggestion was not after all so very implausible. 'That might not be absolutely impossible,' he said. 'But at worst it couldn't be more than a passing phase in the history of humanity.'

'It could last a hundred years or so and do away with civilization for a thousand or so more.' Benson became specially emphatic. 'There will never be real peace until we stop setting our hopes on material progress and begin to aim at a change of heart.'

'A lot of people have been aiming at that for two thousand years and over – it has been the central idea in all the great religions – and what good has it done?'

'It hasn't been given a fair trial yet,' Benson said.

'It has been given too long a trial. We shall never abolish war while we put the things of the spirit before the things of this world. We must believe that external progress can be achieved and we must struggle to achieve it.'

'Struggle?'

'Yes, peacefully if we can. In the long run men will fight only against nature and not at all against other men. But the necessity for struggle will always exist. By struggle, not by turning in upon ourselves and trying to improve our souls, we realize our full potentialities as human beings.'

Alan became aware how incongruous it was that he should be advocating external action whilst Benson – big-boned, earnest, almost the typical muscular Christian – was all for the inner life. The muscles at the corners of Benson's jaws seemed to bunch, as though he was clenching his teeth, and made the skin above it remotely resemble the skin over the knuckles of a fist. However, he gave a slight smile as he said, 'And when this struggle you favour has produced all the material gains that you hope from it, when everyone has been provided with motor-cars, helicopters, houses, greenhouses and so forth, would men still have to go on struggling?'

'They would want to go on. It would be the means whereby they could live most fully.'

'But what external ends would be left for them to struggle for?'

'They could explore and colonize other planets.'

'There would be a limit to that. Even if they discovered how to travel almost as fast as light they would never be able within a human life-span to reach planets in other solar systems than our own.'

'They might learn how to induce a suspension of life in themselves which would allow them to survive for thousands of years.'

'Unless we reject the second law of thermodynamics we must recognize that the whole universe is continually running down to a state of dead inertness. Eventually no life will survive anywhere.'

Alan, wondering what less-than-usually unintelligent Christian tract Benson might have got this idea from, said, 'If the universe is infinite it could go on running down eternally and there's no reason why life should ever come to an end.'

'Life existing in any particular part of the universe must die out. Human life as we know it must die out.'

'We should be conceited if we believed that we are unique and that beings similar to ourselves won't be produced by similar chemical conditions in other parts of the universe. Human life may survive somewhere for ever.'

'What consolation can that be to us if everything men have struggled to achieve on this earth is wholly lost and can be of no benefit to other humans in other solar systems?'

'I don't believe that anything anywhere can be wholly lost.'

After Alan had said this a dissatisfaction with its mystical vagueness grew in him and developed into a distaste for the philosophical turn that the conversation had taken. He woke again to his purpose of getting a signature from Benson, who was now saying with an obviously religious implication, 'In one sense that's very true.'

Alan tried to give the appearance of meditating on this for a short while, then said rather too brightly, 'I wonder how it was we got on to talking about the universe.'

'I think what started us was my questioning the value of material progress.'

'Yes. And we were led to that by this letter.'

Benson, becoming aware that he was still holding it, put it down on the master's desk, and was silent.

Alan asked, 'Do you feel you might perhaps sign it?'

'No,' Benson said placidly. 'I don't like to be disobliging, and I know you're sincere in your opinions, but if I signed I should be insincere and should be going against my principles.'

'I see.'

'Not that I think the letter is likely to have the slightest effect on Chamberlain's policy, if you send it to him. Almost certainly he won't even see it, or if he does it will go straight into his wastepaper basket.'

Alan, knowing he ought not to, allowed himself to retort, 'In my view pacifism at present, however admirable some pacifists may have been during the nineteen-fourteen war, is nothing more than the negative obverse of Fascism.'

He picked up the letter from the desk and went out of the classroom.

In the corridor on his way to the common-room he knew that the House league game he was due to watch must already have started and that he had no time now to try to collect any more signatures. However, the despondency he was beginning to feel did not arise either from a sense of lost time or from disappointment at his failure with Benson but from a cause, at first obscure, which became clearer to him as he was opening the door into the common-room lobby. He was depressed by something he had said to Benson. What was it? It wasn't the parting remark about the obverse of Fascism: Benson had deserved that. It was what Alan had said about the future of humanity, about the continuing necessity for struggle. Could he really be satisfied with the thought of a future in which men would be permanently striving, even though only against nature and not against one another? Wouldn't he prefer to think of a time to come when they would be able to live serenely and pleasurably instead of strenuously and restlessly? Wouldn't he rather have Wordsworthian contemplation than endless external exertion? Wouldn't he perhaps rather have Baudelaire's *'luxe, calme et volupté'*? No; or if he would he was being utterly unMarxist. This was what came of allowing himself to begin to resent the necessity of perpetual struggle. He walked into the common-room from the lobby and went across to his locker. There were five or six of his colleagues in the room. He did not bother to ask himself whether any of them had not yet signed. He put the letter away in his locker. He would take it round once more the next morning. He must go immediately now and watch the league game. His despondency was on him still as he walked out of the room again. To counter it he reminded himself that he had succeeded in getting signatures from three-quarters of the staff, including Brook and the Headmaster, and had had only one refusal. After the many school terms during which his attempts to influence his colleagues politically had seemed to produce if anything a negative result, he had had a triumph, and it was a triumph that he might never have had but for the cumulative effect of all the apparently fruitless political work he had done here in the past, and it ought to make him proud and glad.

.   .   .   .   .

During the following few days before Chamberlain and Daladier signed the Munich agreement with Hitler and Mussolini, increasing anxiety gave Alan an uninhibited energy and he spent all his spare time until late every night on political activity – meetings, local demonstrations, poster parades, selling pamphlets, distributing leaflets, arguing with strangers. When defeat came, and Chamberlain, returning from Munich after having betrayed Czechoslovakia, announced, 'I believe it is peace for our time. Go home and sleep quietly in your beds,' Alan experienced not despair but a consummation of the loathing which had already been aroused in him by this man's earlier sayings – as for instance, 'How horrible, fantastic, incredible it is that we should be digging trenches and trying on gas-masks here because of a quarrel in a far-away country between people of whom we know nothing,' and, viler still than that deliberate appeal to philistine insularity, the coupling of a quotation from Shakespeare, 'Out of this nettle, danger, we pluck this flower, safety,' with, 'When I was a little boy I used to be told, "If at first you don't succeed try, try again." ' How dared this evil old man, who had the mind of a precociously cunning small boy and who represented all that was most diseased in decaying imperialist Britain, attempt to support his criminal policy by quoting from Shakespeare, who stood for England at its best? Even Chamberlain's physical appearance as shown by photographs in newspapers favourable to him – the long scraggy neck sticking out of the stiff butterfly collar like the neck of a strangled turkeycock – was nauseating. What could he be like in private life? If amiable, which Alan found almost impossible to imagine, his amiability would be even more odious than an open sadism could have been, since it would be a villainously hypocritical cover for his encouragement of the Nazis in their war plans – though no doubt he would prefer the war to be unleashed against the women and children of the Soviet Union rather than against those of Britain. The possibility that Chamberlain might not deliberately be working for war between Germany and the Soviet Union did not occur to Alan, who was unable to believe that any eminent and experienced politician could act criminally without meaning to. 'Forgive them not,' Alan thought of the Chamberlain Cabinet, 'for they know what they do.' Hatred buoyed him up in the days after Munich, but not only or even mainly hatred. His certainty that the long struggle for peace had at last failed gave him strangely a feeling of relief, such as he might have had if after a long illness someone dear to him had died. Now a new and more hopeful struggle would begin – to prevent Chamberlain bringing Britain on to the side of Fascism in the coming war, and if possible to force him to make an alliance with the Soviet Union before then – more hopeful because the last few days had shown that large numbers of people here were uneasy about the appeasement of Hitler, and in this new struggle Alan must go all out, must spend without reservation all his free time and energy.

On the morning after the news of the Munich agreement Alan was walking up the gravel drive to the main entrance of the school, when he was overtaken by Benson, who however made no triumphant comment but said 'Good morning' and was then silent.

As they went into the building together Alan said, 'I'm sorry if I sounded offensive the other day when we were having that discussion about the letter I asked you to sign.'

'Offensive?' Benson seemed to try not altogether successfully to recollect, and added, 'Of course you weren't.'

In the common-room some minutes later Alan, not looking to see whether anyone was looking, took out of his pocket the copy of the *Daily Worker* he had been carrying with him and laid it on the table among the other daily newspapers there. He had never brought it in here before. He was going to bring it in every day from today on.

14

On a hot and breezy Sunday nearly ten months after Munich, Alan and Elsie – her mother having agreed to mind the baby for the day – went walking in the country south of London with a group of about twenty others, mainly Party members, most of whom they knew. The ramble was led and had been organized by a young man from the Workers' Theatre Movement named Tommy Pryce, who chose a westward route along and half-way up the escarpment of the downs. Exercise, the bright weather, the presence of girls, the cheerfulness of the men and a sense of being among friends made Alan happily excited. He noted with poetic pleasure how the bursting gorse pods crackled as though on fire, and in one bush how a single spider-thread, stretching between gorse spines and, shaken in the breeze, caught the sunlight which shifted to and fro along it like a shuttle flashing across a loom or like a finger quickly moving on a violin string. And his interest in the other girls had the effect of increasing his affectionate awareness of Elsie at his side. He walked with his arm through hers.

The turf path began to descend towards a wide-curving gap which had been cut through the downs by a river flowing from south to north. The very broad white dual carriageway of a concrete arterial road made the river seem narrow beside it, but was itself made to look small and even inoffensive and perhaps attractive by the big tree-crested hill which rose beyond it at the far side of the valley. On this hill the ramblers would have their lunch, Tommy Pryce had suggested.

They reached the arterial road and entered the concrete tunnel which had been constructed beneath it to enable pedestrians to get across without interrupting the traffic. A heavily glazed skylight was fixed into the ceiling half-way along the tunnel between the two carriageways overhead. Tommy Pryce, who led the way, started singing just before he walked in through the tunnel entrance and he continued more loudly when he was inside. The tune was the tune of the National Anthem but the words, which referred to the bearded King George V, were new to Alan, who was momentarily alarmed lest they should be heard outside the tunnel by someone unconnected with this group, and was then reassured because the noise of the traffic would make the words inaudible, and was then ashamed because he ought to have approved of them even if he'd thought they would be heard by every member of the public within a hundred yards from here.

> 'God shave our hirsute King,
> Bare his receding chin,
>   God shave our King;
> Let him quite hairless be
> That all the world may see
> And no more bow the knee;
>   God shave our King.'

Pryce was out of the tunnel as he sang the last two lines, and when Alan and Elsie were out of it also, and were on the path that sloped up to the level of the arterial road, one of the other ramblers coming from behind them said to her, 'Tommy composed that one a long time ago. I'm surprised he hasn't produced a new one for the new monarch. He's not usually so untopical. He certainly has an amazing facility for turning out lyrics. And good ones too. The W.T.M. are lucky to have him. If he'd been less politically conscious and less honest he could have made money writing for the West End stage.'

It was Willy Lamont. He wore dark glasses, and the left sleeve of his sports-jacket had no arm inside. He had been blinded and maimed in the nineteen-fourteen imperialist war. He was probably aware that he was speaking to a woman, but until Elsie answered him he did not know that he knew her.

'He's a first-rate chess-player too, so they say,' she said of Pryce, and at once Lamont recognized her voice.

'You're Elsie Hutchinson, aren't you?'

'I was. I'm Elsie Sebrill now. Fancy your remembering my voice.'

She did not think of introducing her husband to him; and Alan had never individually met Lamont before but had only listened from the audience to him as a main speaker at several peace meetings.

'Of course I remember you, Elsie. Are you still teaching?'

'I didn't give it up when I was married, but now I've had to for a time because I've got a baby to look after.'

'Congratulations.'

Lamont's pleased face, inclining forward beyond Elsie's, turned towards Alan as though in the expectation that he would now, whether he was Elsie's husband or not, speak and become a distinct person; and Alan might have spoken, but his habit – caught perhaps from poetry-writing – of being over-careful about words before using them made him too slow, so that Lamont gave him up for the time being and went on to Elsie, 'Do you still see a good deal of Enid West-bury and Bertha Carrol?'

'Oh yes. We hold meetings at our flat, and they come. They're with us on this ramble by the way.'

'I know they are. I've been talking to them. Enid is this year's president of her union branch and Bertha is its secretary. That's good.'

A stile, which had a silver-painted, oak-leaf-emblemed National Trust sign on a post beside it, led away from the arterial road into a riverside meadow. Lamont's wife, who always accompanied him wherever he went and who had been walking at his side as silently as Alan at Elsie's, helped him with a not too obtrusive lift of her hand beneath his arm to climb the stile. The river was walled on its far side by the steep cliff, now dark with yew and box, which it had curvingly cut out in the high chalk hill. On its near side also there were trees, among which Alan could name to himself only the chestnut for certain, though he guessed at alder, white poplar and maple, and under these trees there was a winding brown path which the ramblers followed. Lamont, continuing his talk with Elsie, showed that he knew the names of almost everyone on the ramble and had already talked to many of them this morning. People were his interest, Alan thought and was disgusted at himself for having been so mean as not to have spoken a single word to him yet. But Alan's very consciousness of the growing length of his own silence made speaking seem increasingly difficult. He looked at the river brownly moving, pebbled spits jutting into it from the banks here and there, its water at the bends appearing not quite smooth and resembling layers of gelatine. Then Lamont stopped talking about people and began talking about the scene around him, which he seemed to know as well as he knew the people:

'There used to be Himalayan balsam growing at the bottom of the river-bank quite near where we've got to now.' He turned his face towards Alan as though with the slight hope that this remark might find an amateur botanist in him and cause him to talk at last. Alan looked down towards the river-bank, knowing that he wouldn't recognize Himalayan balsam even if it were conspicuous there, and he saw nothing that was likely to be it. Lamont, turning his face away again, said, 'Another name for it is policeman's helmet, but I don't fancy that – and not only because the flower is pink.' He laughed as though he was laughing off the hope of hearing Alan speak, but Alan was determined now to say something, no matter what; however, the first sentence that came into his head – 'I'm afraid I know hardly anything about flowers' – seemed far too tepid and negative, so he did not say it, and there was a desperate pause, and then without forethought and irrelevantly he did say, 'I was at your last meeting in Stepney. I meant to ask a question but thought it might not be suitable.'

'What was it?' Lamont said, with a sudden though transient coldness, like a man reminded of his job while on holiday.

'Well, after Munich I believed war was bound to come within a year. But lately I've wondered whether the rulers of the capitalist countries could really be so foolish as to fight one another instead of combining against the Soviet Union. I'm beginning to suspect that whatever Hitler does Chamberlain will never forcibly oppose him. And Hitler will never initiate a war against Chamberlain's Britain. Both of them must know that war between them might well mean the final destruction of capitalism. I wanted to ask what you think about this idea.'

'I think they may be fully aware of the dangers of an inter-imperialist quarrel; but they may be driven to it, all the same, by economic pressures that are far stronger than their mutual good intentions – stronger even than their shared hostility towards Communism and the Soviet Union.'

A narrow green-painted iron footbridge appeared suddenly beyond the concealing plumes of a weeping willow. Tommy Pryce had already crossed it to the other side of the river. Lamont was held back for a moment by his wife, who signed to Elsie and Alan to go over first, which after briefly hesitating they did, Alan thinking as he went how un-Marxist the views about Chamberlain and Hitler that he had lately been toying with were when compared with Lamont's. Reaching the path at the far side of the bridge, Elsie and Alan walked slowly in the expectation that Lamont would come up with them again, but he didn't, and Alan looking back saw with disappointment that he and his wife had attached themselves to another couple – Len Whiscop and Helena Shields. Perhaps Alan had chanced upon an unwelcome topic to talk to him about; or perhaps Lamont would have detached himself anyway at this point, meaning to give himself time to speak to every one of the ramblers in turn.

On the right of the path was a small field of coarse grass with shrubs, and very close on the left was the thickly-treed hill. Alan noticed some litter that had been deposited under a dogwood bush by eaters who had sat there. He said to Elsie, 'Newspapers in trees, glass in the running brooks.'

'That sounds familiar.'

'It's a misquotation from *As You Like It*. The banished Duke says in the forest of Arden, "And this our life exempt from public haunt Finds tongues in trees, books in the running brooks, Sermons in stones and good in everything." '

'I learnt that in the fifth form. I liked it.'

The path made a right-angled turn to the left and soon rose steeply, exposing along its meandering upward course the grey-white chalk of the hillside. Elsie had difficulty in climbing – she always did have it even on much gentler slopes, and it was quite genuine – and she laughed as he got behind her and pushed her with both his hands in the small of her back. Then the path became easier where half-revealed yew roots extended across and made shallow steps in it. Alan looked at the trees beside the path. There was one yew that had fallen, probably quite a long time ago, but was still alive, and from its trunk numerous small straight branches stuck up vertically and close together like the teeth of a fine-toothed comb. Another yew had a tangle of clematis lianas resting like a huge nest high on its boughs. Another had lost much of its bark and the naked wood beneath was of a Red-Indian colour. Nearer the top of the hill the dead and pale trunk of some different kind of tree stood shadowed by yews and suggested a small monument in the wooded grounds of an eighteenth-century country house. Stopping for a moment at this spot, Elsie and Alan looked back over the heads of the upcoming ramblers who were following them, and he was surprised to see how very far below after his short climb the valley already was. Len Whiscop waved to Elsie and Alan, paused in his walk to droop with mock exhaustion, panted convulsively and protruded his tongue like a dog's. Lamont seemed to be climbing without any difficulty. Alan turned to go on again with Elsie. Almost at once he was aware of something startling about the appearance of the trees that were ahead of him on top of the hill. He did not know precisely what it was, but he knew that it had a connection with the sudden flight of a bird among them – straight and fast and low and level and intermittently visible in the gaps between boles. This passing movement, like the flicking open of a shutter, gave to these trees a significance which he was on the point of grasping and which he felt to be vital for him to grasp but which eluded him. Perhaps they were presenting him with the idea for a poem, were about to set him free at last from whatever it was that had for far too long stopped him writing. 'The genius of the woods,' he thought, trying to get somewhere near to the idea. But this was not near enough.

Then, as he and Elsie reached the top of the hill and followed Tommy Pryce's lead, he began to look closely at individual trees, hoping that by so doing he might make the idea clearer, and he noticed what a variety of shapes and colours the beeches showed. The ridiculous, the graceful, the mad, the podgy, the uncompromisingly grand were there, and one with arms crossed in the posture of a convivial singer of

'Auld Lang Syne'. The bark of some was silvery grey, of some was pastel green, of some was vertically streaked with bands of greenish-black having a pattern-resemblance to the markings of a skunk or a badger or a snake's head (Alan was too zoologically ignorant to be sure which), of some was soot-black. There was one which was growing on a raised bank and which had above-ground roots clawing the soil like the talons of a bird of prey. He saw elsewhere a trunk with a barley-sugar twist in it; another with a rounded ridge running diagonally down beneath its bark like the neck-muscle of a girl who had turned her head to look over her shoulder; a bough like a bent elbow; a protrusion in the shape of a teat and another in the shape of a chancre; several boughs showing a shallow hollow like an armpit where they joined the main trunk, and one of the hollows having a bunchy fuzziness of twigs projecting from it; two trunks lumpy like the torsos of old wrestlers; an ash and a beech, both tall, growing in full-length contact with one another, close-pressed as if in the act of love or murder. He noted the various appearances produced where a small branch had broken off from the trunk and the bark had begun to grow over the injury: craters, and sea anemones, and lead piping protruding from the mouths of gargoyles, and once the dead finger of a decaying hand pointing ominously into the depths of the wood. On one tree a bunchy ganglion-like swelling beneath smooth bark resembled varicose veins. Wavy horizontal lines made the surface of another seem ripple-marked like current-bedded sandstone. The roots of another had been left in the air by the erosion of soil from beneath them and they stuck out all around like a crinoline. A branch hung like a fireman's hose. Black bark with a sheen on it made him think of the sweat-glistening skin of a very dark negro. Split bark widely sundered and with turned-in edges had the look of a sheep's carcase skewered wide-open and hanging in a butcher's shop. A beech with two trunks bifurcating from the bole and ascending vertically and very straight imitated a tuning-fork, and a similar double-trunked tree near-by with a wider fork more curved at the base was like a lyre or a lyre-bird. A tree with a large wrinkled growth swelling heavily out from half-way up its trunk recalled an engraving which Alan had once seen in a book of monsters and which had shown a man in seventeenth-century clothes with a headless parasitic brother hanging out from the middle of his chest. Alan found that the grotesqueness, the arthritic-seeming deformity of some of the trees in this part of the wood made the gracefulness of the others all the more appealing, and in return the gracefulness, the slenderness and the grandeur of some gave to the deformity of the others a beauty it might not have had if seen in isolation. However, his examination of individual beeches did not bring him nearer to clarifying the startling idea which they as a group had at first seemed to present him with. If anything he was further from grasping it now than he had been before. He had lost the excitement of the wood in the interesting detail of the trees.

Tommy Pryce came to where the wood stopped at a big expanse of turf on the south side. Two fallen tree-trunks were near the edge of the grass and these appeared to him as good seats which the ramblers could sit on while eating their sandwiches. With the toe of his shoe he upturned some of the dry brown beech-leaf carpeting close to the tree-trunks: it came up in a compact clot, the underside of which was dark with damp, and among the exposed leaves beneath it white mycelial threads were visible. A fungus was growing against the butt of an unfallen beech next to the fallen ones, and Alan wondered whether it was the honey-tuft fungus, whose name he remembered from his reading both because, like the coral-spot fungus, it was verbally attractive to him and because the honey-tuft was said to kill within two years the tree it began to grow on.

'Nice and wet here,' Pryce said, 'but dry as a bone on top.

Let's sit on these logs and eat.'

Most of the others, when all of the group had arrived here, sat on the tree-trunks, but Alan and Elsie chose the grass, which was warm and thistle-free and had been grazed by rabbits till it was as short as the grass of a lawn. Alan had been carrying his and her lunch in a small rucksack that he now removed from his back and handed to Elsie, who had prepared the food and knew which of the greaseproof-paper-covered packets contained what. She grinned as she gave him the three hard-boiled eggs that he had told her he would want when she had asked him in the flat how many. And he did want them. The walking he had done gave relish to his eating, made it a pleasure so keen that it was like an aesthetic experience. With the eggs there were brown bread-and-butter sandwiches and afterwards he ate a banana and an apple, and he drank hot coffee which she poured out for him from a vacuum flask into a plastic cup. And the pleasure did not end when his appetite was satisfied: it changed, evolved, became a happiness deriving not just from food but also from the presence of the comrades eating and talking around him.

'How fine they are,' he thought. 'How devoted and honest, how different from what anti-Communists say that Communists are, how much better as human beings than their traducers.' He looked at Lamont, conqueror of dreadful disabilities, and at Lamont's wife, whose self-sacrifice for her husband had made possible his outstanding work for the cause; at Len Whiscop, born in a slum, mainly self-educated, who was among the Party's most effective economics tutors and who once, when trespassing on principle, had led a group of ramblers including Alan and Elsie past a game-keeper holding a shotgun; at Sammy Pentire and his Polish wife Rosa, both of them nearer seventy than sixty but slim and fit, who were vegetarians and had been active for socialism since their twenties; at George Farmer, an Old

Etonian who could have made a bourgeois career for himself if he hadn't chosen the Party; at Enid and Bertha, teachers, who had remained loyal to the working class into which they had been born and whose scrupulous intellectual honesty would allow them to accept nothing on faith, not even from the Party leaders. He thought of other comrades who were not here on this ramble: of Wally first of all, and of Eddie Freans, and of Jimmy Anders. Then he thought of people opposed to the Party: of Mrs Greensedge, who cheated at whist drives and who had once said that her husband would be furious if he thought she was getting mixed up with Communists; of a university don who had alluded to Marx and Engels with complacent contempt and in words revealing that he had not bothered to study their writings; of Christian imperialists paying lip-service to the Sermon on the Mount and expressing horror at the Marxist view that the use of force was in certain temporary revolutionary circumstances justifiable; of young careerists despising the working class they had risen from and abhorring Communism because it contradicted the only principle that made sense to them – their own advancement. Such people were of the class which Alan himself had belonged to, but which he had broken with. 'I have cleansed myself of their customs,' he thought, remembering Dante's line: *'da' lor costumi fa che tu ti forbi.'* He belonged at last, without reservation, among these comrades he was sitting with here. They accepted him as one of them, and he knew that in spite of, or perhaps partly because of, his diffidence, they liked him. He loved them, and he would never again allow himself to repine because of the amount of work the Party expected from him, or to hanker back after what he had been fond of in his bourgeois days.

But as soon as he'd thought this he became aware once more of the beech trees. They gave him, just as they had given him when he'd been climbing the hill, the feeling that he was on the very threshold of discovering something important for him. However, this time the feeling did not begin to lose definiteness when he looked more intently at the trees. From his position just outside the wood he was able to see, as he hadn't been able to from inside, the sun on the upper surface of the leaves; and all at once, out of the brightness and the greenery, the idea which had been eluding him came to him clearly. It was not an idea for a poem: it was bigger than that. At first he expressed it to himself excitedly in the words 'This is why I was born'; but then he asked himself, 'How could these trees mean that?' He immediately knew the answer: they meant it not just because of their own beauty but because they represented a different place and time from here and now. They evoked for him the poetic life he had tried to live in the seaside village that Richard had invited him down to years before. They were associated with the white gate under the arched hawthorn, with the path up to the verandah, the glass-chimneyed brass paraffin lamp waiting dim-lit on the bobble-fringed table-cloth, with Richard's reading aloud in the open night air, the morning esplanade, the sun on the tumbling glaucous sea, Basher and the check-capped madman, Peg, the walks with Richard along the shore, the imaginings, the words, the things looked at, the imagery, the poetry, the creative joy. And as Alan sat thinking of that time he had the impression that behind his right shoulder, just out of eyeshot, Richard was sitting here with him, and was saying distinctly and calmly, 'There is no other life on earth to compare with that.'

Alan almost immediately became alert to the anti-Party implications of this imagined remark, and he inwardly set about refuting it. The poetic life, he reminded himself, had brought him near to suicide, was an unlivable delusion. How much more surely disastrous it would be if he tried to live it now under the shadow of looming Fascism and war. How soft-witted, how criminal he would be if he were to abandon for its sake the struggle without which no poetry at all and no remnant of civilization could be saved. He was to blame for having allowed himself even momentarily to think of the poetic life as still a possibility for him. During the past few months he had believed himself cured at last of such illusions. He was disappointed to find that the old weakness remained.

At least, he felt he ought to be disappointed. And yet, as he sat and continued looking up at the trees, he could not suppress a contrary and a stronger feeling, a gladness, a conviction that the poetic life was not a fraud, not a mirage, was good, was possible. It was possible because he knew from within himself that he was capable of it. There was nothing in his nature, or in Nature outside him, that prevented it. If he had so far failed to live it, this had been due not to any lack within him of the potentiality for it but to unnatural external circumstances, to anti-human conditions in human society. And these conditions would worsen; but not for ever.

A time would come when human beings would know how to remove the social obstacles which they themselves had been forced to set up against happiness. Then the poetic life could be lived – though he would be dead – by others whose inborn bent would be similar to his. There would be a world in which everyone would have freedom for self-fulfilment, would be expected, would have the prime social duty to become whatever he was born to be. 'A world not of contemplation,' Alan thought, remembering his argument with Benson and his doubts afterwards about the worthwhileness of perpetual future activity, 'but of the kind of activity in which each individual would be doing what he was best suited for and loved to do.'

The trees were right in what they had seemed to tell him and Richard's imagined voice had not been lying to him.

The poetic life was the finest life. No other, not even the Party life, could compare with it. But it could not be lived now. To try once again to live it would be to retreat towards failure and dishonour, would bring him farther from it than he was at present. There was only one way towards it, and that was the way of constant political effort, of Communist struggle for a struggleless world in which poetic living would at last become actual. True, neither he nor any of his comrades here would be likely ever to reach it. They were separated from it by gulfs of desolation and fire, by plains and towns clogged with the bodies of the millions yet-to-be-killed in imperialism's wars and persecutions. But on the increasing grimness of their struggle would be reflected, as from a mirror far up beyond the outer layers of the earth's atmosphere, the light of the future freedom. He could see the reflection now, in the faces and in the characters of the comrades around him. This was what distinguished all of them from non-Communists, raised them above even those whose abilities were greater than theirs. This in Elsie was what, more than anything else, made him love her.

She sat listening to and laughing at banter that was going on between Tommy Pryce and Len Whiscop. Alan, his shoulder slightly behind and touching hers, wanted to find an immediate way of letting her know his feelings about her. He could have put his chin over her shoulder so that his cheek touched her neck – other couples in the group were being more demonstrative than that; Charlie Webb for instance was lying with his head on Ellie's lap – but this would have failed to express what he needed to. He could have said into her ear, 'My darling, my darling' – the talk was loud and general enough for him to say it without the others hearing – but this would have come very far short of what he meant. At last he pressed his knuckle against her elbow. She turned to him with a pleased and inquiring look, and he told her, 'I've been thinking how admirable you are.'